Gyda wanted her life to be filled with passion, love and children. Everything she knew she would never possess.

She looked over at Thorstein, who pulled relentlessly on his oar, hour after hour. He never seemed to tire, although sweat now beaded his brow. He was strong and young, with a prosperous settlement.

He would make a fine husband.

The thought hit her square in the ribs, and she bit her lip as if it were a wicked desire.

Of course the idea was ridiculous.

Wasn't it?

Thorstein had no desire for her—he thought her shallow and arrogant—and she did not care. At least he showed her respect, and respect kept her safe.

Despite herself, her lips tingled with the memory of his kiss. It had been perfect. Soft, gentle and hot. But he'd made it clear the type of woman he wanted, and it had made her heart heavy to hear it. It reminded her of her own naive desires for marriage, before she'd realized how men could be.

Author Note

History has lived beside me all of my life. I grew up near the beautiful Warwick Castle. I studied in York and saw the York Minster from my bedroom window every morning—if I craned my neck out of it, which I often did! Now, when I take the Tube into the city, I see the Tower of London as I exit the station. Sitting majestically beside the river, not caring about the modern world buzzing around it. There is something so beautiful and enduring about these buildings that always makes me stop and stare. Who walked here before me? Who saw these being built? These questions have always sparked my imagination.

History lives and breathes beside me, and I adore it. I hope to reflect this as accurately as possible in my writing. However, not all facts are known regarding this particular murky period in history, and although I've tried to stay true to the facts, I have filled in the gaps with artistic license.

Thanks go to my long-suffering critique partners Leonie Mack and Lucy Keeling, who always see the first hot, messy drafts of my work. Also to the Romantic Novelists' Association New Writers' Scheme, Essex Writers United and in particular to Virginia Heath, who encouraged me to "just send it" when I was faffing about editing and reediting this novel.

Last but not least, thanks go to you, my reader. I hope you enjoy reading Thorstein and Gyda's story as much as I enjoyed writing it.

LUCY MORRIS

The Viking Chief's Marriage Alliance

HARLEQUIN
HISTORICAL

HARLEQUIN®
HISTORICAL™

Recycling programs for this product may not exist in your area.

ISBN-13: 978-1-335-50627-6

The Viking Chief's Marriage Alliance

Copyright © 2021 by Lucy Morris

This edition published by arrangement with Harlequin Books S.A.

For questions and comments about the quality of this book, please contact us at CustomerService@Harlequin.com.

Harlequin Enterprises ULC
22 Adelaide St. West, 40th Floor
Toronto, Ontario M5H 4E3, Canada
www.Harlequin.com

Printed in U.S.A.

Lucy Morris lives in Essex, UK, with her husband, two young children and two cats. She has a massive sweet tooth and loves gin, bubbly and Irn-Bru. She's a member of the UK Romantic Novelists' Association. She was delighted when Harlequin accepted her manuscript for publication after submitting her story to the Warriors Wanted! submission blitz for Viking, Medieval and Highlander romances. Writing for Harlequin Historical is a dream come true for her and she hopes you enjoy her books!

The Viking Chief's Marriage Alliance is Lucy Morris's debut title for Harlequin Historical.

Look out for more books from Lucy Morris coming soon.

Visit the Author Profile page at Harlequin.com.

For my mum, Moira.

I love writing romance because of you.

Prologue

Gyda watched as her husband's funeral ship caught the wind and sailed out to sea. It burned brightly, a magnificent symbol of Jarl Halvor's power and influence. Her handmaids stood beside her with cool expressions. They would not miss their master and neither would she. They'd all felt the sting of Halvor's hand at one time or another.

'We worry about you,' said Erica, her most trusted handmaid, and friend.

'I'll be fine. I knew this day would come eventually. I've prepared for it.'

'Your tapestries won't be enough for you to escape.'

'My tapestries and some silver. It'll be enough.'

It had to be.

'Be careful, mistress. It won't be long before Baldor makes his move. The people love you and hate him. My Viggo says he lacks support from half the warriors. They suspect a war between the brothers. But if Baldor marries you before his brothers return from trading they won't dare challenge his inheritance. Ah, look…here comes the runt now.'

'Shh!' hissed Gyda, fearing for her friend's safety.

Halvor's son, Baldor, walked towards them. He was the eldest son but had always been weak and sickly, as was his wife, who had died of a chill last summer. A disappointment to his father and a source of amusement to his brothers. If he'd not taken after his father in temperament she might have pitied him.

'It is a shame that you decided against joining my father in the afterlife... Ragnar will be disappointed. He will be home soon...'

He sniffed as he spoke and her stomach churned. He knew how much she despised Ragnar.

'Your father will be welcomed in Valhalla by his first and second wife. He will not miss me.'

'True.' He stepped closer, his stale breath fanning her cheek. 'We have much to discuss.'

She leaned away. 'About...?'

'About how you can keep your position here as mistress. How we can rule together.' He grinned, showing the gaps in his yellow teeth.

'Your father died yesterday.'

'And today we mourn his loss. But tomorrow...'

He let the threat hang in the air, and she knew that was what it was. A threat.

'We'll speak later.'

As he walked away her jaw tightened and her handmaids looked at her with worried eyes. 'I will need a ship,' she said.

Chapter One

North Sea, Coast of Northumbria, 880 AD

Thorstein Bergson's longship crashed through the turbulent waves at a relentless pace. Even so, he feared it would be too late for the survivors of the shipwreck that lay broken upon the rocks. The wind and rain stung his face as mountainous waves threw his boat up and down with merciless fury. But he knew these waters, every dip and every shallow—unlike the unfortunate travellers who'd strayed too close to the broken teeth of land.

Above the wreck, high on an arching cliff, a lonely oak tree burned. Struck by lightning, it blazed from the inside out, its blackened branches reaching up into the storm as if screaming for mercy. Its centre a glowing beacon of death and destruction in the early light of dawn.

A message from the gods that even he could not ignore.

If there were any survivors they should leave an offering at the base of that tree. Without it, Thorstein would never have seen their longship and come to their aid. He was still unsure why he was risking his men's lives, and possibly his own, to help strangers.

At least the storm that had raged throughout the night was beginning to die. Thor no longer beat his hammer in the righteous sky, and the lashing rain was beginning to ease. It wouldn't be long before they reached the horse-shoe of cliffs that surrounded his settlement's harbour.

His friend Magnus came to join him at the prow of the ship. Magnus leaned his shoulder against the intricately carved serpent's head and clicked his tongue against his teeth as he followed Thorstein's gaze. 'We shouldn't sail too close to the rocks, or we might meet a similar fate.'

Thorstein grunted in agreement. The storm was running out of power, but the cliffs were treacherous at the best of times. Currently the tide was coming in, and it was coming in fast.

Magnus eyed his friend thoughtfully. 'They'll probably all be dead before we reach them.'

Thorstein frowned and folded his arms against his barrel chest. The longship slowed as his men turned the vessel to come abreast of the wreck. Both men braced their legs and barely moved as the ship swung to the side. They had been in worse waters than this.

Thorstein's arm ring shone in the amber light of dawn and he stared at the burning oak above the wreck, his facial scar aching in the bitter whip of the wind.

'I'll get as close as I can,' Magnus said, and he nodded.

He frowned at the survivors where they clung to the side of their upturned hull. Their pale, exhausted faces were like skulls in the weak light of dawn.

A cobalt cloak drew his eye. The shade was deep and rare, reserved for only the wealthiest of nobles.

Was this why Thor had brought him here? Was he to save a noble and win a reward?

Thorstein crossed his arms and braced his legs wide as his boat rocked from side to side. He had no need for wealth. His hoard was safely buried beneath his Hall. He had enough for both his future and the afterlife. No, there must be some other reason he'd been called to their rescue.

'Can you swim?' he bellowed, his voice carrying over to the survivors of the wreck. 'We will run aground if we get much closer.'

Their ships were far too close as it was, and he would rather not risk his own men any more than he needed to.

In answer, several of the shipwrecked crew jumped into the rolling sea and began to paddle wearily towards them. He watched with tense shoulders as even the wounded jumped into the water. He relaxed a little when he saw they were being helped along by their more able shipmates.

He threw a rope over the side, and his men did the same.

Thorstein's eyes were pulled back to the cobalt cloak. It was worn by a woman. Some of her ash blonde hair fell limply forward as she raised her face to the sun. As she stood, he saw she had the bearing of a queen. Her head was high and her spine straight. She was tall, he noted. Even for a Norse woman she was well above average in height, her head level with that of a red-haired man who she appeared to be arguing with.

Thorstein felt almost sorry for him as she glared imperiously down her sharp nose and spat words like flaming arrows. He watched as the man snarled back at this woman with the face and stature of a goddess. No doubt the spoilt, pampered wife of this unfortunate traveller. He pitied the man—a wife like that was a curse, no matter how beautiful she was.

She didn't jump into the water like the others. Her jaw

was clenched in a stubborn line as she stared the man down and shook her head.

To Thorstein's surprise, the man let out a bellow of frustration and jumped into the water alone.

The woman looked out towards Thorstein then. Her blue-grey eyes were cool and sharp as she assessed him with a steady gaze. She did not flinch, as some women did when they saw his crucifix scar, and he respected her more for it. Some thought it shameful that he bore the Christian mark of their enemies' religion, although he felt no shame personally.

She turned away, and he lost sight of her. His chest felt suddenly tight. *Where was she going?*

He watched as the wreck groaned and swayed against the tide. Pieces fell and broke up, leaving the boat at a perilous and unsupported angle. He waited with growing impatience for the woman to return, but she didn't.

The red-haired man was being hauled aboard his ship, coughing and choking. Before he'd fully caught his breath Thorstein was demanding an explanation, 'What is your lady doing? The tide is coming in—the wreck will break up!'

The man looked at the boat with a snarl of contempt. 'She's not my lady! May the sea take her and her silver! She has given me nothing but bad fortune since she stepped aboard my ship. If you have any sense you will let the sea take her!'

An odd satisfaction warmed Thorstein's stomach at the knowledge that the man was not her husband. He glanced at the rest of the wretched crew as they fell upon his deck like dead fish. None of the survivors seemed a wealthy enough match for her, and he wondered for a moment if her husband had been lost to the storm.

He scowled at the way his heart beat faster at the thought.

What did he care? She'd be drowning beneath the disintegrating ship if she didn't hurry soon.

A cracking sound followed by a deadly thud drew his attention back to the wreck. The mast had snapped, the top half falling and splitting the deck and hull in two. He couldn't see the lady, but the mast had fallen in her direction.

With a savage curse, Thorstein threw off his heavy cloak and tunic, kicked off his boots and dived into the sea.

Bang!

Gyda stared at the thick mast that had landed inches from her feet with empty lungs and trembling fingers. She'd been moments away from stepping forward to reach her silver chest when the mast had fallen.

Not for the first time she wondered how she was still alive.

She'd been travelling for days in the wind and the rain, soaked to the bone, and then shipwrecked on rocks. Now she understood why the helmsman had ordered everyone as high as possible on the wreck. They would have died from the cold of the sea otherwise. Being seen and saved by those from the shore had been their only hope.

She almost regretted climbing down to save her silver, but what harm would a few moments more in the sea do to her? They'd been rescued—all would be well, surely? She just needed to hurry.

But the heavy mast now lay on top of her silver. Its scarlet sail lay across her cargo like rotten clothes on a long-dead corpse. She shuddered as she remembered the screams of men as they were thrown overboard, swallowed by the black sea never to be seen again.

Would that be her fate now? Had she been foolish to ignore the advice of the helmsman?

All her possessions were lost. Except for her silver. And the silver would make all the difference to her future. She had to get it. Without it, she would once again be at the mercy of men. No, if there was a chance for her to keep her freedom she would take it and damn the risks!

A corpse bobbed in the swelling water around her feet, although she tried not to look too closely, for fear of losing her nerve. The light of the burning tree above coupled with the milky light of dawn had given her hope earlier. She'd seen her silver chest and hoped to retrieve it. But now that she was wading through death and destruction she wondered if she'd lost her sanity as her toes screamed in agony from the deathly chill.

Her fingers ached with cold as she stared at her precious cargo. Chests that had been filled with the fruits of years of her labour now lay thrown across the rocks like dice along with their contents. Beautiful gowns and tunics embellished with precious Byzantine silks or trimmed with arctic fox, intricate vibrant tapestries woven with the finest wool. Luxury goods she could have traded at Jorvik's impressive markets.

Now they were ruined—as was her future.

She'd planned to start a new life in Jorvik. With her cargo, she would have earned an independent living as an artisan weaver and dressmaker—as only a widow could. Now she wondered if she would live to see Jorvik at all.

Surely the gods wouldn't expect more from her? They loved brave women, and leaving Viken had been the bravest thing she'd ever done. Were they angry with her because of her failings as a wife?

Pushing thoughts of her failed marriage and her dead husband aside, she grabbed hold of the halyard rope attached to the mast. If she could pull the mast aside she would be able to reach her small silver chest. All might not be lost.

A great wave ploughed into the side of the wreck, spraying her in icy water from head to toe. The ship cracked and moaned like a dying beast and she tugged on the rope with all her might, her palms burning under the strain.

She choked and spat out mouthfuls of saltwater that made her stomach revolt and her mind spin. The weight of her sodden clothing pulled at her, sapping her strength as the water rose from around her ankles up to her knees with terrifying speed.

She tightened her grip on the rope with bloody fingers and braced her foot against a broken chest for leverage. She would not fail again.

'Woman, are you mad?' a man shouted from above.

She squinted up into the bright light of a new day. It was their rescuer. She had seen him earlier, standing proud at the prow of his ship. His whole body had hummed with the vibrant energy of a commander. He was the sort of man who both thrilled and terrified her.

'You must leave now, or the ship will collapse on top of you!'

She stared at him in shock, sliding her eyes up his impressive form as if trying to confirm to herself that she'd indeed gone mad.

He had long legs, anchored wide, and narrow hips that flared to an impressive torso. His long hair shone in the dawn like a raven's wing, and his branded face was set in a grim frown. The man's soaking wet tunic was moulded to his chest, and she could see the shadow of dark hair and the ripple of muscle beneath the pale linen. He was impressive and frightening at the same time.

She looked away to focus on her task.

She tried, but she could not move the mast, no matter how hard she pulled. Her frozen fingers didn't seem able to grasp any more.

'No possession is worth your life, woman!' bellowed the man.

Gyda's head snapped up at the reprimand. 'Rather than shouting at me, maybe you could help? If you lift the mast, I could pull it free!'

'There's no time. The tide is almost in.'

'Then I suggest you either help me or leave me. Because I will not leave my silver!' she shouted back.

It was a risk, and she held her breath while she waited for his response.

He climbed down towards her.

Although he was scowling darkly, she couldn't help the warm tingle of relief that shivered down her spine as he approached.

She tossed back a few strands of loose hair with what she hoped was an appreciative smile. She had always been awkward around handsome men, never knowing how they would treat her or what they would do.

As this man joined her she noticed he was surprisingly nimble for his size. He placed his bare feet and hands carefully and quickly as he climbed down the broken wreck.

'Now, as I said, if you could just lift the mast—'

She couldn't say any more as she was lifted high in the air by two burly arms and slung over the man's shoulder. Surprise knocked the air out of her lungs, and she took a moment to gather her scattered thoughts. Then her outrage took over.

'What are you doing?' she screamed, her fists pounding into his back with as much strength as she could muster after the exhausting last few hours.

'I'm saving your life! Now, stop wriggling like a damn eel!'

His gruff words were punctuated by a light slap to her rump. It wasn't hard, but the indignity of it made her fists clench. 'How dare you? Put me down!'

He climbed the sheer deck, using whatever ropes and wood came to hand. More than once a piece of the ship broke away in his grasp, or crumpled beneath his weight, and each time the man shifted or moved to a better position with surprising ease. He was a giant bear, with the surefootedness of a goat.

She stilled her movements as she slowly realised how close the wreck truly was to full collapse. She hated to admit it, but she could now see the dangerous predicament they were both in and she began to fear for their lives.

He set her down at the top of the deck on the outer shell of the hull. To her despair, she realised the ship had now tilted completely on its side. As the sea crashed through the rocks it opened up a gaping hole in the hull. The ship flexed and groaned beneath the strain.

She hissed through her teeth as a particularly hard wave vibrated through the timber beneath her numb feet. She grabbed on to the one thing she could rely on in the continually shifting world. Her rescuer's arms. Her fingers gripped his biceps and she swayed towards him, her harbour from the storm. He grabbed her waist, and even through the many layers of wool and linen she could feel the strength and warmth of his fingers. She looked up into his blue eyes. They were as bright as a harvest sky and just as endless.

'Can you swim?' he asked, and she nodded vacantly.

Unbidden memories of long summer days swimming in the fjords with her sisters swept through her mind, only to be quickly carried away on the wind. She couldn't bear to think of those lost days—not now.

Her legs shook under the power of his gaze.

The man's eyes widened slightly and she realised belatedly that it was the hull trembling beneath her feet. His fingers tightened on her waist and he lifted her up off her feet. Something which hadn't happened to her since she was a child had now happened twice in only a handful of moments, and with utter disbelief Gyda cried out as the man threw first her and then himself into the swirling sea below.

Chapter Two

Gyda gasped as the icy water hit her. She just managed to choke out some salty water before her body was dragged beneath the surface. All sound and reason were drowned out as she was tossed around like a child's plaything beneath the waves, unsure of what was up or down, sea or sky. Panic squeezed her chest tight as her cloak and gown became tangled around her limbs like a frozen shroud.

She was drowning.

The sea pulled at her mind and body with a strength she could not hope to fight and she became still, her lungs burning, begging for the mercy of her last breath.

Something grabbed her and tightened sharply around her waist. Her mind was filled with her mother's tales of sea monsters. She fought tentacles, scratching against the beast with blunt nails—only to realise belatedly that the tentacles were, in fact, two strong arms.

She broke the surface, coughing, her body weak and limp. The arms around her were a man's—her rescuer's. Broken fragments of the shattered longship bobbed around them. She frowned as she realised she was once again beholden to this stranger, this bear of a man. He'd saved her life three times since she'd met him.

But although she should be grateful, she could not find it in her heart to thank him.

Without her silver she had nothing.

'I've got you,' he said, holding her head up and out of the water as he swam towards his boat.

His callused but surprisingly gentle hand curved beneath her jaw—a stroke of sunlight against her skin that made her shiver with the longing to be warm once again.

The crew reached down and hauled her quickly up onto the deck. Her teeth chattered so hard she feared she would break a tooth. Blankets were draped over her head and shoulders, and she clutched at them with bone-white knuckles.

The dark-haired stranger climbed aboard shortly after, his long legs swinging onto the deck with a splashing thud. Giving orders to his men without stopping to catch his breath, he quickly peeled off his wet under-tunic and dropped it with a slap.

His left arm was decorated from wrist to shoulder with blue-green knotwork and runes, and Thor's hammer, Mjolnir, covered the thick plate of muscle above his heart. The tattoos appeared to writhe and pulsate under her gaze and she blinked rapidly to clear her head.

He rubbed at his wet trousers with a blanket, before casting it aside and reaching for the dry over-tunic that was being handed to him by one of his men. Next, he tugged on high leather boots and tightened the laces with sharp tugs.

The boat rocked to one side, and she clutched at the clinker-built planks to stop from sprawling at the stranger's feet.

He noticed her then, and crouched down in front of

her. His eyes washed over her in a detached assessment. It was apparent that he didn't like what he saw because he snarled out a curse. Then his hand moved like a striking snake and grabbed hold of her foot.

She kicked out with a shout of protest, flustered by the speed and heat of his touch. 'What are you d-d-d-doing?' she asked, hating how pathetic the cold made her sound.

'Checking your feet,' he said, as he tugged off her shoes and leg wrappings with frightening efficiency.

Her breath came out in a hiss at the sight of her naked feet. They were as pale as bone and there was a frighteningly blue tinge beneath her toenails. The man cursed and pulled the blanket from his own shoulders with a snap of his wrist. He shook it out and wrapped her bare feet and calves in the dry wool, swaddling them until they were wrapped under several layers.

'You should take off all your wet clothing and wrap yourself in dry blankets to avoid a chill.'

He dragged over a nearby pile of blankets and started to rub her hair vigorously with one of them as if she were a child. She felt light-headed from the rough movement as her braids unravelled in a mess around her shoulders. She'd be untangling the knots for hours.

'N-n-no,' she ground out through trembling lips.

'I have seen men lose limbs after being exposed to the sea.'

He was right, of course, and they both knew it. But she was a lone woman in a strange land, with little protection or wealth. Her clothes and jewellery identified her as a jarl's wife. They gave her power in a world ruled by men. They were her sword and her shield. And she would wield them with arrogance and pride—because if these men realised how vulnerable she truly was... Well, it didn't bear thinking about.

'Take off your cloak at least. Otherwise it will only soak the dry blankets and make you ill.'

The idea of being sick as well as destitute made her earlier resolve falter. She looked into his bright blue eyes and wondered if she could trust him. For all his gruffness and huge physique, he seemed genuinely concerned for her health.

Refusing to break eye contact, or back down in the silent battle of wills between them, he stood up and raised one eyebrow in question.

She would concede the cloak, she decided. She could already feel the wind biting into the damp cloth and it made the horrible shivering worse. She shuffled to her feet in a huff, refusing to acknowledge that he was right or had had any say in her decision. The strength of her conviction was somewhat diminished when she wobbled on her numb feet as exhaustion threatened to engulf her.

His large hand snapped out to steady her and out of habit she flinched. His hand hesitated, and then settled gently on her shoulder, steadying her with its warm strength.

She avoided his shocked expression with grim determination and began to fiddle with the bronze brooch on her cloak.

'Let me help...your fingers must be numb,' he said in a soothing tone, as if she were a spooked horse.

He reached for her brooch. The design was intricate and shaped into Odin's ravens of thought and knowledge, both of which had currently flown from her mind as his fingers brushed a welcome flame beneath her jaw.

Her shoulders relaxed as she took a shuffling step towards him, gripping the blanket around her head and shoulders, afraid of the inevitable blast of cold once the cloak was gone. He quickly undid the brooch and her blue cloak pooled at her bundled feet.

She was grateful when he quickly gathered the blankets that were draped over her closer, shielding her from the wind and the eyes of the other men.

'No one will see if you strip down to your shift,' he said, deliberately raising his chin and looking up with great interest at the seagulls weaving through the clouds.

Now that she was free of her wet cloak, the chill of the sea air was making her tremble viciously. She decided to trust the honour of this warrior, for now, and tried to unbuckle the matching brooches that held up her thick woollen gown. But her fingers were raw from the earlier rope burn, and as the wind bit into them she struggled even to grip a brooch without her hands screaming in pain.

She gave up with a sigh of frustration. 'I can't undo the brooches... My fingers...'

'Hold the blanket and I will help you.'

She took hold of the blanket's corners, her fingers brushing against his delicious warmth once again. He avoided her eyes as he bent his head to focus on the clasps. They were tiny in his hands, and he had to bend down significantly to look at them. His hot breath fanned against her neck and she had to bite her lip to stop herself from sighing.

She glanced down and embarrassment clawed up her spine. She imagined she looked terrible, and his unpleasant scowl only confirmed it. He removed each brooch with grim determination, as if he were removing a leech. It was another blow to her already tattered pride.

Gyda squared her shoulders and straightened her spine. She did not care what this man or, in fact, any man thought of her.

No man would ever break her again.

* * *

The soft panting of her breath against his face was a cruel torment. It reminded Thorstein of another type of intimacy—one he'd foregone for far too long, judging by the inappropriate thoughts racing through his head.

It had been a long time since he'd taken a woman to his bed. Since leaving the Great Army he'd spent all his days rebuilding an old Saxon village into a much larger, more prosperous settlement. He'd proved that his Overlord's faith in him had been well placed, and soon he would be rewarded with an alliance and a bride of his Overlord's choosing.

He'd been so focused on ensuring his claim was secure that he'd not noticed the passing of time.

He noticed it now.

As the gown fell to her feet he swallowed the painful knot in his throat. Her wet shift clung to her body, outlining every sweeping curve as well as the shadow of her hard nipples beneath the white linen. She was the fertility goddess Freya made flesh.

A sudden desire pulsed through his veins, its strength making his knees weak. He dragged his eyes up from her body and saw an intricate amber necklace against her collarbone. He focused on it—it was a reminder that she was not his to admire. Another symbol of her wealth and status.

There had been a time when he wouldn't have dared meet the eyes of a woman of her rank. To spite his past he stared her straight in the eye as an equal. She blinked back at him, her eyes as cool and piercing as a blade.

He pushed her brooches into her hands with more force than he'd intended, embarrassed by his sudden desire for her. He was no longer nameless and poor, he reminded himself, with a sharp inhalation of the brisk sea air.

'I am Chieftain of this settlement, Thorstein Bergson. Also known as Thorstein the Burned.'

Her eyes flickered to his burn, but as before she didn't react to the sight of the enemy symbol branded into his face. She looked away from it slowly, with a calm lack of interest, as if he'd mentioned he had dark hair or blue eyes. She observed it without pity or disgust, and for some reason that made him want to know more of her private thoughts.

'Who are you and what brings you to England?'

When she spoke her voice was commanding, despite her obvious exhaustion. 'I am Gyda Ynglingdóttir, widow of Jarl Halvorson of Njardarheimr.'

Warm interest flickered in his chest at the word 'widow' and he tried to ignore it, tried to focus. She'd said so much with very few words. 'Yngling? The royal Rus bloodline, descended from Freya?'

She shrugged. 'A distant relation—but my mother wished for my sisters and me to carry the name.'

A *very* distant relative by the sounds of it, he thought, unable to hide the twist of his lips. 'Ah, I see…'

He imagined her mother had used that distant link to the dynasty to gain her an advantageous marriage with the Jarl. She bit her lip under his knowing gaze, and then frowned into the wind, her face pale against the white of her shift.

He tugged together the sides of her blanket, covering her from his traitorous eyes. 'Sit and rest. Soon we will reach my Hall.'

She swayed slightly before sitting down, and for a moment his worry over her health returned. But she righted herself quickly and tossed her head back in a haughty gesture of defiance.

'I was travelling to Jorvik,' she said. 'Are we close?'

'Less than a day by river from my land.' He paused, thinking of how she'd said she was a widow. 'I have heard of Jarl Halvorson. He prospered well from the first raids in England.'

Thorstein did not know the man personally—he had gone Viking well before Thorstein's time in England—but Sven had spoken of him in passing. His Overlord was a distant relative to the Jarl. Gyda didn't seem moved by his praise of her husband...possibly because his greatest exploits had taken place before she was even born.

From bitter experience, Thorstein understood why a poor woman with no connections or wealth would marry a jarl. But a woman with status and beauty... Surely she could have had her choice of men?

His eyes fell on the ornate amber necklace draped around her throat. Njardarheimr was a prosperous port along the northern trading routes, and as the Jarl's wife she would have the first choice of the finest luxuries the world had to offer. Could women be so shallow? In his experience, they most definitely could. Was that why she'd left her home? To set up a new life in another trading centre, with another man?

'I've met one of your husband's sons... Ragnar. But if you are looking for him, the last I heard he was seeking glory in the battles to the south.'

Jarl Halvorson's son Ragnar was older than her, so couldn't possibly be her son. He'd met him less than a handful of times, at the gatherings of jarls. Ragnar had always struck him as a cruel and self-serving warrior, but he was handsome and rich. He supposed that mattered to most women.

'I know.' Her eyes dropped and her face was expressionless, as if she were shielding him from her thoughts.

He waited for more but she remained silent.

'Did your husband die at sea?' he asked gently, curious as to the reason why she would come to England at all.

'No, he died at home.'

The earlier flicker of warmth he'd felt doubled in size, but he ignored it and crossed his arms, leaning against the side of his boat as he looked down at her. Her face had turned a brighter, healthier colour, although he suspected by her complexion that she was normally pale, and he might need to keep an eye on her to ensure she didn't develop a fever.

'Why come to Jorvik? Why risk the journey?'

'I wished to begin a new life.'

She sighed, and he noticed that she wasn't looking at the approaching shore when she spoke, but at the broken wreck on the rocks. Her eyes were red, but whether from emotion or the sea water he couldn't tell—everything else about her was so calm.

'I have nothing now.'

He found he missed the fire she'd spat earlier...this resignation was unsettling.

He gave a dismissive snort. She would be fine. She wore expensive clothes and jewellery. She was a woman of status, with connections and beauty. She wouldn't be poor for long.

He'd known true hardship. When famine and disease had stolen his family from him. When he'd suffered under the mad bishop's twisted 'baptism of fire'. When Thora had left him, wounded and feverish, unsure if he'd even survive the night.

Losing some possessions and some silver was nothing

in comparison, and yet the way she looked at the wreck he'd have thought she'd lost all her hopes and dreams.

He looked to the horizon and was relieved to see they approached the wooden pier. He pulled his cloak tighter around him as the wind whipped against his face.

His land was always a welcome sight. He'd taken great risks to be noticed by the jarls. Some of his schemes had paid off, others not so much... He'd risen from a nameless youth in the Great Army to a warrior respected by jarls and kings.

Most men fought for glory. But owning land had always been *his* ultimate goal. And for his part in the taking of Jorvik Thorstein had been richly rewarded. The settlement was under his control.

He had gained more than he could have possibly imagined when he'd left Kattegat as a green youth with no training to go raiding in England. This was a rich and fertile land, blessed with forgiving winters and warm summers, and the sea overflowed with fish. All of it was his to reap, to nurture, and it would flourish. It would be a simple and rewarding life.

He knew his future and it did not include a spoilt, shallow beauty from his homeland—especially one who only desired jewels and luxuries. His Overlord would offer him a wife. No doubt a Saxon, related to Sven's own wife. Their alliance would be formalised through marriage, and Thorstein's land and status would be secured for ever.

Thorstein turned and looked away from her towards the approaching harbour, hating how those unshed tears had made his guts twist. He had no need to feel guilty. He had saved her life—it was not his responsibility to look after her future as well.

A person had to look after their own fate.

He cleared his throat loudly and replied, 'Life is full of disappointments.'

Chapter Three

As they moored at the harbour, Gyda saw that several women and children waited with clasped hands and lined, searching faces. As soon as they were assured of their loved ones' safety they went quickly to work, helping the survivors into the warmth of the Great Hall.

Their rescue had not come without its own risk. It was a sobering thought. If Thorstein had not sailed to their aid they would have died out there, of that Gyda was certain.

Her body still shivered, her hands ached and her toes were burning something fierce. She took several deep breaths hoping she could summon enough strength to walk. She stooped down to unwrap the blanket from around her legs to free them, but her hands stilled as Thorstein growled in her ear.

'Leave it. I will carry you.'

She thought about protesting against his offer but, feeling the warmth of his arms as they wrapped around her body and scooped her up, she didn't have the strength to deny him even if she'd wanted to.

He cradled her body against his chest and jumped down on to the pier as if she weighed no more than a bag of feathers. A gust of frigid wind whipped across her face, blowing the blanket from around her head. Unconsciously she tucked her head beneath his chin, to shelter herself from the worst of the sting. She smelt the salt of the sea mixed with a rich, earthy musk on his skin. Free from its braids, her mess of hair swept against his face.

His arms tightened around her and he stumbled a few steps. She clutched the fabric of his over-tunic and the cloth bunched in her fingers, revealing glimpses of his tattooed chest beneath.

'I'm sure I can walk to the Hall by myself,' she whispered, breathless and embarrassed by how awkward he must find carrying her long body. There was no doubt that was why he'd stumbled. Making jests about her height had been one of Halvor's favourite pastimes.

She looked up through her lashes and was surprised to see his face was flushed.

'I'm fine. I misjudged my step, that is all.' He strode towards the Hall with his eyes set firmly ahead.

She glanced around at his settlement as they made their way through it. It was large, with several longhouses and outbuildings surrounding the Great Hall. There was evidence of both fishing and farming wherever she looked, and the people seemed happy and healthy.

It would be a nice place to bring up a family.

Her stomach tightened at the thought.

She wished she had been raised somewhere like this instead of at her ambitious father's court. Maybe then she would have been married to a young, strong farmer like Thorstein instead of a man three times her age. Now she had nothing—not even her silver or her tapestries with which to make a living.

She would have to throw herself on the mercy of her brother-in-law. Dependent on another man's whims, again.

The Hall was newly built, the colour of the timber golden and fresh. There were no decorations or tapestries anywhere—the place was almost austere in its lack of home comforts—but it was large and well planned, with a central firepit that ran down the length of the room.

Either side of the communal space were the usual interior rooms for storage, and judging by the pleasantly fresh smell of the Hall it looked as if the animals were kept in another building. Each interior room had double doors to keep out the draught, but they were low enough to let in the morning light from the large smoke hole above. In fact, the amount of light was a welcome surprise. At the back of the Hall there was a display of weapons on two more double doors, which she presumed marked the entrance to the Chieftain's rooms.

It was a beautiful longhouse. In her mind, she was filling the walls with her own tapestries. Placing *The Stag* here and *The Bear* there. A wave of nausea hit her as she realised that she would never see those tapestries again, let alone hang them in a fine Hall such as this.

'I imagine we are a poor offering compared to the luxury you're used to,' said Thorstein, his mouth twisted in a bitter line.

She opened her mouth to speak, but nothing came out. What could she say to him that wouldn't sound insincere? The truth was that his Hall *was* simple compared to Halvor's home. It did not have the finest furs, the most ornate carvings—or any carvings at all, for that matter. There were no tapestries nor treasures that she could see. But it was still beautiful in its practical simplicity.

How could she tell him that she would be glad of a home like this? That she would happily live in a cave if it meant she no longer had to live with a man who hated her?

She closed her mouth, gave a shrug of indifference and avoided his eyes. She heard him click his tongue in irritation, but stubbornly refused to respond. Better to appear rude than weak. She had to remind this man of her status. Her connections. Without her wealth, she was vulnerable.

He deposited her on one of the benches beside the fire and then walked briskly out of his Hall without a backward glance.

The following hour passed in a frenzy of activity as the women of the settlement fed and clothed the survivors of the storm.

After a bowl of restorative broth, Gyda was ushered into Thorstein's private sleeping area to change.

'You're very tall… I doubt we'll have anything to fit you properly,' said one of the women as she lifted Gyda's shift up and over her head. 'But we can wash your clothing whilst you rest and return it straight away. I've picked up your gown and cloak from the longship and they are already being washed as we speak.'

'Thank you,' Gyda said, swaying on her feet.

Exhaustion had her firmly in its grip now, and her head was swimming with fog. At least she was finally warm again, and her toes had thankfully returned to their normal colour.

'Come, lie down, mistress,' said the woman called Elga, who'd taken charge of helping the survivors.

Gyda guessed by her name that she was Saxon, although she spoke Norse with only a slight accent.

Elga helped her dress in a shift and a coarse wool gown. It was too large at the waist and too short in the leg, but it was warm and well made. Then she led her towards a gigantic bed, simply carved and surrounded by wood on three sides to keep out the chill.

'But this is Chief Thorstein's bed! I can't sleep here.'

It was a weak protest, and her body swayed even as she stared longingly into the sleeping box, with its piles of furs and soft woollen blankets. It did look cosy and inviting…

'Thorstein has no need for it now. He's out salvaging what he can of your wreck.'

'He is?' Bright hope lit within her, but she saw the villager's eyes soften with pity.

'I would not hope for much, if I were you. The sea and the rocks will have taken most of it by now.'

Elga nudged her towards the bed and Gyda climbed in and lay down. It truly was huge and, even as tall as she was, there was plenty of room to stretch out and still not reach the sides. It was definitely a bed built for two, although she'd not been introduced to any wife as yet.

Elga tucked her in as if she were a child—an oddly soothing gesture that reminded Gyda of when she'd used to tuck in her own sisters, long ago.

Elga was plain, but she had strikingly large brown eyes and pretty freckles across her nose. Her rich chestnut curls were barely concealed by a cap. Her clothes were not that of a chieftain's wife, but then again, maybe Thorstein did not see the need to dress his wife in fine clothes. His own were simple and functional.

'Are you his lady?' she asked.

Elga shook her head with a laugh. 'Our Chief is not married.' She paused, and then dipped her head in a conspiratorial way. 'He was married once, but that was a long time ago…before he settled here.'

'She died?' Pity washed through her. She could understand such loss. So many women died too young, most of them during or after childbirth, like her sisters.

'She was like you—a Norse woman. They divorced.'

Elga said this in a hushed tone which caused Gyda to smile. She knew Saxons were not allowed to divorce as easily as the Norse. Divorce in Norse culture was as easy as declaring their marriage dissolved in public and living apart for more than six nights. Halvor had threatened it often enough, but he would have had to admit his own shame as well as hers.

'Get some rest, my lady. I'll bring your clothes back as good as new.'

The room darkened as Elga left and closed the door, and the small firepit in the corner flickered its light across the polished furniture. Gyda sank into the furs with a contented sigh. The mattress was thick and comfortable, and it smelt of aromatic herbs and fresh straw.

Thorstein might not dress in impressive clothes, but he certainly indulged in other luxuries… The thought amused her, and she fell asleep with a smile on her face.

Thorstein stared at the sleeping figure of Gyda curled up in his bed. Blonde hair flowed over the pillows and the furs. She shone like a pearl in the fading glow of the fire and stole the breath from his lungs. Her milky white hands rested beneath her flushed cheeks, and there was a half-smile on her pink lips as she slept.

She was beautiful, it was true. But her pale skin would burn in the summer sun, and her long, elegant hands had never worked the earth, or perhaps even a day in their life!

She did not belong here.

She slept deeply and hadn't even flinched when he'd walked into the room. Her breath was shallow and even.

Before he did something stupid—like take a step closer and run his fingers down the curves of her side—he made a deep coughing sound to clear his throat.

It was not entirely a ruse to wake her. His throat was dry and painfully tight from the sight of her lying in his bed.

Gyda's eyes flickered and then opened. They adjusted to the gloom and then, as she focused on him, her body stiffened. He turned the burned side of his face away from her, so as not to startle her further, using the excuse of stoking the fire.

'It is almost time for the evening meal,' he said.

When he glanced back, he was almost sorry to have woken her as he saw the look of horror on her face.

'*Nattmal?* Already? Have I really slept the whole day?'

'You have had an ordeal. It is to be expected.'

It was a reminder to himself as much as it was to her. She had nearly died. Twice. Three times if he counted her half drowning in the sea. She'd said she'd lost everything, but she wasn't weeping or panicking, and he was grateful for that. He never knew what to do when a woman cried. Gyda was brave, strong-willed, and not intimidated by him in the slightest. There was a lot to admire in her character.

'Did you find my silver?' she asked eagerly as she sat up, the furs flowing down to her lap. 'Elga said you'd gone back to search the rocks.'

He sighed. There it was—the shallowness that reminded him of Thora. Of course she would be asking for her silver.

'We didn't find your silver. Just…bodies.'

'Oh. I'm sorry… I didn't think,' she whispered, her face flaming as she lowered her eyes.

He looked away, poking the fire until sparks flew, not

daring to look back at her or enjoy the enticing way she looked, half dazed in his bed.

'Your longship's helmsman, Orm, wishes to go hunting tomorrow. To help fill our larders in thanks. Then he plans to travel north.' He tried to curb the bitterness in his tone as he said the word 'thanks'. She had still not thanked him.

'To Jorvik,' she said with a decisive nod of her head, as if the destination were obvious.

'No, to his brother's farm... What are your plans?' he asked casually.

There was silence for a long time, and when he risked a glance he was struck by how lost she looked.

She blinked up at him, the vulnerability quickly replaced with outrage. 'I *paid* him to take me to Jorvik! I have nothing but the clothes on my back. He has a duty to take me to my kin.'

He had said as much himself, but Orm had spat a curse on the floor and called her a cold-hearted bitch he should have sacrificed to the sea when he'd had the chance. He'd then gone on to laugh at her expense, making jokes about her husband dying of frostbite and not old age.

'He believes he has delivered you as close to Jorvik as he is able. He has lost his ship and half of his crew.'

'He has no honour!'

They agreed on that, at least.

Thorstein huffed, reaching for the fire poker, but then he hesitated. If he stoked the fire any more the room would be unbearably hot, and the air was already uncomfortably close. He shifted from foot to foot and eventually crossed his arms over his chest and leaned back against the door.

'I will speak with him,' she said.

She rose from his bed and pulled on an ill-fitting

brown gown that looked like a sack on her elegant frame. Even without her fine clothes she was a rare beauty, and she moved with the confidence and grace of a queen.

'Do you have family in Jorvik? Any protection?' he asked.

Her hands stilled on the woven belt she'd pinched tightly at her waist. Her blue-grey eyes were an icy storm of brittle defiance. 'I have connections…a brother-in-law. Sven Leifson. He's one of King Guthrum's men and one of the city's leaders. He will look after me. At least until I can make other arrangements…'

She faltered at her last words, as if she were unsure what to do, and the sudden doubt in her eyes made him shift uncomfortably.

He sighed, levering himself away from the door. Now he was certain of what he had to do.

'I know Sven Leifson,' he said, and noticed how her face fell at his words.

'You do?' she asked, already masking her surprise with a quick tug on her already tight belt.

'His current wife is a Saxon. Was your sister his first wife or his second?'

She brushed the invisible creases from her gown with a flick of her wrist. 'His first. My sister Astrid died giving birth to their son.'

'I see. He has seven children now. All of them boys.'

'I shall be sure to congratulate him when I see him.'

Her voice was clipped and sharp. He wondered if she was angry that Sven was married or if she disapproved of him taking a Saxon wife.

'What is your connection with Sven?' she asked.

'He is my Overlord.'

Her eyes widened and she stepped closer with apparent

interest. Like a dumb ox he lumbered on, hating himself for feeling the need to justify his connection.

'We fought together in the taking of Jorvik. King Guthrum has been dealing with much discontent since his treaty with King Alfred. I imagine Sven is...busy.'

He thought it best to prepare her. He doubted the pragmatic Sven would have time for his dead wife's sister. Whatever had possessed her to leave the safety of her home and travel to Jorvik? Unless she thought to marry Sven?

The thought hit him like an axe to the head.

Sven wasn't much older than him and was still strong. Marrying an older man had not bothered her in the past. Did she imagine Sven would cast his wife aside for her?

Sven was wealthy and powerful...the type of man who could provide for a woman like her. Unlike him, who could only work the land for his reward.

Thora had wanted wealth, and no matter how much land he'd won, it had never been enough. She'd left him for a rich jarl.

He saw Gyda's hand stray to her amber necklace, her long, elegant fingers stroking the stones thoughtfully as they flashed in the firelight and she stared into the flames.

'I will need an escort to reach Jorvik safely.'

He stared at her fingers as they stroked her pale collarbone and wondered what she would do if he kissed her. No doubt she would slap him for daring to touch her and demand his hand be cut off in payment. Judging from her earlier disdain, she obviously considered herself above him and his settlement.

She blushed when she caught him staring and her hand dropped to her side. 'I could pay you.'

She was closer now. He could reach her within a couple of steps if he wanted to.

His knees locked and he forced himself to remain still. He tried to keep his voice casual, although it sounded husky to his own ears. 'No need to pay me. I must travel to Jorvik anyway. You may as well join me.'

Her entire face lit up, as if he had offered her his weight in gold. 'I am in your debt, Chief Thorstein.'

She closed the gap between them, then reached out and touched his forearm. It was the lightest of touches, but coupled with the brightness of her smile it was breathtaking. Her eyes sparkled like snowflakes in the sunshine, leaving him dazzled.

The spell was quickly broken, however, when she added, 'I'm sure Sven will compensate you well for your service.'

He wasn't her true target.

Dark clouds gathered in his mind and jealousy writhed within his stomach like a serpent. It was Sven she wanted, not him, and she was obviously a woman used to manipulating men to get what she wanted.

He shrugged away her touch as he turned away and opened the door. 'We have no need for court manners here. I am Thorstein.'

He would ignore her now, and eat and drink until she retired—no doubt without even asking his permission to use his bed again, as she'd done earlier that day. Such a woman could not be trusted, and yet he wanted her. More so since she'd given him that bright smile and gentle touch. But he was mad even to imagine that there was any true feeling behind it.

Maybe he should have kissed her? At least then her

inevitable rejection would have put this strange desire to rest.

How could he want her? She'd still not even thanked him for saving her life.

Chapter Four

Gyda sat beside Thorstein in silence throughout the meal. She'd given up talking after her attempts at light conversation had led nowhere.

Benches had been dragged out for *nattmal*. The Hall heaved merrily with conversation and people. Children ran between the tables, making their mothers curse as they struggled to balance platters of meat and piles of bread, or ladle steaming stew from the cauldrons above the fire into bowls. The men laughed, drank ale and talked amongst themselves, sharing stories with mutual acquaintances, occasionally ruffling an errant child's hair as it passed.

He ate relentlessly, only speaking to her if he wanted her to pass the bread or the jug of mead. She didn't mind. At least she had an escort to Jorvik now. One she trusted far more than her previous choice.

What did it matter if he didn't like her? Once she was under Sven's protection she needn't worry about Thorstein or his lack of manners ever again.

Nattmal lumbered to an end and the shipwrecked crew began to settle on piles of blankets around the Hall. The light faded, and Gyda could see the stars through the smoke hole. It was quieter now, with the last few conversations disappearing with the twilight into the gloom.

She stroked the amber necklace at her throat and wondered where she was going to sleep.

Orm was giving her bitter looks that unsettled her. She knew he blamed her for the shipwreck because she'd refused to sacrifice her necklace to the sea gods. She'd reasoned at the time that the gods had already received several sea chests full of her beautiful tapestries—what difference would one necklace make?

It had been a bridal gift from her husband. He'd given her many gifts over the years, but nothing ever as fine as this. Those other tokens had been given not out of love, but because they reinforced his own status, power and wealth. She'd accepted them all gladly, knowing that when the time came she would receive little from his family for her future. After all, she was his third wife, and childless.

She sighed. Her thoughts were taking a dark turn and she didn't have the strength to face them. She wanted to go to bed. But would Thorstein offer his bed again, or would she be forced to settle with the others around the Hall?

She would have to wait and see.

She sat with a painfully rigid back, refusing to show weakness by slumping. She was a woman of status—it was what had kept her safe before and it would do so again.

She glanced at Thorstein, who had finished yet another large portion of stew. He was handsome except for the large crucifix burned into his cheek. Its significance was not lost on her. He must have been captured and tortured by a Christian enemy at some point.

She knew many warriors who would find the enemy's

religious symbol branded onto their skin shameful. But this man hadn't grown a thick beard to cover his scars— instead, he wore them openly. It struck her as honest and brave, and she admired those qualities.

But, despite his kind offer of escorting her to Jorvik without payment, he'd somehow turned cold towards her. Ignoring her for the entirety of the meal as if she'd offended him in some way. She was particularly confused that he'd not yet offered her his private rooms again.

Soon they were the only two people left at the table. Everyone else had gone to find a bed at the sides of the Hall.

'Are you not tired?'

His husky voice startled her and she paused before answering, tasting the words in her mind to see if they were palatable.

'May I sleep in your rooms?' The question felt bitter on her tongue.

A satisfied smile spread across his face and he leaned forward, as if to get a better look at her in the dying light of the fire.

'Are you offering to join me in my bed?'

'Of course not!'

He laughed again, the sound rumbling like distant thunder, and it caused shivers to run down her spine.

'Well, at least you asked my permission this time.'

Her cheeks heated at his words. 'Elga said you would not mind.'

His eyes flashed with surprise and then softened. 'She was right. I was only teasing you… You may sleep in my bed until we travel to Jorvik.'

She frowned. She did not like to be teased. It was cruel and unnecessary, and sometimes it led to terrible things.

'Alone?' she asked.

'Of course.' His look was one the trickster god Loki would have been proud of. 'Although…'

He paused, and it took all her pride not to lean forward and demand him to release her from the torment. He was taking his time to reply. *Beast!* He sighed deeply with feigned regret, and there was a mischievous glint in his eye that set her teeth on edge.

'I will require something in return,' he said at last.

Her hand flew to her necklace. 'But you said you didn't require any payment to take me to Jorvik!'

'And I don't. But the use of a man's bed…that is another matter entirely.'

His face was suddenly grim, all previous humour gone. He had her in his trap and her chest tightened painfully under his predatory gaze as it lowered to the necklace resting against her collarbone.

It was a pity, but she doubted it would be the first sacrifice she would have to make if her brother-in-law did not take pity on her…

She gritted her teeth and pushed the dark thought out of her mind. She lifted the necklace from her collar.

'That is not what I want.' His voice cut through the air like a blade.

'What *do* you want, then?' Her whisper was barely audible above the crackling fire.

'You must know what I want.' He sighed as he looked at her lips.

She frowned, her hands frozen at her throat. It was as if he were weaving a magic spell on her. Her limbs tingled and her breath felt heavy.

He leaned forward and rested his hand on his cheek, the scarred side of his face hidden from view. He looked devastating. But if anything she preferred to see his scars. It reminded her that he was only a man.

He was close to her now—so close that his breath caressed her skin and caused her to shiver.

'You might consider it a high price, but it's one that even a beggar can pay,' he said, in a voice so low she wondered if she'd heard him correctly.

She could think of only one thing both she and a beggar could give a man freely.

A kiss.

She stared into his face and told herself there was no truth to his words.

And yet she found herself leaning towards him... Or was he leaning towards her? She couldn't tell any more.

He smiled lazily. 'It will only take a moment, and it will cost you nothing but your pride. But if you insist... I could take your necklace as payment. Your choice.'

Despite his words, there was a teasing quirk to his smile. There was no real payment to be made, only an offer. One she wasn't sure she dared to take.

The silence between them grew thick with possibility. A fire sparked within her chest and she felt both angry and excited at the same time. She wanted to defy him so badly...to press her lips against his smug smile. Dare to do the unexpected.

She stared at his mouth, her heart thumping wildly in her chest. Did she dare?

She heard the taunts of Halvor in her mind. How he'd called her 'cold' and 'passionless'. But she had not always been so brittle. Her marriage had beaten and tempered her like a blade in the fire.

'The gods love brave women,' Astrid's sweet voice whispered inside her.

She lurched forward, driven by the need to defy all the men who'd tormented her in the past. She *wasn't* cold and unfeeling. Here was a man who wanted to kiss her—a young, virile warrior. Maybe he could make her feel what her husband had not?

She grabbed his face with both hands for balance and then pressed her mouth against his, almost bruising her lips with the clumsy force of it.

Thorstein, surprised by her sudden decision, rocked backwards and had to brace himself against the bench so they wouldn't fall in a heap on the rushes.

She stared into his wide eyes as both pleasure and triumph made her light-headed. His lips were firm and plump beneath her mouth, and she closed her eyes as she pressed her breasts against the hard muscles of his chest. The sensation was delicious, and she wondered if she would melt in a puddle at his feet. *This* was what she imagined when she'd heard her sisters giggling about the marriage bed.

She opened her mouth, gasping for air, and he pressed forward, wrapping his arms around her waist and pulling her close, his own breathing shallow and fast. Their lips touched again, more softly than before, and she felt the wet heat of his tongue slide against her own. It was gentle and sensual—nothing like the kisses she'd endured before.

She pulled away, her body aching. Her lips tingled with a longing to return to him. It had been the most perfect kiss.

And then he ruined everything by opening his mouth to speak. 'I only wanted a thank-you.'

Her world tilted and she felt sick. 'What? You said… But…' She squirmed like an eel on the end of his mocking hook. Blood drained from her face, leaving her cheeks numb with cold.

'What an eventful night. A kiss from a queen! I suppose it's a thank-you of sorts…' He laughed.

Bitter memories rose like ravenous beasts in her mind. *'You will all be queen of your lovers' hearts.'* She blinked, forcing down the twisted words of the Oracle who'd made a cruel mockery of her sisters' dreams.

'I'm not a queen,' she retorted, her voice brittle.

It was not only embarrassment that she felt, but fear as well. She'd played a game with a handsome man and lost—again. She was a terrible judge of character. She saw deceit in good men and love in bad ones. When would she ever learn?

'Really? You act like one,' he said mildly, although his eyes were still as hot as fire.

She scowled at him, felt her spine stiffening even further—which she had thought impossible until now. She jumped to her feet, almost toppling the table in her haste and causing the remains of *nattmal* to wobble and shake.

She stilled it with a firm slap of her palms against the wood. The pain made her flinch, but she welcomed it. She stared down at a bemused Thorstein, who looked as if he'd been dropped from a great height. She raised her chin and drew up her invisible shield, pretending indifference when in truth she was shaken to the core.

'Goodnight, Thorstein.'

Odin's teeth! What had he done to summon her wrath now?

She strode away like a shieldmaiden going into battle. Fearless, powerful and utterly unattainable.

It wasn't his fault she'd presumed the worst about him. He'd only wanted a thank-you—something anyone would have given to a man who'd saved her life!

She'd got her way, and yet she was still unsatisfied.

As was he.

He took several deep breaths to calm his blood and shifted awkwardly on the bench. Her kiss had been clumsy and heated—the sort of kiss he would have stolen from a maiden back when he'd been young and enthusiastic, when his face and his heart had been unmarked by war and betrayal.

He'd never known a woman who melted with desire one moment and then snapped into frozen steel within the blink of an eye. Had she really taken such offence at being described as a queen? Or had it been embarrassment after realising how low she'd stooped by kissing him, the chieftain of a small settlement, a man with no family name or wealthy kin?

As the wife of a powerful jarl she'd been only one step away from being a queen. It must have hurt her pride to be forced to beg for a bed. How bitterly she must have felt that humiliation.

He smiled, sensing for the first time that Gyda was not as cold beneath the surface as she appeared. She would be a challenging wife. A man would never know what to expect from one day to the next. It would be both maddening and thrilling.

A movement caught his eye and he realised Orm was grinning at him from his pile of furs. Then the helmsman snorted with derision and rolled over.

The hairs on Thorstein's neck bristled, and he searched the dim light for any others who might have seen him behaving like a lovesick pup. If Magnus heard about it he'd never hear the end of it. To his relief, no one else appeared awake. The Hall had settled down into a quiet chorus of snores and snorts.

He stood with a lurch and went over to the box of blankets and furs that had been brought out for their guests.

There was only one thin blanket left, the better ones having been taken long before his conversation with Gyda.

He picked it up with a huff and walked towards an empty bench that had been pressed up against the wall. He lay down, his feet dangling over the end.

He could have slept on the floor, but the rushes were filthy from the feast and he didn't want to wake with a rat nibbling his nose. He'd slept in worse conditions over the years. During his youth in the Great Army he'd endured nights out in the open with only his shield as cover from the elements.

He pulled the blanket up to his neck and tried to ignore the discomfort.

Had he really become so pampered?

The thought made him more uncomfortable than the bench.

Gyda would be horrified if she knew his roots. His parents had died when he was young, leaving him to be cared for by his uncle. He'd been a good man, but a simple farmer, with his own hungry mouths to feed.

When Thorstein had set sail from Kattegat he'd kissed his aunt's and his uncle's hands and thanked them for their kindness, but he'd not looked back as his boat had set sail. There had been nothing for him there, and he'd known even then that he would never return to his homeland, though he'd had nothing more than hope and the naive confidence of youth.

Now he wondered how he'd survived those first years. No doubt the fear of failure had kept death from taking him on the battlefield. He'd wanted land, security, the home and the family he'd never fully experienced for himself. If he earned honour, silver and glory along the way, then he'd consider himself lucky.

Then he'd met Thora. Beautiful Thora. The daughter of a camp follower and a thrall. She'd had ambitions too, but he'd realised too late that hers were not the same as his.

He had known that she took the herbs her mother used to prevent children. He'd thought it wise—they'd barely had enough to feed and clothe themselves, let alone a child. But then she'd confessed that she never wanted children at all. He should have believed her. Instead he'd thought she would change her mind in time. When he'd secured enough wealth for their future.

She'd pushed him to take greater risks, to challenge other men, and he'd done it, desperate to please the woman he loved. She'd appealed to his pride and manipulated him. He'd thought it was to build their future, but she'd always shrugged when he'd mentioned farming the land as his ultimate goal.

'Let us see where fate takes us,' she'd always said, her eyes never quite meeting his.

Fate had taken her to a rich jarl's bed, and he'd realised that he'd only been a stepping stone towards a greater ambition.

Who could blame her? The daughter of a thrall, she'd had even less than him. Marriage had given her respectability and freedom.

He didn't blame her—not really—but he would never make the same mistake again.

Now the fates had been kind to them both. Thora had left the life she'd despised and he'd learnt to guard his heart against manipulative, ambitious women.

He was as much to blame as she.

A wife should be picked like land. A pretty meadow meant nothing. You had to dig deep to check if the land was fertile or filled with rocks.

He needed a woman used to hard work and life in a

simple settlement. She'd be attractive, if possible, but that wasn't vital. She would have to want children most of all. She didn't need to have the stunning beauty of Gyda, for example, she just needed to be kind and loyal.

'Sounds like a damn dog,' he muttered quietly to himself, shifting awkwardly on the bench until he almost fell off.

He cursed loudly and pressed his back closer to the cool wall. It appeared he needed to think more about his requirements.

He had land, he had status, and when he had them his children would be valued and loved. They would have warm, soft beds that smelt of spring and a loving mother who kissed their hair and told them sagas as they drifted off to sleep. They wouldn't feel like a burden and they would always have a home, no matter how far away they travelled.

He was so close to living his dream. To the future he'd planned on those miserable nights beneath his shield in the rain. He just needed the right woman.

It took Thorstein a long time to fall asleep. He kept listing his new wife's requirements—a good cook, a homemaker, maternal, hardworking…

The list went on and on until his eyelids grew heavy.

Then he dreamt of silver-blue eyes and hair as soft as a feather stroking across his cheek.

Chapter Five

Gyda watched the sunrise filter in around the door frame of Thorstein's chambers. The milky light slowly turned brighter as the occupants of the Hall rose and began to prepare for the day. She planned to avoid Thorstein, especially after the misunderstanding and the searing kiss of last night.

He'd only wanted a thank-you.

The embarrassment burned her face all over again and she groaned into her pillow. She couldn't bring herself to leave the aromatic warmth of his furs. To see his knowing smile. Why was she always such an awkward idiot in front of handsome men?

Gyda thumped the pillow hard, until feathers flew and her breath was laboured. Exhausted, she slumped onto her back and forced her clenched fingers to slowly relax.

Pretend nothing had happened—that was the best course of action. She couldn't control how he treated her, but she could hide her own feelings easily enough. Retreat behind her cool and pragmatic facade. There she would be safe, even from herself.

A big sigh escaped her.

Despite the comfortable bed, she'd spent most of the

night restlessly tossing and turning. So many worries had crowded her thoughts and threatened to overwhelm her. Her meeting with Sven…her future…not to mention Thorstein's opinion of her.

She groaned at the memory of his mocking jibe. He'd teased her by calling her 'a queen', mocked the very manner that had kept her heart safe all these years. And all after giving her a kiss that had made her heart leap and her toes curl.

She felt as if she'd never been kissed until last night. Maybe she hadn't—not really.

The thought made her heart sink.

She threw aside the covers. She was no victim, and her pride wouldn't allow her to remain in bed all day, ashamed of herself. She refused to be ashamed of herself.

She rose and dressed quickly in the same ill-fitting gown she'd been provided with the day before. Better to save her own gown for when she travelled to meet Sven, she decided. She washed in the basin of water provided, and braided her hair in a long rope down her back. There was no polished plate to look in, to check her appearance, but she felt stronger and more confident. She had faced worse men and lived. A calm and confident attitude had got her through many awkward moments.

As she walked into the Hall her eyes immediately sought out Thorstein. He was in the centre of a group, standing with a mixture of his own people and the crew from the shipwreck. His eyes locked on hers and her step faltered for a moment. Only when his eyes moved away was she able to breathe again. He'd clearly chosen to ignore her for the time being and she could live with that—in fact she was grateful for it.

She walked towards the fire to see what was on offer

for *dagmal*. Elga stood there, stirring a pot over the low flames.

'There's still some stew and bread left,' Elga said as she handed her a bowl and a spoon.

'Do you have any porridge?' asked Gyda.

'Of course—over there.' Elga pointed towards a group of children and mothers at the opposite end of the firepit.

Gyda walked over to the pot beside them and ladled a portion of thick, creamy oats into her bowl. Then she settled down with the children and began to eat.

'Don't you like fruit, lady?' asked a small girl beside her with a cap of blonde curls. She must have only seen five or six winters.

'Oh, I didn't see any.'

'I know where the fruit is!' cried the little girl, putting down her bowl with a thump and running off to a sack on the other side of the fire that Gyda hadn't spotted until now.

'Using a child as your own personal slave?'

Thorstein's sardonic voice rolled across her senses like thunder, prickling her skin and making her shiver as if against an approaching storm. She turned slowly to face him, and had to crane her neck to meet his accusing glare.

'Must you always think the worst of me?'

'Prove me wrong, then.'

'She's just helping me.'

She turned away from him, her head down, unable to meet his eyes. She had not behaved well since she'd met Thorstein. Although it had not been her intention, she had put him in danger on the wreck…and then she'd kissed him as payment when all he'd wanted was a thank-you.

She watched as the little girl rummaged around in the sack for a moment, then pulled out a heaped ladle of dried fruits and berries that gleamed like jewels. Taking great care, the child walked back to her, dropping about half of the ladle's contents on the rushes.

'What are you doing with that, Frida?' asked a flaxen-haired woman who was feeding a baby at her breast.

The woman looked tired and at the edge of her patience. At least Gyda didn't have children keeping her up all night. Although for some reason that didn't comfort her…

'It's for the lady!'

She caught the exasperated eyes of the child's mother and gave her a knowing smile; she'd seen similarly frayed mothers over the years. 'Frida is helping me with my *dagmal*. Don't worry—feed your baby. We'll be fine.'

The woman relaxed and gave her a grateful nod. 'Thank you, mistress.'

Frida eventually reached her and tipped the ladle into Gyda's bowl. Even after she'd dropped so much on the rushes, her bowl overflowed with fruit.

'Oh! That's a lot!' said Frida, her eyes wide.

The bench creaked as Thorstein settled in the seat beside her.

'I'll help her eat it,' he said, and to Gyda's horror he reached into her bowl and grabbed a fistful of fruit. He threw some into his mouth with a smile, before adding, with his mouth full, 'You should return the ladle to the sack so the next person can use it, Frida.'

Frida nodded, and dutifully ran back to the sack to replace the ladle.

Gyda looked at the child's bowl beside her. There was still a lot of porridge in there, but not much fruit, so she placed some of her own into the bowl.

'Don't give her too much. She'll never eat all her porridge and then she'll moan to everyone she's hungry later,' he said, although he seemed more amused by the prospect than irritated.

'My sister Astrid used to do the same.' Gyda smiled at the memory, but then her stomach tightened. 'I told you she was Sven's wife. Have you met her son Ivar...? My nephew? He must only be a few years older than Frida...'

She'd never met Ivar, but she was going to see him soon. A sadness tightened in her chest as she realised how much time had passed her by.

'No... He must be older than that... He must have seen eleven, maybe twelve winters?'

'Yes,' he said, taking a moment to assess her. 'He looks a lot like you.'

His eyes continued to caress her hair, her eyes, her lips, until she felt hot under his inspection. 'Astrid was my twin.'

His eyes narrowed. 'I see. That's why you're so keen to meet with Sven.'

The bitterness of his tone was like a slap in the face. 'I have no other kin. Where else am I supposed to go?'

He scoffed at her words and her shock turned to anger.

'What woman hurt you so much that you must curse me with her shadow?'

It was only meant to be a salty swipe at him, but she knew the second it hit home. His face paled and his body tensed. But he didn't bellow or strike out, as Halvor might have done.

'My first wife,' he answered.

His voice was quiet, savage, and for some reason that only made her feel worse.

She swallowed down her guilt, but it stuck in her throat. 'I didn't mean... I'm—'

Frida returned and sat on the bench beside her. 'Oh!

Thank you, lady!' she exclaimed at the sight of the berries in her bowl.

'You're welcome… Be sure to eat all of your porridge as well, though.'

The child gave a bobbing nod as she licked her lips. 'Yes, mistress.'

Gyda dared to look at Thorstein, but he'd risen to talk to a group of men who were passing. They appeared to be preparing for a hunt. They were armed with spears, bows and knives. It was then that she noticed Thorstein had several blades strapped to his hips, including a lethal axe strapped to his back.

No doubt they would be gone for most of the day, which suited her. Although she wished she'd not angered him, and instead had asked when they would be leaving for Jorvik.

Why could she not be sensible around him?

Maybe she should go and speak to him before he left? Clear the air between them?

They seemed constantly at war with each other and she couldn't understand why. She was certain the kiss had affected her far more than him, which explained why she was so brittle with him. In contrast, she'd probably only surprised him with her…enthusiasm. He'd not even mentioned it, so it couldn't matter to him at all.

She felt a little nauseous and looked down to stir her porridge again, unsure if she could take another bite.

'Are you from the north?'

Frida's chatter was a welcome distraction and she turned towards her on the bench to listen better.

'My father is from the north,' Frida went on. 'He says it's beautiful…with big mountains surrounded by the sea called forges. And there's always snow on some of the mountains—even in summer!'

'Fjords,' she corrected softly.

'Fy-orges,' Frida repeated, with an adorable frown of concentration.

'Close enough.' Gyda laughed. 'Yes, I'm from the north—from Viken.'

'Do you miss it? Father says it's a very beautiful place. But he doesn't think he'll see it again.'

The question startled her. Throughout her long, miserable marriage she'd been focused purely on planning her eventual independence. Running the port well, increasing her wealth and working on her craft. Dreaming of a new life, free from the cruelties of angry men. She'd not taken the time to think about what she would lose. Her homeland.

'It is beautiful…'

'*Your eyes are like the fjords in winter.*' The memory of those words from her distant past made her stiffen.

'But it's beautiful in a cold and harsh way. The land is unforgiving when the harvest is poor.'

No, she would not miss it. She missed her sisters—but she'd lost them long before she'd set sail to Northumbria.

'Father says there are giants, trolls, wood elves, dwarfs and all sorts of creatures that live in the fy-orges. Have you ever seen any of them?'

'No, but I have heard many tales about them from my mother.'

'I like stories.'

'So do I. Maybe I can tell you some before I leave?'

'Oh, yes, please!'

Thorstein and his party of hunters were making their way out of the Hall. She wondered if he would pass her without speaking, but then he caught her looking and stopped.

'We will travel to Jorvik at dawn tomorrow. Be ready early. No lying in my bed all morning.'

'I'll be ready,' she replied sharply.

Did he consider her lazy because she'd woken later than his villagers, his hunting party? What difference did it make? The man seemed to find fault with her no matter what she did. What was the point in arguing?

'Good.' He swung his bow over his shoulder and gave her a grunt of acknowledgement as he walked past. But then he paused and turned back towards her. 'Ask Elga for anything you need,' he said.

Then he was gone, sweeping out of the Hall before she could open her mouth to reply.

What had possessed her to kiss him? Men were all the same, even the ones who gave perfect kisses. They cared for nothing and only used a woman for their own pleasure or gain. No matter what promises or kindness they appeared to give, they would be forgotten by the light of dawn.

She stayed for a while with Frida, telling her the tale of when Thor had a competition with a giant, over who could eat and drink the most. Afterwards, she sought out Elga and asked for some sewing supplies. She'd decided to use her free time to embroider a belt for Frida as a parting gift. The child was curious and sweet. She reminded her of her youth.

With her basket of tools and her thick blue cloak, she walked down to the wooden pier and settled herself on a blanket to sew in the sunshine. It was summer, and the days here were bright and fresh, perfect for the intricate work of embroidery.

As always, she sat alone, letting the work and the lapping of the waves soothe her nerves. She could see the settlement from where she sat, and the productive work of Thorstein's people as they tended fields and animals. There was even smoke from a forge, billowing in the cloudless sky.

She couldn't help but admire the hard work that must have gone into building this community. There were no politics here, and everyone appeared to be working towards the common good, rather than for personal gain or power. It was so different from Halvor's Hall—or her father's, for that matter.

For the child's belt, she decided to sew mountains interspersed with the mystical creatures Frida had been so enamoured of. A troll with a thick head and a heavy club, a dwarf with a hammer, a mischievous woodland elf and finally a small hunched-up old woman—the Angel of Death or the Volva, the Oracle—all names used to describe the woman who chose to wander from Hall to Hall, divining fates. It was the Angel of Death who took the lives of the sacrifices, whether they be goat, horse or human.

Gyda depicted her as she remembered her when she'd visited her father's Hall and divined their fates. A dark, looming figure, curled in on herself like a dead leaf. A pale, skeletal hand outstretched, clutching bones and runes with yellow clawlike nails.

'Four beautiful daughters,' she'd proclaimed, with the voice of a strangled crow. 'Four different fates, and yet mostly the same. All shall be the queen of their true love's heart, and one shall live across the sea.'

They'd presumed she'd meant Astrid—after all, she had been about to marry Sven, who at the time had been under King Ivar and King Halfdan's command and due to set sail to England in the spring. But by then Astrid had been too heavily pregnant to travel, and had died before she could join her husband.

Now it appeared that Gyda was the one to travel across the sea…not that she placed much faith in the old woman's prophecies. She'd probably only sought the favour of her parents' Hall for the night.

Gyda had been the queen of no man's heart. Her father had ruled her with an iron fist. Someone had to marry for the family's benefit, he'd told her, and as the eldest, and with no sweetheart to speak of, it might as well be her.

She had not begrudged the sacrifice. Without it, none of her sisters could have married men of their choosing. She would never regret her choice, no matter how cruel the fate of her sisters. She had allowed each of them to be blissfully happy…for a short time at least.

Yes, at first she'd believed it was worthwhile, that marrying Halvor had meant her sisters' happiness. But time had revealed the cruel joke of her fate.

Her marriage had been a political match, combining the strength of two jarls to increase their power and profit. Her father had had illustrious ancestry but very little land. But eventually—and the irony was not lost on her—all her father's land, including the land given to her as her bride price, had been owned by Halvor anyway. Her sisters had all been dead, and when her parents had died their land had been swallowed up by Halvor's estate, his claim strengthened through his marriage to her.

She'd given her family nothing.

As she completed the last stitches to Frida's belt, she saw Thorstein and the hunting party returning to the settlement. She looked on in a daze. Hours had passed while she'd sewn and brooded.

The hunters carried two large hogs and two deer carcasses on poles, the meat swinging from side to side as they entered the settlement to be surrounded by cheers. Tonight there would be a grand feast.

The sun was low in the sky, casting its balmy light on the end of a long day. She packed up her sewing materials and stood with a wince. Her muscles ached from sitting down for so long. She rolled her shoulders and shook the tension out of her limbs before heading back towards Thorstein's Hall.

As she walked through the settlement she kept an eye out for little Frida, and found her furiously digging up weeds in one of the vegetable patches outside a family home. Her mother was chopping vegetables at a table by the door, the babe asleep and strapped to her back, and she gave Gyda a bright smile and a wave as she approached.

'I have a gift for Frida. With your permission?' She handed her the belt.

The woman gave her a beaming smile and then looked at the stitch work. 'Mistress, it's beautiful! That's so kind of you—you really shouldn't have gone to the trouble.' She wiped her hands on her apron before taking it off and carefully placing it in a basket of fresh-smelling laundry.

'It was my pleasure. I enjoyed Frida's company this morning. She's such a sweet child. She will grow to be a fine woman, I'm sure.' Her heart melted at the sight of the tender face of the sleeping baby pressed against its mother's shoulder. 'The gods have been good to give you such beautiful children.'

'Thank you, mistress. Your skill with a needle is incredible.' Her fingers traced along the stitching in reverence. 'My name is Hilda. If there's anything you need before you leave for Jorvik…?'

'I'm sure I will be fine. But thank you anyway.'

Gyda left them, giving the distracted Frida a wave as

she passed, her heart filled with a calm joy she'd not felt in many years. She was healthy and not too old. Having children of her own was still a possibility if she wanted them—and she did, desperately.

But when she looked to the future she wanted to see independence, security. A husband would not give her that, but a livelihood would.

One day, if Sven was kind, maybe she could have both? Her own income and independence. But if she met the right man she could have a family too.

Maybe all was not lost.

Chapter Six

A shadow fell across Thorstein's face as he cleaned and sharpened his blades. Someone stood in the open doorway of his Hall and momentarily blocked the light. A prickle of heat ran down his spine and he knew who it was straight away.

He couldn't help himself. He looked up.

Gyda stood in the doorway, still and hesitant. An outsider.

Why did she always look so alone? Even in a crowd.

For a mad moment he wanted to draw her close and offer her a place in his settlement. Take away that hesitation and loneliness, give her a reason to smile, to be at ease. He'd spent so many years fighting for his own home that he felt her absence of one keenly.

She squared her shoulders and raised her elegant chin. The embodiment of feminine strength. Her eyes found his and a flash of fire ignited between them. He released the breath he'd not realised he'd been holding. She was a Valkyrie...an ethereal beauty who decided a warrior's fate. The idea that he could offer her anything was laughable.

'What has she done with her day?' he asked Magnus

quietly, unable to look away as he almost basked in the sight of her shining brighter than the sun.

His trusted friend shook his head. 'She spent most of her day on the landing pier... The women seem to like her.'

So she'd wasted an entire day doing nothing but pining over her lost possessions. Why was he not surprised?

To think he'd worried about her...

He must be mad.

A single kiss had addled his mind. But, then again, she wasn't the only one who'd spent the day fixated on a lost cause. He'd missed the killing shot on one of the boars. Too distracted by the memory of her soft body crushed against his the night before. Her desperate lips had been begging for a connection, for passion, and he'd answered with an unsettling longing of his own.

He needed to focus, to push aside these idiotic romantic notions.

'Gyda!' he barked, and several of his people stopped their own conversations and stared in surprise at his uncharacteristic anger.

So much for remaining focused.

At his sharp tone her eyes narrowed and her nostrils flared. A perverse part of him liked it that he brought her emotions so close to the surface—even the negative ones. She wasn't as cold as she liked to appear.

He tried to improve his voice, but it still sounded like a rumbling threat. 'Come sit with me a moment...please.'

He was sure that if it hadn't been for the final 'please' she would have refused him. As it was, she made her way over calmly, her hands neatly folded in front of her. She had to sidestep a few groups of men, but she ignored their stares. Her gown looked terrible, but somehow she still managed to walk with grace and confidence.

He had to admit that some things were not dependent on wealth. And she'd been born with elegance, and a presence that could command a room whether she wore rags or silk—no one could take that from her.

She settled beside Thorstein, taking a moment to re-arrange the skirts of her badly fitted gown and place a basket of meagre sewing supplies at their feet. What on earth did she hope to make with those few scraps? He'd instructed Elga to give her anything she wanted from the stores.

'I hear you spent the day alone on the landing pier. Please tell me you are not still hoping for your silver to be washed up on the beach?' He tried and failed to mask his irritation.

'Of course not. I was sewing.'

Thorstein glanced down at her basket with a cocked eyebrow, and although she visibly bristled she did not comment further.

'Maybe you should go and help with preparing to-night's feast. I'm sure Elga will find something useful for you to do.'

He gestured towards the open doors of the side room where the women were busy at work. Gyda had the de-cency to look guilty as she saw the flurry of activity and the sweat on their brows.

She opened her mouth as if to speak, but was cut off by a raucous bellowed laugh from Orm, who sat with two other men who were staring at her with wolfish expres-sions from across the fire.

Liquid rage raced up his spine and he gripped his blade so tightly that sparks flared as he ran it down the whetstone with a savage jerk.

Orm's eyes narrowed slightly, but then he raised his horn of mead and shouted cheerfully, 'To easy prey!'

An uneasy cheer trickled through the Hall.

Thorstein looked at Gyda's pale face and kept his voice low as he spoke. 'I think it best that you work with the women for now, and sit by my side during the feast.'

With a stiff nod she walked towards the women, her steps a little quicker than usual.

He turned to Magnus and gave a lazy tilt of his knife towards two golden-haired brothers who stood a little apart from Orm and his men. They were watching the women preparing the meal with great interest, occasionally murmuring something to each other while remaining a respectful distance away.

They were skilled, respectful and quiet—qualities Thorstein favoured in young men. He had too much land and not enough men to work it properly. However, he needed people he could trust, and he was careful about who he chose to join his settlement.

'Those two are decent bowmen and good hunters. Find out what you can about them. Why do they travel with Orm? What do they want in life?'

He watched as Elga accidentally knocked a basket of herbs off the table, and the two brothers practically fell over themselves, rushing to help her gather them.

Magnus chuckled as he watched the scene unfold. 'What do all men want in life? You were wise to treat the Saxon widows and orphans well. They will be our best recruiters!'

Many considered Saxons to be no better than thralls— the spoils of war without any rights. But these women were not slaves; they were free and they lived under his protection.

'Tell everyone to keep an eye on Orm and his men. I want no trouble for *any* of my people tonight.'

'Of course,' said Magnus, losing some of his humour.

Gyda came to join him as the feast was served. She kept to her own thoughts, but he saw her sharp eyes watching him from time to time as they ate.

As he'd instructed, the women and children were kept separate from the strangers as much as possible without alerting suspicion, and no one left the Hall without a companion.

He resolved to encourage more marriages in his settlement.

A chore he was not looking forward to...

He leaned in close to Gyda, inhaling the scent of heather and fresh salty air that lingered on her neck. 'You're safe. I'm just being cautious.'

She closed her eyes and inclined her head softly. 'I know.'

Had she just shivered?

His body hardened at the thought.

Before he was tempted to move closer, and taste the pale skin of her neck, someone thumped down on the bench at his other side.

'Those three are loyal to Orm,' Magnus said. He pointed at the group surrounding Orm, then nodded to another group of men who played dice by the fire. 'The two brothers and those three all have a return contract. You're right. The brothers would make a good addition to the settlement, but they will not go back on their word to Orm.'

Thorstein nodded. He was not surprised. Many crews were bought with such contracts of honour. Families were indebted to the helmsman for taking their sons as crew, and in return they received part of the boat's profits. It was a matter of family honour to fulfil their contracts.

'But they're not opposed to leaving?' he asked, taking a sip of mead and trying to ignore the silent curiosity of Gyda at his side.

'No. In fact, they are asking for permission to return here after their contracts are paid.'

'Good—'

Suddenly Orm's shout rang across the Hall. He was holding dice in his meaty fists. 'Thorstein! Do you play?'

He shook his head as he sized up Orm. The man was big and burly from many years of rowing, and a good wrestler judging by the way he'd held down one of the wild hogs on the hunt earlier today. 'I prefer more physical sport.'

Orm grinned. 'A contest, perhaps?'

'Perhaps…' Thorstein shrugged. 'Axe-throwing?'

'I prefer wrestling.'

Thorstein nodded and pretended not to notice the sly glint in Orm's eyes. Contests and wrestling were common entertainment in most Halls, but Orm looked as if he took such matches more seriously than most.

'First one to be thrown to the ground?'

'And held down until a count of five.'

'Ten.'

'Ten—why not?'

'Now, the prize… I like the skills of your two archers.' He nodded to the two brothers. 'If I win, you gift the remainder of their contracts to me?'

The two brothers exchanged a look of surprise, but nodded when he looked at them. They were willing.

Orm scratched at his red beard. 'I would consider one of them…not both.'

'Two, or it's hardly worth the risk.'

'Very well. But if I win you will give me your bedchamber for the night…' A cruel smile slashed across

Orm's face. 'I believe that comes with a kiss from the lady?'

A few of the men sniggered, and Thorstein heard Gyda gasp at his side.

'That is not up to me to give,' he said lightly, ignoring the fire in his belly that made him want to rip out Orm's throat.

He dampened it down with logic. This was a negotiation, nothing more. After all, Orm had nothing of value to offer. He'd suspected Orm would ask for his beautifully carved axe—it was a prize he'd no doubt had his eye on from the start. But Thorstein had no intention of losing, so he wouldn't mind it being part of the wager.

Orm made a great show of boredom as he looked around the room at the meagre decorations on display. 'There does not seem much else to win...except maybe one of your Saxon women for the night? What about that one? She has no husband,' Orm said, pointing at a horrified Elga.

Several of Thorstein's men, including the usually easygoing Magnus, tensed at the insult to one of their own.

But before Thorstein could open his mouth to deny such an offensive request Gyda stood up, and in a clear voice proclaimed, 'Both men's contracts. And *if* you win, you may have Thorstein's bedchamber for the night and a kiss from me. Nothing more, of course... But that is only if you win.'

Orm threw back his head with a triumphant laugh, 'Both men it is!'

He stood up and began to remove his cloak and shirt.

Gyda sat back down on the bench with a soft thud that shook Thorstein to the core. Was the woman mad, to offer herself like that as a reward? And how dared she believe he would not protect the women of his settlement?

'If I needed your counsel I would have asked for it!' he snarled, his teeth clenched tight in a smile for Orm's benefit.

She sniffed the air haughtily, as if she believed he had very much needed her intervention. 'I will not allow you to barter Elga's body as if she were a prize sow.'

He scowled at her and spat on the floor. The wager suddenly became bitter on his tongue. 'But you would barter your own? Who says I would have allowed him to have Elga, or any of the women for that matter? You, however, seem very free with your own affections. Kisses are not trinkets you can sell or give away without consequence!'

She turned to him, her eyes hard. 'I know that! And I have no intention of giving anything away, freely or otherwise. I am trusting you not to lose this match... Tell me you won't lose it.'

Her expression became uneasy at the end of her tirade.

'Of course not!' he growled, throwing off his tunic as he stood.

Some of Gyda's fears subsided at his proud response, and she was able to relax the tension in her shoulders as she watched him prepare to fight.

He stripped to bare feet and bare chest, his dark leggings the only piece of clothing remaining. All young Norse men were powerfully built. But Thorstein up close took her breath away. His powerful body was a weapon, and her thoughts scattered like sparks of fire. Muscles rolled beneath his tattooed skin—even his shoulders were inked with the dark blue wings of a raven.

A strange warmth began to build beneath her skin. She couldn't help but compare his impressive physique to that of her late husband. Halvor had been so much older than her, his belly soft from too much meat, mead and wealthy living. She had never felt love-lust for Halvor, as her sisters had felt for their husbands. She had never expected to. But when she looked at Thorstein heat unfurled within her, making her bite back a sigh of pleasure.

She looked to Orm, whose muscles were equally thick, but they made her cringe. She imagined those thick fingers wrapped around her throat, crushing the breath out of her. In contrast, she remembered the warmth and gentle touch of Thorstein's fingers as he'd held her head out of the water and wrapped her frozen feet in soft wool. He had the strength of a bear, but she somehow knew that, unlike Orm, he would never use his physical power against her.

She prayed she had not made another stupid mistake by offering her kiss as a prize.

Thorstein walked over and said something quietly to Magnus, who then glanced towards her and nodded.

Then Orm and Thorstein faced each other, bare-chested and with arms spread. Everyone gathered around them, cheering their chosen man and offering wagers amongst themselves.

'Begin!' shouted Magnus, and the two men charged at each other like two stags clashing antlers.

There was a smack of muscle against muscle as they grabbed each other in bear holds and then twisted from each other's grip. The crowd roared in response, and Gyda noticed that Magnus had joined her at her side, occasionally pushing away anyone who got too close or jostled her by mistake. She wondered if that was what Thorstein had asked him to do. It made the heat in her stomach spread a little more.

Orm had grabbed Thorstein's waistband, but after a moment of grappling together they pulled apart and began to circle each other once again, prowling like wolves, waiting for the opportunity to give the killing strike.

They clashed again.

Cheers raged around them as more bets were placed and every man shouted support to their chosen fighter. Gyda was pleased to note that nearly everyone supported Thorstein.

They grunted, and the rushes bunched and scraped beneath their feet as they struggled to maintain their stance. Neither man relented in his hold upon the other. When Orm adjusted his grip slightly, she winced at the red welts left on Thorstein's skin by Orm's brutish fingers.

Then Orm whipped out an arm and slammed an elbow into the side of Thorstein's head. Thorstein barely flinched, only grunted as he bore down against his opponent. Gyda had to choke down the cry of fear that escaped from her throat. She squeezed her hands into fists, ignoring the pinching crescents of her nails that would bruise her skin.

Thorstein seemed almost beaten, and he leaned precariously to one side as Orm pressed him further down. A flash of horror and fear swept through her—not only for herself, although the idea of kissing Orm made her want to retch, but for Thorstein's safety too. His spine was bending like a tightly pulled bow and she prayed that his knees wouldn't buckle, that he would hold on and push back.

But Orm had better leverage and continued to push down with a vicious strength. He used all his weight and muscle against Thorstein, until the veins on his neck bulged with the strain and his breath snarled through gritted teeth.

Just when she thought all was lost Thorstein roared.

He reared up and twisted his body, turning Orm suddenly in an impressive trick that unbalanced him and swept the man's legs from beneath him. He lifted him up into the air with a powerful thrust of his shoulder and then slammed him down onto his back with a deafening bang, throwing reeds and dust into the air.

Orm groaned like a falling tree and her spirit soared with triumph and pride. She cheered, and Magnus glanced at her in surprise. She felt the hot scald of a blush on her cheeks and looked away, quickly regaining her composure.

Thorstein waited a moment, as if to prove beyond doubt that he was the victor of the match, before slamming on top of Orm to win the wager.

Pinned to the ground and dazed, Orm struggled in vain to release himself, bucking and cursing beneath Thorstein's weight. Magnus and Orm's second both dropped to their knees to make the ruling, Magnus thumping the ground with each count.

'Ten, nine, eight, seven, six…'

Orm tried to strike out, but Thorstein punched him with a sharp jab to the face and then pushed him down harder, sweat beading his brow as he grunted and struggled to hold the equally fierce man.

'Five, four, three, two, one! Thorstein wins!' bellowed Magnus.

A cheer thundered through the Hall and Thorstein rocked back on his heels as wagers were paid and bitter curses spat by the losers.

Orm gave a wheezing cough as he struggled to stand, his nose bloody and his feet skidding, as if he were trying to stand on frozen ice.

Thorstein rose and grabbed him by the bicep, righting him to stand on his feet. He pulled him close and muttered something in his ear that made him scowl, but eventually the loser gave a curt nod of agreement.

Orm and his men returned to the fire, and two more men took to the floor, to begin a more friendly wrestling contest.

Thorstein returned to her side and pulled on his under-tunic with sharp angry tugs.

'What did you say to him?' she asked.

He turned to face her, blocking the light with his big body. His jaw clenched as he moved closer and bent his head slightly, so that she could feel his breath against her cheek. His eyes looked almost black with the fire against his back.

'I told him that I do not share what is mine, and that I will kill any man who dares to take without asking.'

Gyda shivered, although not from fear. 'I think I will retire for the night,' she whispered, barely able to form words in her dry throat.

She licked her lips and watched as his dark eyes snapped to her mouth with predatory intensity.

He shrugged lightly, though his voice was rough. 'As you wish.'

She shut the door to his chambers with a quiet click and wondered why his possessive words had affected her so much. Surely he'd spoken only of protecting Elga and the other women of his settlement? Why, then, had it felt as if he was talking about her? And why had that possessiveness filled her with molten heat and excitement, not fear?

She shook her head. It was better not to dwell on such madness. Tomorrow she would be travelling to meet Sven. She would have new battles to win and greater obstacles to overcome. Soon Thorstein and her time at his settlement would become a distant memory.

She closed her eyes and sighed as she remembered him stripping to prepare for the match. At least all her memories of Thorstein wouldn't be unpleasant. Some she might even cherish.

Chapter Seven

Excluding the two brothers who were now sworn under Thorstein's shield, Orm and his men were gone before dawn the next day. A tracker had been sent after them, to ensure they continued on their way and didn't think to return while he was in Jorvik, although it was a precaution Thorstein doubted was necessary—besides, the settlement's defences would be in Magnus's capable hands while he was gone.

The ship was almost ready to set sail. Several men prepared the rigging and oars while he helped load the cargo. Rowing up the rivers to Jorvik wouldn't take long. They would be at Sven's Hall before the evening meal, and then Gyda would no longer be his responsibility.

His skin itched as he worked. He could feel her watching him—no doubt judging him. She stood regally amongst the piles of fleeces and furs he'd absently tossed aboard, doing nothing to straighten them. The cargo was a pitiful amount to trade with—but then again this trip had not been planned.

He'd be glad when she was gone. Soon he would once again have the peace and order he craved.

He rolled the soreness from his shoulders as they cast

off. The ache was a timely reminder of the very different ache she'd caused with her kiss that first night. He'd thought about that kiss for far longer than he should have…

To ease his irritation, he set to work rowing the boat with his men. He preferred to work alongside his men than steer. Although the labour wouldn't help as much as he'd hoped, because the only remaining seat at the oar faced her.

He managed to ignore her for a time, but then his eyes betrayed him and he watched her despite himself. Her face was turned towards the sun, her eyes closed. She was wearing the same clothes she'd been rescued in. He clenched his teeth against the urge to reprimand her. How stubborn that she would reject the clothing offered by the people of his settlement in lieu of ostentatious damaged garments. Granted, the gown she'd been given hadn't fitted—but she could have spent her day altering another, instead of wasting it sulking over her lost silver.

Still, in spite of everything, he couldn't deny her beauty. It was a pleasure to look at her—which only irritated him further.

She spoke, and it was almost a relief, because he'd been waiting to hear her voice since she'd walked on board and he'd given her a curt nod of acknowledgment.

'It is so much warmer here…and brighter,' she murmured, basking in the warmth of the light.

He half wondered if she was talking to herself. But then she opened her silver-blue eyes and looked straight at him with unnerving certainty, as if she knew he'd been admiring her the whole time. Maybe he had?

He cleared his throat and squinted into the horizon. He'd rather look directly at the sun than be blinded by her knowing eyes. And at least the rhythm of rowing was a welcome excuse for appearing distracted.

'The summers are longer and warmer, that's true. But, while the north has snow all winter, Northumbria must deal with months of rain interspersed with storms, snow, frost and sometimes unseasonably sunny days. England's weather is as cunning as a wolf.'

She looked out at the horizon again, her gaze seeming to caress the mouth of the river with a tenderness that should be reserved for a lover.

'England's weather is certainly full of surprises… Excellent for crops and livestock, though. Fertile…'

When her eyes returned to him he felt as if she had him gripped tightly in her fist. Did she always have to make him think of fertility and sex?

Thora, his first wife, had used her beauty like that. Wielded it like a weapon to get whatever she wanted. He didn't want a seductress—a woman who offered kisses like flowers to doe-eyed men stupid enough to be chained by them. He'd been enthralled by a beautiful woman before. He'd never be so stupid again.

'Yes.'

He wondered how to end this misery. Should he stop rowing? Make some excuse to go to the prow? Leave her to her thoughts? She'd already tormented him enough as it was—why was he loitering?

Because one thing was certain.

He needed a wife.

If any good came from her presence it would be that.

Not just to sate his lust—although he'd felt that keenly since he'd met her. No, his Hall needed more of the home comforts provided by a wife. The feast last night had highlighted how lacking his Hall was as the heart of his community. It needed to reflect the prosperity and pride of his people, not diminish it.

If Odin willed it, he would gladly fight and die for every one of his people, and enter Valhalla considering himself blessed. In truth, marriage was an easy sacrifice to make in comparison. Although the thought made him more uneasy than the idea of battle.

'You seem keen to reach Jorvik, Thorstein.'

It took him a moment to understand what she meant. She was looking pointedly at his arms. Then he realised. His rowing pace had quickened. The man beside him was breathing heavily as he struggled to match him. Thorstein slowed, heat spreading up his neck and face.

'I tire of sleeping on a bench,' he replied, more forcefully than he'd intended.

At his surly response she smiled, as if she knew how restless he'd been and took pleasure in his suffering. Maybe she did know and delighted in teasing him further? Had she been admiring his arms as he rowed? He couldn't be sure, but a twisted part of him hoped so.

'It was only for two nights. Surely you've had worse, a big strong warrior like you?'

Her eyes flashed with mild amusement, and it made him feel like a lust-addled youth. Hot blood pulsed through the scarred flesh of his cheek with every stroke of the oar.

'Of course—worse than a jarl's wife could ever imagine.'

She ignored his barb and looked out to the riverbanks. 'Well, then… Will you be trading in Jorvik? I see you have brought a few fleeces and furs.'

'This is nothing compared to what we usually take to market. These are things we no longer have use for. I thought it best to bring them along for trade… But my main reason for travelling is because I have a debt to collect from Sven. I was going to wait until the autumn to collect, but I may as well take the opportunity now,' he answered briskly.

'A debt? Really? What kind of debt?'

Her gaze dropped to the small piles of fur and fleece around their feet. It caused him to grind his teeth. Why did everything she say blister his skin?

'You think a man like Sven could never be indebted to a man like me?' Did she really think him so low? He might not be a jarl, but he was a chieftain and a fine warrior. 'He owes me a blood debt. I saved his life when we retook Jorvik, and I was branded by our enemies for it.' He tapped his ruined cheek for emphasis.

Her words tumbled like loose rocks. 'I… I did not mean…'

'You presume that a rich man like Sven could not possibly be indebted to a man like me? A raider without an honourable family name? You will learn quickly, Gyda Ynglingdóttir, widow of Jarl Halvor Halvorson. This is a new land, where all men can prosper regardless of whether they are the first son or the seventh. A man with courage can take whatever he wants here, but only a man with strength will be able to hold it. If I were you, I would beg Sven to buy your passage back home. This land is no place for a woman like you!'

Her eyes froze, the light that had twinkled there earlier becoming hard and brittle before his gaze. But he preferred her anger—he could not bear her teasing looks.

'I presume nothing.'

She gave a cool tilt of her head that suggested she would never think much of him.

'I am to be married.'

What had possessed him to tell her that? To his hor-

ror he continued, groping in the dark for the respect he
shouldn't want or need.

'Sven wants a family alliance between us bound by
marriage. You and I will soon be kin…loosely.' He smiled
at the way she shifted in her seat. It was nice to tease her
for a change.

'And who will be the lucky lady?' Gyda sniffed,
smoothing her skirts.

'I do not know. No doubt one of his many nieces. He
implied as much when we last spoke. I trust Sven's judgement on the matter. He knows my requirements.'

A rich chuckle escaped her lips. '*Requirements?* What
are they, I wonder?'

He scowled, not liking the sound of her amusement,
and felt his scar twitching again. He tried to remember the faces of Sven's nieces. They were plain, pleasant women, nothing remarkable, but for some reason he
found himself carried away with his answer.

'I want a woman who is gentle and kind. Someone who
prefers the comfort of warm wool to cold silver. She'll
need to be strong and hardworking, so she can help work
the land, and she must be able to brew ale or some other
useful skill. A pleasant woman, who'll happily curl up by
my side and keep me warm through the long dark nights
of winter. She'll also be young and healthy enough to give
me fierce sons and daughters. But most of all she will
be a devoted wife…reserving her kisses for me alone.'

If he'd hoped to offend her, he'd failed. She merely
smiled indulgently at him, as if he were a green youth
talking of battles to be won.

Had he misjudged her? There was something so bittersweet in her eyes…almost sad. What did he truly know
of her past or her pain? He remembered the way she'd

flinched from him on the ship, and it made him uneasy in his judgement.

'She sounds like a fine woman… I hope you prove worthy of her.'

His heart hardened in his chest. She would never think him worthy of anything. A jarl's daughter and a jarl's widow, she had the blood of kings running through her veins. Of course his 'requirements' would seem naive and simple to her.

She looked away from him then, leaning towards the side of the boat and settling herself amongst the piles of pelts as if she were going to take a nap. Cool and dismissive, as always.

He concentrated on rowing, focusing on the rhythm of the men around him and increasing their speed and power with each pull of the oars. The sooner she was gone, the better.

Despite swearing to himself that he would ignore her for the rest of the journey, he found his eyes wandering back to her regularly—fleeting glances she never returned. He presumed she was sleeping, but as the hours passed he risked longer looks and noticed that she would occasionally open her eyes and stare into the water.

She wasn't sleeping. She was thinking.

Deeply.

He looked into the rippling water of the river and saw her gazing at her reflection. His eyes lingered on the sweep of her neck and the perfect lines of her jaw and nose. Her expression was happy, transformed from its usual cool dismissal into girlish innocence. It was her, but not her. Yet another mask. Except this one didn't hold the disdain he was so familiar with.

This mask was pretty, flirtatious and deeply unsettling.

Of course!

His stomach curdled with bitterness. She was a seductress, preparing to meet a powerful man. She was preening and practising.

It caused a confusing rush of rage to boil through his veins. Had their kiss been a pretence of passion too? The idea offended him more than it should.

Of course it had!

She was a woman who was used to getting her own way and had wrongly presumed he'd expect a sexual favour in return. Suddenly an unwelcome and sickening realisation hit him between the eyes. How awful that must be for her…to presume that all men would only want her in that way. It made a strange pity shroud his earlier feelings of anger towards her.

He wished she'd come to him *wanting* the pleasure of his touch, not feeling as if she had to offer it in payment.

Her mask dropped again and he sucked in a painful breath. No longer a coquettish girl, this was a beautiful woman weathered by battles unseen. Grief and despair burned across her face as surely as the crucifix had branded his cheek. Her fingers touched the corners of her eyes and he wondered if she mourned the passing of time—which was ridiculous. She was the most beautiful creature he had ever seen. Even in her old age he imagined she would still be regal and breathtaking.

It was strange to see her so vulnerable. Somehow he knew this was a side of herself she showed no one.

He looked away, feeling like a thief.

The river flowed past serenely and Gyda became lost in thought. The water was so calm she could see her reflection on its surface. If only she felt as calm.

It wouldn't be long until they reached Jorvik and she

met with her brother-in-law Sven. How should she approach their reunion?

He would remember her, of course—she was her twin sister's reflection, and he had loved Astrid deeply.

But how should she behave? Beg for pity?

No.

Tears were impossible for her. She had sworn never again to cry in front of a man.

Flirt?

Thorstein seemed to think of her as a seductress. She snorted—if only he knew the truth of it! Her 'feminine charms' had been useless when she'd been far younger and far prettier. She doubted anything would have improved after ten years of a loveless marriage.

Besides, the idea of seducing Sven didn't sit right with her. He was Astrid's first and only love. To corrupt that love would be repugnant... But if she could remind him of her...if only a little...maybe he would be kind to her. Give her a loan to set up her workshop, possibly?

But what would she do if he denied their connection and cast her out? Beg Thorstein for help? She doubted that would go down well. Although there did seem something inherently good about him. After all, he'd sailed to the aid of strangers, he'd fought for a woman's honour and now he was taking her to Sven, as promised.

Even so, Sven was her best hope for independence. *Should* she use her similarity to Astrid for her own advantage? Sprinkle in some of Astrid's mannerisms and gestures to remind Sven of his first love? If not to seduce, then perhaps to remind him of the debt he owed her, Gyda? Without her marriage to Halvor her father would never have accepted young Sven as Astrid's husband.

She focused on the water and shifted her features into

an expression both strange and familiar. Timidly she lowered her eyes, so that like two moons they peeked up from beneath pale lashes, shining with a glint of mischief. She spread a shy, whimsical smile across her lips, and as the boat slowed and the water smoothed like polished metal she once again saw the face of her sister. For a moment Astrid was with her again.

But then she noticed the lack of a dimple on her left cheek, and the tiny lines of age forming in the slant of her eyes. She'd seen thirty winters, while Astrid had died before she'd seen twenty-one.

She reached up with her fingers and smoothed the wrinkles with a featherlight touch and sighed deeply. Her own face returned, and the sweet face of her sister fell away like an ill-fitting shift.

Every season her face aged and weathered more.

Every year she lost more of her sister.

Before grief could overwhelm her, she looked away. She was a poor imitation of Astrid. Her sister should have lived, her life filled with passion, love and children. Everything Gyda knew she would never possess.

She looked over at Thorstein, who pulled relentlessly on his oar, hour after hour. He never seemed to tire, although sweat now beaded his brow. He was strong and young, with a prosperous settlement. He would make a fine husband.

The thought hit her square in the ribs and she bit her lip as if it were a wicked desire.

Of course the idea was ridiculous.

Wasn't it?

Thorstein had no desire for her—he thought her shallow and arrogant, and she did not care. At least he showed her respect, and respect kept her safe.

Despite herself, she felt her lips tingle with the memory of his kiss. It had been perfect. Soft, gentle and hot. But he'd made it clear the type of woman he wanted, and it had made her heart heavy to hear him. It had reminded her of her own naive desire for marriage, before she'd realised how cruel men could be.

No, she would be better off pleading with Sven. With him, she still had the chance of freedom—even if he didn't agree to a loan. She would ask to join his household as a companion to his wife and children. She would sell her necklace and buy tools and cloth. She would work every hour she could. Make gowns for Sven's wife and children, as well as tapestries to sell.

Eventually she might earn enough to buy a workshop in the city and live as she'd originally intended.

She might even be able to repay the debt she owed Thorstein. He'd saved her life more than once, and even though she sensed he expected nothing in return she always repaid her debts.

Maybe once she was settled she would make him a tapestry for his Hall? Something wild and symbolic. The wolf Fenrir fighting his chains, perhaps? Or Thor beating with his hammer? She liked the idea of the latter, but when she thought of how she would illustrate Thor only a dark-haired warrior with a scarred face standing in the light of dawn came to mind.

Heat raced through her thoughts like lightning and her dress felt tight against her chest. Why did Thorstein affect her so badly? She had not felt like this since her youth…and look how badly that had turned out.

Her eyes locked with Thorstein's. There was a frown on his hard face. She looked away, smoothing her skirts, determined not to look up again until they reached Jorvik.

He must think her mad. Maybe she was? Astrid was

long gone. Sven might not remember her twin sister or care about her plight.

Who was she really?

Nothing more than a poor reflection of an old, dead love.

Chapter Eight

The river twisted like a serpent through fields and forests and the landscape was a green blur. Or at least it felt like that to Gyda, whose nerves increased with every stroke of the oars.

Then they reached it.

The Norse capital of England and the centre of her new world. Jorvik.

She stared open-mouthed as they sailed between two walls of freshly heaped earth. The mounds were topped by a wooden palisade that surrounded the city. The high spiked fence obstructed her view, but she could still hear the voices and clatter of a bustling city beyond. Northmen and Saxons walked along the wall, their clothing slightly different from each other's in both colour and style.

Thorstein came to stand beside her and she couldn't deny her curiosity. 'I have heard there are ancient stone walls here.'

Thorstein nodded. 'There are.' He pointed to the steep slope of the mounds. 'They're impressive walls of rock, but too old. They're crumbling and weak in places. We have covered them with earth to create a stronger defence.'

'Oh, of course,' she answered, although in truth she was disappointed. She had hoped to see the giant walls of ancient rock she'd heard stories about.

At the next bend they approached a large wooden mooring that seemed to allow entrance into the city. Many ships were tied up along the bank, or jostled for a free space against the pier.

Thorstein set to work, instructing his men as he guided the boat into a narrow space.

Gyda climbed as high onto the pelts as she dared, and from her slightly raised vantage point she could see out over the city, from the banks of the river to the opposite city walls in the far distance. A sea of buildings dipped and swelled within, from low huts to high towers, including several stone Halls with thatched roofs.

Did Sven live in one of those? Or were they used by the Saxon priests?

She knew that the Saxons built stone homes for their God—it was their gilded churches that had first enticed Northmen to raid. She'd heard that some even had tapestries made of coloured glass set into their walls. She would love to see something as impressive as that.

The rest of the buildings, however, were a disappointment, small and closely built. Little wooden homes and workshops nestled together, with walls of wattle and daub and thatched roofs the colour of mud.

A hundred smells assaulted her nose as the boat thudded against the pier—none of them pleasant. Smoke, rot, and the sweat and excrement of hundreds of people. The smell clung to the air and she braced herself against it, pinching her nose until she'd adjusted to the foul odour.

Even Njardarheimr had not smelt as wretched as Jorvik. Being a sea port, its sea breeze had cleared the air more often than not. But Jorvik had no breeze as far as she could tell—just acrid smoke that burned the eyes.

Thorstein laughed as he helped her off the boat with a steady arm. 'Going back home is looking much more appealing, I imagine.'

She scowled at his perceptive words and matched his long strides with her own as she tried her best to avoid the worst of the muck. 'Any centre of commerce and trade is expected to be a little rough on the senses. I look forward to experiencing all that Jorvik has to offer... Once I meet with Sven, of course.'

'Of course.'

He walked away, instructing his men to remain and guard the ship while they went into the city alone.

She tried to pretend nonchalance, but in truth a thrill shot down her spine. She had never seen so many buildings and people. They crowded the city in a jumble that made it difficult to see the horizon. And as she grew accustomed to the unpleasant smells and the clamour of noise, she began to appreciate the industry around her.

Smoke billowed out into the blue sky from crowded workshops as they made their way through the warren of streets to the centre of the city. She stared in wonder at the sights around her, and stopped so often that Thorstein tapped his foot with impatience more than once. But she paid him no heed.

Every type of craftsman and merchant was present in the filthy streets of Jorvik.

A glassblower called out to her, strings of brightly coloured beads draped along his sleeve. Rainbows danced across her fingers as she admired them. The hammering of metal workers filled her ears, creating strange music as they tapped lightly on intricate rings and golden thread, or banged loudly, forging weapons. Every now and then she would hear the gust of a bellows or the hiss of hot metal as it was plunged into troughs of water.

Each new path took them on another road to discovery. She had thought Njardarheimr a busy centre of commerce. It seemed like a farmstead in comparison to Jorvik.

Next, they passed wood-turners and bone-carvers, who were making the most of the remaining daylight to produce polished combs, sharp needles, hairpins, spoons and dice.

She passed a beautifully carved Tables board made of walrus tusk. It reminded her of the set Halvor had kept beside the bed, gathering dust. She passed by with a smile. She would not miss the sight of it. She would not miss the sight of Halvor or his Tables board or his broken teeth or his swollen gut. She was free of him and his family.

People bartered animals and goods in the street. A goat was passed to a leatherworker in exchange for a set of new boots. A few scraps of silver were exchanged for a beautiful bundle of lush reindeer pelts. She felt as if the whole world was mixed into the cauldron of Jorvik, with people from every known land present in its tiny streets, meeting and trading with one another.

Her pace slowed as they passed weavers and cloth-workers. Many sold finished garments and tapestries, trimmed with a variety of silks and furs. The array was breathtaking, and the skills impressive, but her pieces would not have looked out of place amongst them.

Gyda swallowed down a painful lump in her throat. Her precious tapestries would have shone here. They would have been admired, bought and treasured. Instead they lay at the bottom of the sea, rotting.

She pushed aside her melancholy and focused on the

styles and trims available. She noted the pieces she liked. She stopped at one colourful stall in particular and admired the vibrant bolts of cloth and thread on display.

She noticed that Thorstein was staring at her with a strange look upon his face. 'Please can I stop here for a moment?' she asked him. 'It's… It's why I wanted to come here. Originally, I mean.'

He gave a slow nod, and for once she thought he understood her. He knew this wasn't just about admiring the goods. This was what she'd wanted when she'd crossed the North Sea.

A sturdy woman with sharp eyes wiped her hands on her apron and greeted her with a wide smile. 'Admiring the purple, my lady? It's a pretty colour that would suit your complexion.'

'How do you get such a vibrant colour?'

'Oakmoss,' replied the woman with a smile.

Gyda frowned as she stared back at the cloth. 'But shouldn't that make it yellow?'

The woman cocked her head and gave her a shrewd look. 'Are you sure you want to know, mistress?'

She turned towards the woman and caught a spark of mischief in her eyes. 'I'd love to recreate it if possible… But I'll understand if you don't wish to share your secret.'

The woman laughed, and it sounded as rich and as vibrant as her bolts of cloth. 'It's no secret, so I don't mind telling you… Urine. The oakmoss is left to steep in urine for at least three months.'

She felt the shadow of Thorstein beside her.

'Delightful—and you charge a premium for piss-stained clothes, no doubt?' he said.

Gyda laughed, and she thought she caught the twitch of a smile at the corner of his lips. 'Such things don't bother me,' she said. 'Any clothmaker worth her salt knows how to use urine to bleach and fix dyes. Although I've never achieved anything like this. Three months, you say?'

'Yes, and stir once a day. It needs the air to get to it. Now, this one,' she said, reaching for a piece of cloth the colour of summer twilight, 'is from a special lichen found far north of here, from the land of the Picts.'

'It's beautiful.'

'Thank you, my lady. My name's Edith. Is that your work? It's impressive,' said the woman, pointing to the embroidery on her neckline.

'Thank you—yes, it is. I'm Gyda.'

'Well, Gyda, I'd be happy to trade embroidery with you for cloth, dye or lichen. If you're interested?'

She could tell Edith was a shrewd businesswoman. She'd noticed Gyda's skill with a needle, but she'd also noticed the tattered state of her gown. She didn't mind. Far from it. She was delighted to have made such a useful contact—and on her first day in Jorvik.

Her dreams were not so distant after all. But they would depend on how her meeting with Sven went...

No more avoidance. She needed to face her future.

She noticed Thorstein was slowly walking away.

'I'm so glad to have met you, Edith. I have to go now, but I will certainly come and see you again soon. I have nothing to sell at the moment, but I hope to in the future.'

'Well, I look forward to seeing you, then, mistress. Remember, you will find me here by the church.' Edith pointed to a large building at the end of the road, with high open doors.

After a quick goodbye, Gyda quickly hurried after Thorstein. He didn't comment on her tardiness and continued at the same leisurely pace. It was considerate of him, and it reminded her of her own manners.

She took a deep breath and kept her eyes firmly ahead as she spoke. 'If I don't get a chance to tell you before we part... I want you to know that I am grateful...for everything you've done.'

'It was my duty—'

'No.' She stopped walking and turned to face him abruptly. She doubted anyone would dare knock into a warrior as intimidating as Thorstein, and she was right. The people flowed around them as if they were rocks in a stream. 'You have saved my life and protected me as if I were your kin. I have never been very good at... at expressing myself, but I want you to know that you have my thanks.'

He didn't say anything at first, just stared at her in bewilderment, his blue eyes as bright as the beads she'd seen earlier. Finally he said, 'You're welcome. That's all that I wanted...before.'

She couldn't speak. She knew she should, to apologise for her earlier assumptions, to clear the air between them at least. But she couldn't. Her pride, her fear—whatever it was—wouldn't allow it. If he knew how weak she really was then he would use it against her, as all men did.

She gave a curt nod and his nostrils flared with irritation, but to her relief he didn't press her further. Instead they walked on, an arm's width between them.

They passed the church, but she couldn't see any glass tapestries, no matter how much she strained her neck as they passed.

To avoid the embarrassment of looking at Thorstein again, she looked instead at the clothing of the people around her. It reminded her that many different tastes and traditions were blended together in her new home, and that she would need to bear that in mind with the clothes she made.

This was a Norse city, in a land ruled by Danes, but the Saxons and their Christianity were still present everywhere—in the faces of the people and in the large Christian church they'd passed.

Her people were adventurous and curious, but they were also cunning. Why kill an enemy when you could demand a ransom for them? Why burn a city when you could use it for trade?

No, her people would make their mark on this land, of that she was certain. They might have come here by force, but they would rule through flexibility and commerce. This was a land in constant change and renewal. Everything she wanted for herself.

She only hoped she would have the chance to remain.

Chapter Nine

After a while the hustle and bustle of the workshops and traders eased and the distance between the buildings grew, allowing better air to circulate. Sadly, this cleaner air didn't reflect in the tightness of Gyda's lungs, which grew more suffocating with each step.

Her doubts and fears escalated, until all she could hear was the pulsing of the blood in her ears.

Would Sven help her?

They'd reached a huge empty square of well-trodden earth, surrounded by several longhouses. Each Hall had a small plot of land for livestock and vegetables. She guessed with so much food available at the markets the wealthy owners of these Halls would have less need to grow their own.

Thorstein pointed to a Hall on the opposite side of the square—it was one of the largest. 'Sven's Hall is over there.'

Goosebumps shivered down her arms and she tugged her cloak closer.

'Come,' growled Thorstein, striding towards it.

As they approached, a female thrall tending the herb

garden looked up and hurried inside. A few moments later a couple emerged.

Gyda recognised Sven immediately, with his dark blond hair and the long beard that tapered to his narrow waist. It was plaited and wrapped in gold rings. The hair on his head was tied back and shaved at the sides to reveal rune tattoos. His build was much thicker than that of the slim youth she remembered, and his hair was streaked with a few strands of grey, but that was to be expected. She'd last seen him over ten years ago—before battles and conquests, when Astrid had still been alive and all he'd spoken of was new lands filled with treasure.

Sven raised his hand to shield his eyes from the late afternoon light as they approached. 'Thorstein! It's good to see you! And who is your companion…? Is that…? Odin's teeth! Is it… *Gyda*?'

His face was uncertain and pained at first. She was her sister's double, and she knew that seeing her after all these years would hurt him in ways she could only imagine.

But then his face brightened. 'Gyda! Welcome!'

She smiled with relief at his joyful shout. He remembered her kindly. It was an auspicious start.

She sucked in a breath and readied herself for what was to come. The way she behaved and spoke now would determine her fate for ever. She couldn't mimic her sister—of that she was certain—but maybe Sven still had enough feelings for Astrid that he would be willing to help her.

'Oh, Sven! It is such a relief to see you. I have had such bad fortune, brother.'

Although she hated to do it, she tried her best to appear pitiful and sweet. It sounded stiff even to her ears. Thorstein gave her a dark look, but she ignored him.

The small dark-haired woman next to Sven spoke with a confused frown. 'I thought my husband had no sisters living?'

Tread carefully.

Gyda smiled warmly and tried her best to put the woman at ease. 'Oh, mistress, I am an old relic from the distant past. I am Astrid's eldest sister—Sven's first wife.'

She made sure to emphasise the word 'eldest', hoping it would reassure the woman of her intentions. No man would lust after his dead wife's *eldest* sister. The lady didn't need to know she was the eldest by only a handful of breaths, or that they had been identical twins.

If Sven had any sense he wouldn't offer her that information either. A woman could be quite bitter about such things. Thankfully, Sven had always been a master of diplomacy.

'Gyda, it is a pleasure to see you after so long. This is my beautiful wife Brunhild. Come in...warm yourself by our fire. Thorstein, my friend, will you join us? We have much to discuss.'

Brunhild and Sven showed them into the Hall. It was sumptuously furnished, with furs, tapestries and ornately carved furniture. It reminded her of her own Hall in Viken, and a bittersweet melancholy washed over her. She missed the comforts of home, if not her husband and his family.

Brunhild stood aside and held out an arm to beckon her towards a bench by the fire. Her lips were pursed and Gyda feared she might have failed to convince the woman that her presence was harmless.

No matter. It was Sven's good opinion she required. She would work on Brunhild later.

Once they were all settled by the fire with horns of

mead, Sven asked, 'You travel alone? What about your husband, Jarl Halvorson?'

'He died this winter,' she replied. There seemed no reason to elaborate. Sven would know of Halvor's advanced age.

'I see.'

Sven's eyes became hooded as he threw another log onto the fire. She wondered if he already knew what she was going to ask of him. Nerves began to tangle in her stomach, clawing up her throat and threatening to spill her guts at his feet. She pushed them down and focused on her composure.

She smoothed her skirts and tried her best to sound confident. 'I came to Jorvik to sell my tapestries. If you remember, I am an excellent weaver and seamstress.'

'I remember.'

He sipped at his mead and avoided her eyes. She noticed Thorstein looking at her from the corner of her eye, but she ignored him again.

She took a deep breath and studied Sven's face, waiting hopelessly for him to look at her. 'My longship was caught in a storm and wrecked upon the rocks. I have lost all my cargo... I come to you, brother, to plead for your aid.'

After a pause, he finally looked at her, but it was a look without warmth. 'What of your stepsons and your family?'

'My family are all dead—taken by disease or war over the years. Halvor's sons made it clear they expected me to join their father on the funeral pyre...'

She was careful to rein in the bitterness of her tone. It would not do to appear ungracious in front of Sven. She was sick of sacrificing her life to Jarl Halvorson and his family. But a man would not understand her lack of feeling for her husband. Especially a man like Sven, who loved with an open heart.

'I declined the honour… I believe the gods have another fate in mind for me. I wish to be a merchant and a craftswoman, but now… Now I will need support until I can live independently.'

Sven leaned back and folded his arms across his chest as he studied her. His face was blank, cool and detached. Fear swelled in her chest. This was not the passionate youth she remembered. She dragged in a shaky breath through her teeth, trying her best to remain serene, even though she felt like throwing herself at his feet or screaming and shaking him.

Instead, she said quietly, in almost a whisper, 'Please, Sven… Help me. You are my only kinsman now.'

After a long pause that set her teeth on edge, he laughed. 'Of course!'

He reached across and gave her shoulder a brotherly squeeze. She flinched at the unexpected touch but managed a smile. This was nothing. She would gladly crawl naked across the square if it meant she could live independently.

Sven glanced at Brunhild, who was looking at him with narrowed eyes and a clenched jaw. His laugh died under his wife's dark stare and he cleared his throat. 'But let me think on how best I can help you…'

The fear in Gyda's chest returned, and she looked at the quiet Brunhild with renewed respect. Maybe she shouldn't have dismissed her influence after all? Not all husbands were like Halvor.

Thorstein's voice cut through the tension like a blade. 'How are your talks with the rest of the jarls?'

Sven spat a curse into the fire, causing it to hiss. 'The jarls are behaving like children! King Guthrum's treaty with King Alfred will give us peace and time—two things we surely need to build this city into a prosperous trading capital—yet they mither and moan...'

The two men spoke of politics for some time. Gyda pretended to listen as her mind churned with worry. She had hoped Sven would immediately offer her a place in his household, but he'd not even offered her a room for the night. He'd said he would 'think on' how best to help her. What did that mean?

Then Thorstein said, 'I have decided to marry.'

Her curiosity piqued, she listened more closely.

Sven grinned and glanced at her, then Thorstein, which made both of them shift awkwardly. 'You have? Now? I thought you wished to wait until late autumn or Yule. What has changed your mind?'

'We need to encourage settlement and alliances between chieftains. As I was bringing Gyda here to you anyway, I thought it best to arrange my alliance now. I believe you have several suggestions for me?'

Gyda tried to hide her smile at his smug tone.

Sven took another sip of mead. 'I have.'

'Have you spoken with their fathers regarding a bride price?'

'Yes, and I'm sure we can agree on your bride by the end of the evening. But...let's eat first.'

Something in Sven's calculated smile made her nervous, but the evening meal was being served and the rest of his household joined them, disrupting their quiet conversation with a raucous noise.

Amongst the crowd of warriors, wives and thralls, a group of young boys entered the Hall, falling over each other like puppies. All of them had brown hair except one, the eldest and tallest amongst them, who had hair as pale as milk and eyes like silver coins.

The breath ran from her lungs like a receding wave, leaving her heart hammering, bereft in her chest. Then in a rush all her senses returned, threatening to drown her. She stiffened in her seat and gripped her skirts, unsure of whether to run towards or away from her nephew. She had hoped she would see him, but now he was here she was bewildered as to what to do.

Thorstein caught the flash of desperate longing that had struck Gyda's face like lightning. It was gone almost as quickly as it had arrived, smoothed like the imaginary wrinkles on her gown that she so often brushed away. But he'd seen it, and it had reminded him of the look of grief he'd seen so fleetingly once before.

Not the same emotion. But the same honesty.

The same truth.

He followed her gaze, searching for the cause of her pain, and saw a pale-haired willowy boy he recognised immediately.

'Is that my nephew?' she asked, her voice cool, no longer betraying the inner turmoil he'd seen.

She'd covered her feelings so quickly he wondered for a moment if he'd imagined it. But, no, there had been no mistaking that bittersweet pain. He'd caught a glimpse of something similar on the boat earlier that morning.

It was another blow to the wall of certainty he'd built up around her. He'd thought her cold and arrogant. But there was emotion within her, deep and as wild as the sea. He'd tasted it that first night, when she'd pressed herself against him with longing and passion, as if she were the only thing she wanted in this world or the next, only to withdraw with arrogant indifference within the next heartbeat.

It was a mask.

He knew the truth now. There was another woman beneath. A woman in pain. A woman who flinched from the touch of men—even from her brother-in-law. She'd not flinched when they'd kissed, but then she'd been the one in control. Would she flinch if he held her again? Kissed her? Or would she kiss him back passionately? As she'd done that night?

Ridiculous!

She was arrogant and vain. What did it matter that she had hidden depths? It was nothing to him. She was no longer his responsibility.

Except he kept remembering how she'd spoken so enthusiastically with the cloth merchant earlier. Not as a wealthy customer, but with the respect and genuine interest of a fellow craftswoman. She hadn't been lying about wanting to start a business. She wanted independence. And he could not hold that against her. It was all he'd dreamed of for years after Thora had left.

The discovery was so different from his earlier beliefs that he struggled to reconcile them. One minute she was subtly flirting with Sven...the next proposing a business venture.

Sven called over to the youth. 'Ivar, come here! I want you to meet your Aunt Gyda... She has the face of your mother. They were twins.'

Thorstein caught the nervous glance Gyda gave Brunhild at Sven's mention of her being Astrid's twin. Of course! She'd said she was the eldest, hadn't she? Brunhild raised a sable brow at her and she visibly swallowed. He almost felt sorry for her. Brunhild was not a woman to cross.

As her nephew approached, Gyda stood and dipped elegantly, as if she were meeting a prince. 'Ivar, I am delighted to meet you.'

Ivar bowed with the easy confidence of a firstborn son and heir. 'Father said my mother was beautiful and tall. And look, my aunt is almost as big as you, father. Soon I'll be a man even taller than Thorstein.'

'You've got to become a man first, boy,' Thorstein said, and he gave him a light punch to the shoulder.

Ivar grinned. 'Soon I will be old enough to raid and fight.'

'It can take a long time to become a man...some never manage it,' quipped Gyda, and a teasing smile whispered at the edge of her cool expression.

Sven bellowed with laughter and rose to pull his son into a bear hug. He ruffled his pale hair and then playfully pushed him away. 'Perhaps you will be taller than me. But *I* will say when you are old enough to raid and fight. Now, go and eat with your brothers. You can speak more with your aunt later.'

Ivar gave Gyda a brilliant smile before running back to the other boys. Thorstein saw a momentary flicker of disappointment on her face, but she quickly covered it with a cool smile.

Odin's teeth! She was fascinating to watch. He was half afraid to look away in case he missed another glimpse into her heart.

Sven returned to his seat with an indulgent smile. 'I named him after my friend King Ivar the Boneless. I am sure he will prove worthy of that honour. He's a strong boy. Fierce as Fenrir! I swear I will find him howling at the moon one of these nights.'

After the meal, musicians began to play on some pipes, drums and a lyre. The music soared into the air, creating an ethereal song that vibrated through Gyda's soul and evoked the spirits of the gods. She loved music, and only wished she could sing or play herself, but she didn't have any natural talent for it. Astrid and Inga had been the musicians of her family. She'd always been content to sit and listen to them as she sewed. But here she had nothing to occupy her hands, and she found herself feeling awkward and restless.

Thorstein and Sven played a game of Tables, and she sat alone on a bench beside the fire. The household had settled quietly into a hum of conversation, and she watched her nephew playing and laughing with his brothers with growing affection. He was so full of life…

Brunhild came to sit beside her on the bench, a length of embroidery held idly in her hands. 'He was only a baby when I married Sven.'

Gyda blinked at this unusual start to a conversation. 'It must have been hard for you,' she answered carefully, unsure of Brunhild's motivation and hoping there was no malice in her.

She smiled. 'Not really. I was heavily pregnant with another man's child when I married Sven.'

Gyda tried her best not to look too shocked as Brunhild continued.

'No other man would have had me… But Sven was desperate for a mother for Ivar and he promised to take good care of my child. He kept his promise. That's Ceolwulf.' She pointed to the second tallest boy besides Ivar. He was rocking with laughter at something Ivar had said. 'It took time for me to love and trust Sven. But Ivar… I loved him straight away.'

Gyda let out a sigh of relief. There was no duplicity in Brunhild's eyes. She meant every word. 'I am glad my nephew has you.'

'He always will,' she replied firmly.

Gyda swallowed, unsure if this was a warning. 'But I

would like to get to know him better, if I may? He is the only surviving child of my sister…of any of my sisters.'

Brunhild leaned back and studied her, as if trying to read her thoughts. 'I can see your likeness in Ivar… You were Astrid's twin?'

'Yes, but not her equal… I am not my sister. Sven knows that.'

The other woman tilted her head in contemplation. 'Sven loved your sister deeply. It took a long time for him to mourn her. Your presence here will be…difficult for him.'

Gyda raised her chin slightly. 'Sven has known me since I was a child. He knows I'm not my sister and could never hope to be. He also knows that Astrid would have wanted him to remarry. She would have wanted happiness for both him and Ivar after she was gone. I would do nothing to harm your family, I swear it… But I have nowhere else to go.'

Brunhild nodded and Gyda relaxed a little.

'I have no quarrel with you, or with you getting to know your nephew better. But remember, I am Ivar's mother now.'

Gyda's heart softened at Brunhild's words. She was only protecting those she loved—as she would have done if the roles had been reversed.

'Thank you. Sven and Ivar are fortunate to have you… I believe Astrid would agree with me on that.'

Brunhild nodded, then moved away from her to sit beside Sven. She murmured something in Sven's ear and Gyda wondered if she'd passed some kind of test.

She was startled to notice that Thorstein was staring at her. His perceptive eyes missed nothing. It was as if he could see past her skin and bones to the bleeding heart within. She looked away, afraid that there would be nothing left of her privacy if he looked at her long enough.

A short time later she was pulled away from her thoughts by Sven's brisk voice.

'Come, Gyda. I wish to speak with you.' He was already walking towards his private chambers as he passed her. He didn't even pause to see if she followed him.

She glanced over at Brunhild, who gave her a reassuring smile. The time had come. She would learn her fate.

She rose and clasped her hands firmly in front of her, to stop them from shaking, and followed him. As she passed Thorstein's bench he raised his eyes and lowered his horn of mead. He wiped his lower lip with a slow stroke of his thumb and heat raced up her spine.

There was a knowingness to his gaze that set her teeth on edge. Did he know what was to become of her? Did he even care?

She swallowed and looked away from him, hoping she appeared strong even if she didn't feel it.

Sven's private rooms were divided from the rest of the Hall by large frames of colourful tapestries, and the area he took her to served as an antechamber, with two fur-covered chairs placed in front of a small fire. No doubt a cosy place to sit with his wife on a cold winter's night.

If the fates had been kinder maybe she would have been sitting here laughing with Astrid instead. As it was, she stood slightly away from the fire, unsure of whether to sit or stand. An unwelcome guest.

'I'm sorry to bring my troubles to your door. I bet you wish I'd never left Njardarheimr,' she said with a weak laugh, praying that Sven would disagree with her...and mean it.

'No, I'm glad you came,' he said with a dismissive

wave as he moved into a darkened corner. 'There's something I want to give you.'

Her curiosity piqued, Gyda stepped closer so that she could see him better.

Sven had moved to a large chest, and after a moment of rummaging pulled out a smaller box. The firelight flickered over the polished wood and its carvings. It had a depiction of Freya combined with Valkyrie wings upon its lid.

She recognised it immediately and felt as if she'd been struck in the chest. All the air rushed out of her in a single choked breath.

Sven held it out to her. 'She would have wanted you to have it.'

'But…' Despite herself she reached forward, and with her fingers traced the wood with the tenderest of caresses.

'It should have been yours. You were the eldest.'

'By a handful of moments… And I had no need for it then. Halvor wouldn't have approved.' *Then. Now.* Now she felt a burning need to cradle her past and never let it go.

'Call it a bride price if you wish.'

Her fingers stilled. 'What do you mean by that, brother?'

Sven laughed. 'Do not judge me so harshly, Gyda. I speak only of practicalities.'

'Practicalities?' Her mind raced, but she failed to understand his meaning.

'Thorstein would make a fine husband for any woman.'

'Thorstein?' She took a step back, her feet sluggish and unbalanced.

'Yes, Thorstein,' he replied firmly, still holding the box towards her.

'Thorstein?'

'Yes, Gyda.' Sven sighed. 'Is it really so shocking? As I've said, he'd make a fine husband.'

'I do not doubt it… But I have been married before—for *ten years* with no issue! I am hardly a good match for him. Besides, as a widow, I had hoped to start a business, as other widows have been allowed to do—'

'Other *wealthy* widows, yes. But you are not wealthy.'

'My tapestries are the finest in all of Viken!'

'They are also at the bottom of the North Sea…with all your other possessions.'

'You refuse to help me?'

'I have already offered help! Marry Thorstein. He is a good man with a promising settlement. You will be the lady of a fine Hall once again.'

She scowled and looked away. 'I have been the lady of a fine Hall once before, and I have nothing to show for it! Must I sell myself to the first man who plucks me from the sea?'

'Be reasonable, Gyda!'

'I *am* being reasonable. Take me in—if only for a few months…'

'You need to marry. Brunhild is a good woman, but she will not accept my dead wife's twin in her home. And a woman living alone during this unrest… Surely, you must see…?'

Her body slumped. 'I had hoped…'

He laughed—not unkindly, but with a glint in his eye as he shook his head. 'I know… You always had such strange ambitions.'

Her smile was weak in response. She took the small box from his hands. 'I only married Halvor because it strengthened my family's alliances.'

'Yes… And it gave your sisters the freedom to marry men of their own choosing—men like me, who at the time had nothing to their names but courage. I will not forget that, and I'm sure that if Astrid had lived we would still be very happy together. In fact, I am certain of it.'

He paused, his eyes clouded with memory. He plucked an errant strand of hair away from her face and tucked it behind her ear.

'It hurts my heart to see you. The likeness is startling. You are the same, and yet...not.' His hand dropped down to his side.

Gyda took a step backwards and clutched the box tightly to her chest. It was Sven, not his wife who did not want her here. Not in his city...not in his home.

But she was pragmatic about her fate. Without his support she would have to marry. Better to a man like Thorstein, and better yet with her family's jewellery back in her possession.

'Thorstein might not have me. Have you considered that?'

Sven laughed, and dismissed her with a wave of his hand. 'I doubt it.'

Chapter Ten

'Absolutely not,' said Thorstein, throwing down a duck bone with a snap of his wrist. He'd managed to talk Brunhild into giving him some leftovers, but the tender meat suddenly tasted sour on his tongue.

'She's beautiful,' said Sven, looking towards the guest chamber with a melancholy smile.

Brunhild and Gyda had entered there earlier, presumably to prepare it for Gyda's stay.

He'd never seen Sven like this, with his eyes clouded by bittersweet memories. Sven was a warrior, a leader and a political advisor to King Guthrum. He'd been an advisor to King Ivar and King Halfdan before that. He was resilient, intelligent and coldly ruthless when necessary. It was a timely reminder that beauty could rob any man of his senses.

'And?' he said, scowling in the same direction.

Sven laughed. 'And you want more? Fine! Gyda is from an ancient dynasty. The—'

'I know! And such things do not impress me. I have no need for royal bloodlines or grand titles.'

'You should. It is no accident that Halvor's port doubled in size after he married Gyda. There is magic in her veins. She will run your settlement as if it were a kingdom, and she has the skill to bring prosperity to all she manages. Her sister Astrid… She was a lady of light.'

'You think I care about lineage or beauty? I have no ambition for power nor thirst for shallow pleasure.'

'You said you wanted a wife,' snapped Sven.

'For an heir. I have land. I should start a family.'

'I agree—long past time. That Thora stole more than years from you.'

'That's forgotten.' Thorstein eased back into his seat. 'I am happy with my simple life. Working the land… building my settlement. I want a wife suited to that life. Not one forced to accept me because of her misfortune.'

'Hmm…' Sven paused, his eyes piercing. 'She wants you.'

Thorstein snorted. 'Impossible.'

A strange thrill shivered through his veins, but he dismissed it with a roll of his shoulders. His bones popped and cracked without relief.

'Why impossible? You are a young man of status now, with far more to offer Gyda than her previous husband. She has already told me that she would welcome the match.'

Thorstein laughed. 'Welcome it? I doubt she welcomes anything besides silver and fine clothes.'

'With you she can have children, a secure future…'

'She does not strike me as maternal. Only the other day I saw her ordering a small child to fetch porridge for her. I think you have judged her purely on the merits of her sister. Gyda would be much happier with a rich, fat jarl to keep her warm in silks and gold.'

'I may have loved only one, but I knew both sisters well and you are too harsh on her. How can you blame a widow for trying to save her only means of protection in a new land? She has no family here except me—and I am a tenuous connection at best. She told me her stepsons wished her to join their father on the pyre. A woman in the prime of her life—joining him with his previous wives? Outrageous! When I first knew Gyda she was a romantic and kind girl—a little distant sometimes, but her sisters all adored her... It is true she has changed greatly in the years since her marriage to Halvor. But I suspect it is only maturity and wisdom that has cooled her temperament. The base metal, I'm sure, remains the same.'

'I do not want her,' Thorstein muttered.

But he could sense that Sven's mind was set, and he would be in for a long battle of wills if he decided to thwart him on this.

Would marrying Gyda be so terrible?

He bristled at the unwelcome thought. Of course it would be a disaster! They were not suited to each other. Gyda was a woman who belonged in a jarl's court, not on a farm.

Sven's bark of laughter interrupted his thoughts. 'Ha! Now, *that* is a lie! I have seen you staring. I know she seems indifferent at times...'

'She is not indifferent! She blows hot and cold like a tempest.'

'There, then. You want her. She wants you. And you both have no family allegiances or obligations standing in your way. A perfect match.'

'I have told you I do not want her. Keep her in your household if you fear for her safety.'

'Impossible. Brunhild will never accept it. I may command Jorvik, but I am still a Northman and my wife rules the household.'

'Then marry her to another.'

Sven's face darkened considerably. 'I have gifted you with land, status and wealth. Do not make me regret my choice. You asked me to find you a wife and I have offered you an excellent match. Take her. I will pay the bride price and she will cost you nothing.'

At Thorstein's dismissive shake of his head Sven spat on the floor and thumped his fist on the table, causing the cups to jump and spill.

'Thorstein Bergson! You are not the only one I owe a blood debt to. Without Gyda I could never have married her sister or had my son. I will honour her sacrifice and repay her with a man more worthy of her. *You* are that man. Stop behaving as if I have offered you an old sow and accept this gift with gratitude!'

Thorstein dismissed Sven's words. A wealthy woman's idea of sacrifice was not the same as his. She had traded one gilded bed for another. Yes, her marriage to Halvor might have helped Sven secure his match, but he doubted she had done it for her sister—more likely she had done it for silver, jewels and power.

A quiet cough at the doorway drew both men's eyes to the two women who stood there. Sven's wife Brunhild and Gyda were side by side. Gyda's face was cool and inscrutable. She towered over the Saxon woman beside her, her body still and poised—except for her hands, he noted, which were clasped tightly in front of her in a strangling grip.

Thorstein's chest tightened with shame.

Brunhild gave both men a reproachful glare as she passed them on the way to her chambers. 'It is late, and our household is trying to get some rest.' She waved her hand at some of the people resting on piles of furs at the side of the room. 'I am retiring for the night, husband.'

'I shall join you,' answered Sven. He leaned into Thorstein's ear, so the women wouldn't hear his words. 'If you were any other man this would not be a request, it would be an order.'

He stood and followed his wife to their chamber.

Gyda walked towards Thorstein, her steps measured and calm. She sat in the chair Sven had vacated and smoothed the lines of her woollen dress. He noticed the gown was shorter than before, revealing a sliver of skin between her boot and the carefully stitched hem. Presumably to cover the damage caused by the shipwreck.

'You do not want me.'

Her words shocked him with their brutal honesty. She said them without censure or anger but with a steady gaze, as if she could see into his mind and read his thoughts like runes.

Ashamed, he struggled to find words. He would have been happier in battle, with only his fists as weapons, than seated here, talking to Gyda at this moment.

'I need a farmer's wife, not a lady.'

'Is that your only objection?' she asked, her eyes never once retreating from his.

'Yes. My settlement is in its infancy. Its prosperity depends on hard work and strength.'

'Did Sven mention my family?'

'As impressive as that is…'

'It's not what you need in a wife,' she answered with a nod.

He wondered at her calmness. He almost missed the outrage and passion he'd seen on the shipwreck. This quiet, logical woman was harder to argue with.

'Many claim similar lineage regarding their family's lines. It is understandable. They are links to our legends and our paths to power. The claim is still revered even when its origins are lost from memory. My family is no different—but we were farmers once. Freya's fertility poured from my ancestor's hands into our crops. Maybe it was in our blood…maybe not. But it was what initially gave my father his power and wealth. I may not be descended from a goddess, but I know what I am capable of—and I am not daunted by the prospect of being a farmer's wife. I swear I will do all I can to prove that to you.'

His breath froze in his lungs and he had to summon all his wits to sound normal. 'You surprise me, Gyda. I thought you would object to marrying me.'

She leaned forward and placed a hand lightly on his forearm. 'Why? You are a better man than my late husband. Marry me, Thorstein… Please… Give me a chance to prove myself.'

He stiffened at the unexpected touch and saw that she became flustered, moving away quickly.

'If by Yule you still find me unsuitable, then I will accept divorce and use the bride price Sven has offered to return to Viken.'

'You would accept such terms?'

He was dumbfounded. Why would she plead with him to marry her and then in the next breath offer him a divorce? He'd been divorced once before—it was not something he wished to repeat.

'Gladly. I believe we are better suited than you think.'

Her cheeks became stained with a blush, and he thought back to their kiss. His lips ached to taste her again.

'It's Friday tomorrow,' she added casually, not meeting his eyes, her voice quiet and hesitant.

'Weddings should always take place on Frigga's day,'

he agreed, his mind spinning from the surprising turn of events.

Was he really agreeing to this?

'I'm sure Sven could arrange for a *gothi* to perform the ceremony. The dowry and the bride price have been agreed, and Sven already has your allegiance, so there are no further terms to negotiate.'

He decided to test her resolve. 'As this is not your first marriage I presume you won't require the usual ceremonies and rituals?'

A flash of disappointment crossed Gyda's face, but she quickly covered it with a cool smile. 'Of course not—just the essentials.'

Had he really done it? Agreed to marry a woman when only moments ago he'd considered her wholly unsuitable?

But Sven was right. It was a good match. He would be related by blood to his Overlord's heir and it would cost him nothing but a beautiful wife. Gyda seemed willing, and he couldn't deny his attraction to her. Maybe he had been harsh in his judgement of her. He was older and wiser than the youth who'd loved Thora without wisdom.

If Gyda was willing to live a simpler life, then he was willing to give her a chance.

After all, there was no possibility of him making the same mistakes again.

She would never have his heart, as Thora had.

Their alliance would be purely political and for their mutual benefit.

He would never lose his heart and mind to her, but he would enjoy her beauty and strength.

She was a force of nature, and he couldn't help the spark of pride that fluttered in his chest when he thought about calling her his wife.

Chapter Eleven

Gyda sat in front of the polished plate which leaned up against the wall. Brunhild had kindly placed it in her chamber so that she could prepare for the wedding.

She held a golden crown lightly between the palms of her hands. It was her family's bridal *kransen*. She'd never worn it. It symbolised a bride's virginity and purity, and when she'd wed Halvor she'd not had either, so she'd refused.

Inga had been the first to wear it. A winter bride marrying her childhood sweetheart. She'd woven ivy through its golden knots and runes, and the Valkyrie wings had flanked either side of her temples, with the three-pronged symbol of Freya carefully placed at the centre of her forehead. Her pale hair had flowed down her back like a river of snow, and there had been a shy smile on her sweet lips.

Astrid had married next. Her twin had looked the same as her, but they had been as different as the sun and the moon. Laughing Astrid had danced all night to the beat of the drums, never wanting the celebration to end. Sven had carried her out in the end, the bridal crown askew in her braids.

Sigga had been the last, and she'd giggled with Astrid

as they'd dressed her in the blue gown Gyda had made especially—a gown fit for a goddess. Sigga had wept with joy when she'd seen herself in the polished plate…

That was the last time all four of them had been together. They'd embraced, and cried, and promised to visit. But they were all gone before Gyda's wedding had been finalised. Each one taken by the birthing bed in one way or another.

Inga's babe had come too soon, taking her life as well as the child's. Astrid had survived the birth of her son, but had died of a fever only days later. Sigga had struggled with terrible sickness throughout her pregnancy and had been too weak to survive the trials of labour. Her baby girl had died the following winter.

'Men would risk their lives on treacherous seas and raid lands for glory. But a woman's battle is as dangerous as theirs. You carry the honour of your sisters with you now,' her mother had told her.

The Volva had prophesied that Gyda would be fruitless in marriage until she was crowned the queen of her husband's heart. Well, there had been no chance of her being the queen of Halvor's heart. She'd taken comfort in that, grateful that she would never fall pregnant with his child.

Now the idea made her blood run cold.

Her fingers tightened around the crown. It was always so easy to wander into dark thoughts. She sighed. Grief was her constant companion, and even after all these years it would never let her forget.

She spoke aloud, hoping her sisters and mother could hear her. 'I have a second chance. I have learnt my lesson. I won't fail again. I'll be a dutiful wife. Thorstein is a good man. I'm certain of it. I'll make him proud. I'll make you all proud.'

With trembling fingers she placed the crown upon her head and stared at her reflection. In the top half of her hair she'd created many small braids, tied off with thin strips of leather, while the lower part was loose, a symbol of her sexuality, the tips of her hair almost reaching her waist.

Gyda looked down at her gown with a sigh. It was the same gown she'd worn on the night of the shipwreck, and despite several washes and careful repairs it still looked worn and tarnished. Not her first choice for wedding attire, but she cheered herself with the thought that soon she would be able to make new gowns. She would ask Thorstein to buy her some material before they left. There would be a good range of fabric, dyes and needles in Jorvik. Maybe she could buy some of that sunset colour? She'd like to meet that interesting cloth merchant, Edith, again…

Brunhild poked her head into the room. 'Are you ready? Oh, you look beautiful!'

Gyda smiled, turning away from her reflection. 'Has a sacrifice been made?'

She hoped they'd made a sacrifice. She wanted nothing to harm this marriage—bad spirits most of all. She'd been haunted by prophecy for too long as it was.

'Yes, a goat has been sacrificed to your gods.'

'You're Christian?'

'Yes, I'm Saxon, remember?' Brunhild laughed, although not unkindly.

'And… Sven doesn't mind that?'

'Marriage is all about compromise. But I'm sure you already know that.'

Gyda's cheeks burned with shame. 'Halvor didn't compromise much.' Most of the time he'd avoided her, and if they'd disagreed on a subject he'd either shouted at her or slapped her, depending on how stubborn she had decided to be.

Brunhild seemed to understand. She took a step closer and rested a hand on her shoulder. 'Thorstein is stubborn at times. But he's still a decent man.'

The kindness made her uncomfortable. It reminded her too much of what she'd lost.

She reached for her family chest. 'I'm almost ready. I won't be much longer.'

Brunhild remained still. 'Are you sure about this? Marrying Thorstein.'

'Shouldn't I be? Is there something I should know? I thought Thorstein was an honourable man.' Alarm raced through her body and old wounds began to sting.

'Oh, he is,' Brunhild assured her. 'But I fear you have been pushed into this match by my husband. Sven is a good man, but he believes he knows what is best for everyone. This marriage is so sudden...'

'My first marriage took five years to arrange, and I still wasn't happy.'

Brunhild frowned with concern and Gyda put on a light smile.

'Who is to say how happy we shall be? I hope only for companionship, children, and a man who is honourable and kind.'

Brunhild laughed with a shake of her head. 'I hoped for the same. I fell in love instead... It hurt so much more than being alone at first. A man who lives in the past is impossible to love in the present. But thankfully that changed.'

Gyda looked away. Had it changed because Brunhild had accepted Sven's lack of love, or had it changed because he'd decided to forget the past? Was Brunhild worried that Thorstein would be unable to love Gyda because of his first wife?

She was too afraid of the answers to ask.

She began to fiddle with the placement of her crown, hoping to feign indifference. 'Love is a fantasy for young maidens who know little of the real world. I know Thorstein was married before. That he is divorced. I have no desire to win his heart. This is an alliance. I hope to have children and live in peace with a good man. That's all.'

Liar...you want to be loved, whispered a voice inside her, making her heart beat faster.

It was a reckless thought. What was wrong with her? More likely she would win his approval—even Halvor had begrudgingly accepted her after she'd proved so capable in managing the port.

'Maybe you should want more than that,' said Brunhild, and shrugged at her startled look. 'Thorstein and Sven are quite similar in temperament. It is why they get along so well. And both of them always believe they're right, once their mind's set. Sven once believed he could never love again...it took me a long time to make him realise the truth.'

'And what is the truth?'

Brunhild smiled, carefully repositioning Gyda's crown until it sat straight on her head. 'Love is not an object to own. Our hearts are not bound by weight or value. There is always more love we can give and receive. We just need to allow room for it to grow. Thorstein is a good man... be patient with him.'

Gyda couldn't speak. She nodded, and with a knowing smile Brunhild left the room.

She opened the chest; she'd only removed the crown from it earlier. Not quite ready to face all of her memories straightaway. Tears pricked at her eyes until she had to take a deep breath to force them back down. As if they were beloved pets, she stroked the chest's contents. There were bracelets, brooches and beads in a variety of materials, from precious silver and gold to polished amber and glass. There were even a few wooden beads and bracelets, some intricately carved and painted, others more rustic, but all as well-loved and valued as the rest.

Each piece captured a treasured memory of her family. Each piece had been worn by all of them at one time or another. It was painful to look at them, but more painful to choose between them. She had thought never to see them again. As she would never see her sisters or her mother again.

She poured the jewellery into her lap, its weight reassuringly solid, as if she carried the hearts of her family with her.

It would be excessive to wear so much, but as she put on each bracelet, brooch and pin she felt closer to her sisters. She no longer felt alone, or afraid, because each piece symbolised not only her family's love but security—in herself more than anything. Each piece reminded her of happier times. When she'd been loved and valued.

She put everything on—even the glass beads which clashed horribly with her amber necklace. She tucked them beneath her linen shift, patting the beads gently, so they were not visible beneath her gown but would lie close to her heart. The amber had been a gift from Halvor, but it had been her mother who had spent hours carefully threading them into an ornate design. She had to wear them too.

She couldn't choose between any of the pieces of jewellery and she didn't want to. It would be like choosing which memories of her family to honour and which ones to discard.

She would start her new life wearing every single piece.

Their memories close to her skin.

Chapter Twelve

Thorstein drummed his fingers against the head of his axe. Its handle rested on the floor between his legs, its height almost up to his waist. It was a lethal weapon he'd spent months learning to wield, and he usually carried it strapped to his back.

He was glad that it had been years since it had tasted blood. But a man should have a symbol of Thor or Odin on his wedding day, and the axe was by far his most impressive weapon. He'd brought it for this very reason, although he'd thought his bride would be different, and he'd risen early so that he could fetch it from his boat.

However, there'd been no need to hurry. Gyda was still 'preparing herself'.

He felt like an idiot for racing across the city. Here he was, still waiting for his bride well after the midday sun had passed.

She'd insisted on a bath—which seemed madness as she'd been nearly drowned twice in as many days. How much water did a woman need? That had taken most of the morning to prepare, although Brunhild hadn't seemed to mind. Maybe because she would be getting rid of Gyda once and for all.

He dismissed that thought as quickly as it had come to him. Brunhild was not a petty woman.

'What's taking her so long?' he growled.

Was she having doubts? Because he certainly was.

Sven grinned at him. 'Eager to take your bride? And there I was, thinking I'd have to drag you to your own wedding.'

'There's only a few hours of daylight left. There'll be no wedding at all if she doesn't make haste.'

The three men stood at a hastily decorated altar in the centre of the square, surrounded by a handful of Thorstein's men and about as many of Sven's retinue. Everyone was bored and irritable in equal measure.

The *gothi* gave Sven a worried look and squinted at the sun, low in the sky and just visible above the Halls surrounding the square. 'I have another wedding to perform before sundown,' he grumbled.

'It can wait,' Thorstein said coldly with narrowed eyes, and the *gothi* nodded with a visible swallow.

Sven laughed with a dismissive wave of his hand. 'She has to bathe and dress…all these things take time.'

Thorstein rolled his eyes with a vicious snarl. 'She agreed on no unnecessary ritual! Then suddenly she's calling for a bath and for her clothes to be cleaned.'

'Hmm…yes, clean clothes are a *very* unnecessary ritual,' answered Sven, looking pointedly at the axe.

Thorstein ignored him.

'It's your fault we're waiting, Thorstein,' Sven went on. 'She said she'd be ready before sunset. You were the one to insist on a noon ceremony.'

The *gothi* raised his eyebrows at that revelation, but wisely said nothing.

Sven laughed and looked over Thorstein's shoulder at

the opening doors of his Hall. 'Ah, look—here she comes. Some might say…early.'

Thorstein spun on his heel and stared as Brunhild strode to Sven's side and shrugged at Thorstein's displeasure. 'She's ready.'

'Finally!' responded Thorstein sharply.

But Gyda still didn't emerge from the Hall.

As the silence stretched, so did Thorstein's patience. Flies buzzed and the smell of roasting meat filled the square, making his stomach growl.

Thralls scurried around the wedding party. They had the bare minimum of six witnesses, including Sven and his wife, most of whom were Thorstein's men. But some of the people from the surrounding Halls had come out to watch. He felt their knowing stares with every heartbeat that passed and they pressed down on his chest like a shield wall.

Did they all know about Thora?

Would he be rejected once again?

Were they all waiting to watch his inevitable humiliation?

Had he made yet another reckless decision when it came to marriage?

The soft thud of a closing door grabbed his attention and the deep breath he hadn't realised he'd been holding was released in a rush as he saw Gyda step out of the gloom. Her hair glinted in the sunlight, ribbons of braid beneath a crown of gold.

Gold!

The precious metal sparkled, setting aflame her pale, elaborately braided hair. She wore her amber necklace, as well as bronze and silver brooches and pins. Bracelets clicked at her wrists and ankles as she walked, and rings with gems glinted off nearly every finger. The woman was draped in so much jewellery he was surprised she had the strength to walk.

Thorstein cursed under his breath and turned away. If she wished to cover herself from head to toe in Sven's wife's jewellery, then so be it. It would be the last time she wore gold. Maybe that was why she'd done it. Weddings were rituals of change and renewal after all.

As she moved to his side, he asked quietly, 'Are you sure you still wish to be a simple farmer's wife?'

'Yes, I swear it,' she replied, clasping his arm with those slender fingers trimmed with silver and precious jewels.

With a huff, he nodded and looked at the *gothi* expectantly. 'Get on with it, then.'

The *gothi* jumped with fright and began sweeping through the ceremony as if he were clearing out dirty rushes from a stable.

In no time the ceremony was drawn to a close. They handed each other plain silver rings, although no ceremonial swords were exchanged. They made their vows with efficient speed.

The *gothi* flicked the sacrificial blood over their heads. 'You are now bound in marriage!' he proclaimed.

His work done, he quickly packed up his things and shuffled out of the square with an uninterested wave of blessing.

Thorstein stared at the beauty in front of him and felt his face grow numb. She stared back at him expectantly. Her lips were full and delicately pink. She waited, her breath shallow, as she stared at his mouth expectantly.

He should kiss her. But for some reason he couldn't move. And as the silence grew, the moment became thick with awkward tension.

'Come, let us feast!' shouted Sven, snapping him out of his stupor.

Sven grabbed him by the arm and guided him into the Hall, where he was taken to a large table and thrust down onto a bench. Gyda joined him in dignified silence, arranging her skirts as she sat and then stroking her fingers lightly over the engravings of one of her bracelets.

Would she touch him like that tonight? Trace the lines of his body with those lingering fingers?

The thought caught him by surprise and hot need rushed down to his groin. He pulled the table closer, wincing at the loud scrape it made against the floor.

'It's not a specially brewed wedding ale, but it's the best I have,' said Sven, passing a jug of mead to Gyda.

'Thank you,' she said as she accepted the jug and turned to face Thorstein.

She poured the golden liquid into a cup and held it up to his lips. 'For Odin!' he said, and a cheer rang out.

He leaned forward and wrapped his hand around Gyda's silky fingers as he took a deep drink from the cup. His eyes lingered on her lips as the liquid was tipped gently into his mouth. The mead was earthy and rich, with a delicious sweetness, but the taste only added to his thirst for her touch.

With their warm hands still entwined, he moved the cup towards Gyda's lips. She sucked in a breath and he breathed her in. Anticipation threatened to drive him mad.

'For Freya!' she said, and another cheer filled the Hall.

She parted her lips and took the cup to her mouth. Thorstein eased it up a little, so she could drink the remainder of the mead. As he lowered it a stray drop ran down her chin. He reached forward with his other hand and wiped away the liquid with a brush of his thumb. She stared at him, her pupils wide in the gloom, dark pools surrounded by molten silver.

His fingers swept to the back of her head and he pulled her close, pressing his lips against hers as another cheer rang out.

Her lips parted under his and he couldn't resist deepening the kiss to taste more of her. She tasted like winter berries and honey.

He felt her soft palm against his chest, but whether it was to push him away or steady herself he couldn't be sure. Regardless, he moved away, and she let out a sigh, her cheeks flushed.

'Will you place your axe across my lap now?' she asked, her cheeks flushing darker by the second.

He frowned and looked dumbly at the axe he'd leaned against the table when he'd sat down.

He coughed as he felt heat rise in his own face. 'Of course.'

It was a symbol of Thor, and as such should be placed in a bride's lap to promote strong and healthy children. He laid the axe head across her lap, careful to bear the weight of the handle across his own thighs.

'You desire children?' he asked, immediately feeling like an idiot for asking.

Sudden fear washed over her face. 'Yes... Do you?'

He nodded, and her shoulders relaxed slightly.

He'd had no children with Thora. She'd not wanted any children until they were 'better settled', as she'd put it, although of course that time had never come. They'd both realised how ill-suited they were to each other long before they'd separated. Although it had taken him a long time to accept it.

'Well, then, let's hope the gods will it,' she answered

lightly, patting the head of the axe and then reaching towards the platter of roasted meats and vegetables in front of her.

He would have thought her carefree, except her fingers trembled.

The feast was never-ending. If he'd thought the time waiting for the ceremony long it had been nothing compared to this. The food kept coming—platter after platter of succulent meats and extravagantly spiced dishes. He wondered how he could ever repay Sven and Brunhild.

Except, of course, the feast wasn't only to celebrate his marriage with Gyda. It was an excuse to show the other leaders of the city Sven's strength and alliances. Thorstein was Sven's man. He'd sworn himself to his Overlord and would not break his word. But others weren't to know that, and this marriage bound him by blood to his Overlord and his heir, Ivar.

Still, as the evening progressed, with music, entertainment and enough food to sate even Thorstein's huge appetite, he couldn't help but feel humbled by the effort they'd made, especially at such short notice.

He looked at Gyda beside him. She seemed so distant as she watched the musicians play. There was a fragile smile on her lips and her eyes were half closed in thought.

He hoped she realised the significance of such an honour.

No doubt her first wedding had been a grand feast over several days, with attendance from all the Jarls of Viken. Very grand compared to his own first wedding, made in haste after a victory feast.

He'd been a battle-hardened youth, seeking comfort from a girl who had barely known her own mind. His marriage to Thora had been based on lust and promises they hadn't been able to keep. Thora had wanted more than the life of a simple farmer's wife... Had he made the same mistake again by marrying Gyda?

'It was generous of Brunhild to let you borrow her jewellery today,' he said, not hiding the censure in his tone as he added, 'Especially so much of it. I know how wounded you were to lose yours to the sea...but such is fate.'

'Oh, but it is mine,' she said with a beaming smile as she fingered the ornate crown with a tilt of her pretty head.

'What...? How?' If the roof had caved in he could not have been more surprised.

'It is my family jewellery. Sven gave it to me as my bridal dowry.'

Thorstein stared at her until his knuckles ached from clenching his fists, but he refused to yield. Instead he took three deep breaths, stood up and strode towards Sven, who was leaning against a pillar and laughing at Ivar's attempt to wrestle a much older youth.

'You *paid* her to marry me?' he challenged Sven, whose horn of mead stilled in mid-air.

After a pause, Sven took a swig and slurred, 'The jewellery?'

'Yes! The jewellery! How could you even imagine I would accept—'

'Peace, Thorstein!' he said, with a wave of his drink.

Half of his mead slopped onto the reeds by Thorstein's boot, which only further darkened his mood.

'She is a fine woman! Just like her sister. Look at the way she smiles... I only thought to treat her well.'

Thorstein didn't look. He didn't want to look at her. To see her covered in the trinkets that had bought her acceptance.

He opened his mouth, but then promptly snapped it shut. What could he say? That he'd thought she'd married him because of a kiss?

Chapter Thirteen

The tables and benches had been cleared away to allow room for dancing and wrestling. Gyda had danced with some of the men out of politeness, but had quickly withdrawn at the end of each song. Thorstein had not asked her to dance once, which irritated her greatly, but she refused to show it.

His mood had darkened throughout the evening. She couldn't understand why he was becoming so ill-tempered. But she saw it approaching as clearly as a storm rolling in from the sea. He spoke less and less as the evening progressed, and scowled more and more.

Not that anyone apart from her seemed to notice—they were all deep in their cups.

Two men—one Thorstein's, the other Sven's—were in the middle of a wrestling match. They writhed on the floor, their legs and arms locked together, as each man struggled to gain dominion over the other. It would have been an impressive contest if she'd not already seen Thorstein fight.

She sighed as she looked around the Hall absently. She wished she had something to work on. Although no doubt they would look even odder as a couple if the bride set about sewing at her own wedding feast.

At first she'd been nervous about the end of the evening, and the inevitable bedding. Then, after Thorstein had kissed her, she'd been excited, hoping to feel the pleasure her sisters had whispered about.

She could not deny she found him pleasing to the eye…more than pleasing, in fact. Something about the way he moved always drew her. But when Thorstein had abruptly walked away from her she'd feared the worst.

He was obviously annoyed that she'd accepted the jewellery.

But what else had he expected?

They were family heirlooms. Of course she would accept them—and gratefully. Halvor had hated any evidence of her family's wealth. He'd claimed that his wife would only ever need gifts from her husband. It was one of the reasons she'd refused the chest after her sisters had all died. Halvor would probably have thrown it away out of spite.

She hoped Thorstein was better than that… Maybe if she didn't wear quite so much of it he wouldn't object? Wearing all of it had been a mistake. She should have known. Men never liked their wives appearing grander than themselves.

Sven stopped beside her. His voice was thick with drink and his fingers wrapped tightly around her wrist as he pulled her close.

'Thorstein is a good man, Gyda. A good man. Loyal… but that loyalty takes time to earn, and he has been deceived by love in the past. Love him as Astrid loved me and you will be the happiest of women.'

She leaned away from the sickly smell of mead on his breath. It reminded her too much of Halvor's infrequent and disastrous attempts at lovemaking. His horrible breath and fumbling hands, the awkward touches that had made her cringe, followed by the inevitable frustration, the angry words and vicious slaps.

Something she did not wish to be reminded of tonight.

'I will do my best,' Gyda said, patting Sven's arm as she carefully peeled herself away from his grip.

Sven looked down, as if surprised to realise he'd been holding her so tightly. He quickly stepped away, almost stumbling into Thorstein, who approached from behind.

Thorstein steadied him with a heavy palm. He glared at her and she worried that he would think she'd welcomed Sven's touch. Surely not?

'Come, wife, it is time to rest.'

She blinked at the command and glanced at Sven, who sniggered on swaying feet. 'You are eager, Thorstein! But who could blame you? I'll gather the witnesses.'

'No need. It's not as if she's a virgin,' barked Thorstein, and a hush fell upon the room.

Gyda covered her momentary humiliation with a nod. 'Thorstein is right. I'm a widow. There's no need for the witnesses to follow us.'

She clasped her arm around Thorstein's in an attempt at unity, although his muscles tensed under her fingertips. Ignoring it, she walked with her new husband to their bedchamber, her head held high.

It was happening again. Lust was making him stupid. He had sworn that he wouldn't make the same mistake again. That the next woman he married would have no desire for wealth. She would be a hardworking farmer's wife, simple and honest. And what had he done? He'd married a beautiful woman who cared only for jewellery and fine clothes.

At least Thora had had the sense to covet status as well as wealth. Gyda didn't even care that she would be taking a step down by marrying him, so consumed by fickle greed was she.

He watched in agony as she slowly and carefully removed each piece of her jewellery and placed it in the waiting chest. It seemed to take an eternity for her to undress, and the whole time he stood in front of the door, unsure of whether to stay or leave.

The final brooches and pins were unclipped and the apron of her gown pooled at her feet, to reveal a more tightly fitted shift beneath. She picked up the tattered gown and draped it over a nearby chair.

It reminded him of the time he'd seen her undress on his boat. A surge of lust raced through his body, making his breath shallow and his knees weak.

She still wore her *kransen*. It shone in the flickering light of the fire like a living crown of flame. She lifted her foot and placed it on a stool. The shift was too short on her frame and it revealed the pale, slender skin between the top of her boot and her shapely calf. She loosened the ties on her boot and slipped it off. She did the same with the other boot, placing them neatly next to each other.

As she straightened she glanced over at him, her head tilted in a knowing manner that made him burn. How could she do that? Entice and mock him in equal measure, as if she knew him to be nothing more than a dumb beast that awaited her bidding.

She continued to stare at him as her fingers slipped beneath the neckline of her shift to tease out a string of glass beads.

Disbelief and disgust hit him with equal measure. 'Did you fear Sven would demand you return anything you did not wear? Each of your necklaces could feed a family for a month... Do you honestly expect me to believe you will be content as a farmer's wife?'

She stiffened, fear sliding across her features. It was only there for a moment and then the cool, detached mask returned. 'They are mine. What I do with them is not your concern.'

She did think of him as a beast. Guilt washed over him, making him shift on the balls of his feet. He had not meant to imply he would take the jewellery away from her. He knew Saxon men took the bridal dowry as part of their right, but that was not the Norse way.

'They are yours.'

He scowled at the way her shoulders relaxed at his words. How could she make him bend to her will with a simple look?

'We will leave Jorvik at first light.'

'But the feast! Brunhild has planned for three days of feasting!' she cried.

'It can continue without us.'

'A wedding feast without the bride and groom?'

'A feast is unnecessary, don't you think?'

'I suppose... But...'

She paused, as if grasping for a coherent thought, and he took a strange pleasure in seeing her flustered for a change.

'I will need to buy some essentials before we leave... I have no clothing.'

'You can get everything you need at the settlement. There is no need to buy expensive clothing if you are to become a farmer's wife.'

An exasperated huff burst from her lips and she looked at him with silver-blue daggers. 'I do not wear this tat-

tered gown over and over out of love for it! The women of
your settlement had nothing appropriate for me to wear!'

'As I have already said…as a farmer's wife, you will
need more simple clothing. I'm sure there'll be something you can alter.'

She stalked towards him, her fists clenched. He almost found it amusing.

'Do I look *anything* like one of the Saxon women of
your settlement, Thorstein? And do not say that I must
wear more "simple" clothing again! I can see that is what
you are about to say! Look at me! Really look at me. I
am tall! Some of the women in your settlement barely
reach my shoulder! Their gowns do not fit! I need fabric
to make new ones!'

He swallowed the knot in his throat. She was nothing
like the women of his settlement. She was magnificent.

'I will arrange for some fabric to be bought for you.'

He supposed he would be able to arrange something
before they left…

'Thank you, but I am a skilled seamstress and I would
rather choose my own materials.'

More wasted time in Jorvik? He couldn't wait to be
rid of this stinking city and yet she was desperate to stay.

He gritted his teeth. 'No.'

'I cannot understand why you are behaving like this!'
she hissed.

They glared at each other, neither willing to back
down. The heat in the room was making him sweat.

'I suspect we will never understand each other…' he
said. 'This was a mistake. I shall arrange a divorce immediately. The dowry silver can be yours too. I have no
need for it.'

He turned to leave but a hand gripped his bicep with
surprising strength.

'No!'

He turned to face her, felt her panicked breath mingling with his own shallow breathing.

'What?'

'I do not want a divorce. You gave me until Yule.'

'Yes, but…'

'I have until Yule to convince you that I will make a suitable wife.'

'Yes… Unless you change your mind.'

'I won't.'

She lifted her arms and reached behind her neck to the ties of her shift. Her eyes were clear and bright with determination. She was so perfect and so wrong for him all at the same time.

'Don't.'

She frowned, her hands dropping to her waist. 'But I am your wife!'

'I won't bring a child into this marriage until I'm sure it's what we both want.'

Her jaw clenched tight at his words. 'I will not be humiliated. If you leave now they will assume you found me lacking. If we divorce later it will only confirm that I did not…satisfy you.'

He stared into her eyes, the colour of storms and swords. They stole all thought and reason, and he had to look away before he drowned.

She was right. No matter his regrets, he would not humiliate or shame her in front of her only kinsman. Especially if it ruined all chances of a future match for her.

'Then let us sleep. We have an early start tomorrow.'

He walked towards the bed, taking great satisfaction in kicking off his boots in a haphazard manner and tossing his dirty tunic on top of her gown. He dropped onto the bed with a huff and winced as he hit the thin mattress with a bang. The wooden planks groaned and cracked a little under his weight and he rolled his eyes at his own stupidity.

Imagine the embarrassment if he had to explain a broken bed to Sven. He always missed the comfort of his own bed. That was no doubt why he'd been so ill-tempered these last few days.

She sauntered over and primly eased into a space beside him. Together they lay side by side, not touching, but staring at the ceiling late into the night.

Thorstein had fallen asleep, his heavy breathing soft and regular. He didn't snore like Halvor, so that was something.

To think her second marriage was already a failure. The spirits who had woven her fate were truly cruel. Her first long and fruitless marriage had been cold and devoid of all respect and kindness. It, too, had been murdered before her wedding night. And now what did she have? Another loveless match with no hope.

Her nephew's face came to mind, and the pride which had kept her warm on the bitterest of nights reared its ugly head. She would survive this. And, as with Halvor, she would triumph in her own way.

She'd taken Halvor's mediocre port and made it a centre for export and commerce. Now she would have the family she deserved! Her mind and will were firmly set. Curse the Oracle and her cruel words. She had a man in the prime of his life and she would ensure this marriage worked.

She turned to face her sleeping husband. His big body filled the bed, warmth radiating off him in waves. She stifled a sigh of pleasure. She was always cold at night, and it was pure bliss to have his warmth beside her. Her own personal sun. He was handsome, too, in a hardened warrior sort of way.

He was nothing like Halvor. No, Thorstein was no impotent, jealous old man like Halvor. He might never love her, that was true. But she was no young, inexperienced virgin, as Thorstein had quite rudely pointed out. She had never found pleasure in the marriage bed, but she knew attraction when she saw it, and for all Thorstein's bluster and denial, he wanted her.

She would prove to him that she could be a good, dutiful wife, and in return he would give her children. Damn the Oracle and her lies! She was the mistress of her own fate. She only needed to wield courage. And courage was easy to find when you wanted your goal desperately enough.

Children.

She wanted them more than anything—even more than her dream of being an artisan. Even if she had to give up her dreams of enterprise, she would not give up on her only chance to be a mother.

It was before dawn when Gyda awoke to the sounds of Thorstein moving about the chamber.

'Thorstein, is that you?' she croaked, her voice husky after a restless night. Several times she'd woken to find herself being rolled back to her side of the bed.

The bedchamber was cold now. She could see her breath rising in the air, but very little else.

'Did you hope for someone else?' came a bitter voice from the gloom.

She heard him curse as he tripped over something, and she allowed herself a vengeful smile. It would serve him right for throwing his clothes around.

'Brunhild has gone to a lot of trouble. It would be rude to leave without saying goodbye.'

'Brunhild will be glad to see the back of you,' snapped Thorstein as he thumped at the fire's embers with some kindling. He stirred up enough heat for the kindling to catch and soon the room was lit up enough to dress by.

She ignored his comment. She refused to argue with her new husband on the first day of their marriage. She hoped he wasn't right about Brunhild—she'd hoped to build some bridges with her, if only for the sake of her nephew.

So she got up, dressed in her clothes from the day before and picked up her jewellery chest with as much pride as she could muster. Thorstein would soon see what she was made of.

As she looked up from tying her boots she noticed his scowl was even darker than before.

It turned out that they passed Sven as they left. He was only just retiring, and was weaving from side to side. When Thorstein told him they were returning to his settlement Sven laughed, slapping him on the shoulder with three good-natured thumps, and slurred something about enjoying his treasure in peace.

Dawn was only just beginning to peek over the workshops. Even so, the city was awake, and craftsmen were already setting up their tables outside to make full use of the long summer days.

He didn't have to slow his pace to accommodate Gyda, as he'd had to do with Thora. Her long legs could keep up with him. It was only now, as she was slowing down, that he realised how pleasant it was to walk side by side with a woman who could match him step for step.

As they passed the Christian church, he noticed Gyda

hesitate. He followed her gaze to the clothmaker stall. The craftswoman was there, helped by a young man who, judging by his features, might be her son.

Irritation sparked within his gut, and for once it wasn't directed at his bride. Gyda was right. She was not like the women of his settlement. He doubted there was any woman on earth quite like her. The garments she'd borrowed had been ill-fitting and too short. If buying her some cloth saved him from the tormenting sight of her bare ankles every morning then it was a price he was willing to pay. Even though it was like a deep splinter in his thumb to admit it.

'Choose what you need,' he said, pausing to toss her his silver pouch.

The leather slapped against her breast and flopped onto the jewellery chest she still clutched in her arms. Thorstein frowned at his own stupidity—he'd forgotten she was carrying that.

But her expression was serene as she took a step towards him and held out the chest. 'Thank you.'

He took the chest. With an imperious inclination of her head she calmly took his silver pouch from the top, as if it were her due payment and he'd finally seen sense.

'Only simple fabrics—nothing ostentatious. Cloth fit for a farmer's wife,' he growled, hating how petty she made him feel. But he couldn't resist goading her further, adding dryly, 'If that's what you still want…wife?'

She paused and raised her chin a fraction to meet his eyes. Her hair shone in the light of the dawn and glowed with vitality like fresh milk, taking his thoughts and scattering them like leaves.

'Yes, Thorstein. I still want to be your wife.' She tilted her head slightly as she continued to assess him. She looked at him as if he were a puzzle box she wasn't quite sure how to unlock. Her eyes sparkled with mischief as she added coolly, 'You will want me too...eventually. I am sure of it. I will make an excellent wife.'

The air rushed from his lungs as if he'd been punched in the gut, leaving him winded and silent.

She sauntered towards the cloth merchant in triumph, without giving him a backward glance.

He must guard himself against such mercenary tactics as that. A woman who used her sexuality as a weapon had the coldest of hearts, in his experience.

Gyda felt warmth loosen the muscles of her shoulders. Thorstein was not as inflexible or as obstinate as he'd first appeared. There was kindness there, and consideration—more than she'd ever had from her first husband.

She was confident in her words. She was a good homemaker and, for all Thorstein's bluster, there was hope for them, however thin the thread. She was hardworking, skilled and, above all things, patient.

Time and persistence—that was all she needed to be happy.

Chapter Fourteen

Time and persistence.

Those words caused a bitter taste in her mouth. It was three days since their wedding. All she'd had was time, but that time had been mostly spent alone.

After their hasty departure from Jorvik, they'd arrived back at Thorstein's settlement before nightfall. The villagers had been bewildered by her return. She'd been bewildered too.

By Thorstein's silence.

He'd helped her down from the boat, but his hand had slipped away from her palm as soon as her feet had touched the weathered wood. Her sacks of market goods had followed soon after, with even less respect, tossed onto the pier beside her feet. He'd had a short word with Magnus, and then she'd learnt he was going fishing and would be away for a couple of days.

The sail had unfurled with a slap and he'd been gone, his boat sailing out into the harvest sky that reminded her so much of his eyes.

She'd been left to explain her presence to everyone. Explain her marriage.

That had been humiliating in the extreme. Oh, he'd

muttered something to Magnus, but where were her introductions, the announcement, the celebration?

She sighed. She didn't need all those things really… but it would have been nice, and it would have made her transition from guest to mistress so much easier.

That first day *nattmal* had been a sombre affair, with the villagers not quite sure what to do with themselves or her. She'd retired early, hoping that the dawn would burn away this new humiliation and she'd be able to start her new life afresh.

She'd awoken not refreshed, but with a fire in her belly. On her first day as mistress of her new home she'd worked with Elga, learning about the household. The stores, the animals and the families.

Elga had done well at managing the settlement's silver and goods. But there was room for improvement, and Elga had seemed relieved to hand over the burden. Gyda had taken the responsibility gladly, noting plans for future improvements and reorganising the stores to her liking. She'd worked well into the night, only pausing for a simple meal before falling into Thorstein's empty bed exhausted. It had felt good to have a purpose, a household and a home once again.

The second day she'd spent sewing her new wardrobe. She'd decided she would use the offcuts to make belts for some of the village children. She'd kept her word to Thorstein. The cloth she'd bought was plain, but well made, practical, the colours simple. But she knew the artist inside her wouldn't be appeased. She would add embroidery slowly…over time.

She'd sat outside in the sunshine and talked with all who had passed by. She'd made a point of learning everyone's names, and she'd found the day far more pleasant than she'd expected. After their initial shock at Thorstein's absence, the villagers seemed content to make their own judgement about her, and for that she was grateful.

And now, on the third day, as the sun hung low in the sky, Thorstein's boat had returned.

'Ho! Stranger!' Magnus called cheerfully as he approached and embraced Thorstein with a mighty hug, only to reel back. 'You stink!'

Thorstein gave a half-hearted grunt and continued to unload the boat, unaffected by his friend's comment. The haul was good—several chests were heavy with salted cod and herring.

It had taken two nights on the open sea for him to forget the scent of Gyda's hair.

'Is your hunger sated?' asked Magnus.

Thorstein blinked and straightened slowly. 'What?'

'I presume you had a hunger for herring? I cannot think why else you would leave your beautiful new wife.'

'The settlement needs feeding whether I take a wife or not.'

'Hmm…' Magnus nodded, unconvinced.

Thorstein dropped a chest at his feet. 'You should take a wife. There are too many unmarried women here as it is. Look at what nearly happened to Elga, for example. Now, help me carry these to the stores.'

Magnus scowled at that, and Thorstein took some satisfaction in his friend's discomfort.

They walked up to the village and he headed straight towards one of the empty stores.

'Not that one. It's full,' said Magnus, passing the store he'd approached.

'There's plenty of room.' Thorstein frowned.

'It's full. Gyda has been hard at work reorganising the stores. That's the brewing house now.'

He moved towards another store, but was interrupted once more.

'That's being used for dyes and fleeces. Not that one either. That one's being used for—'

'Tell me where I can go or I'll drop this fish on your head!' Thorstein's bellow caused a nearby horse to prance in its stall.

'That one.' Magnus pointed with a barely concealed smirk.

He entered the open doorway holding the chest tightly. The peace of the last couple of days was already lost, like water through his fingers.

He pulled up short when he realised he wasn't alone. It was her. She'd done this.

Gyda stood with her back facing him. She wore a rusty red gown that clung to her hips and waist. He thought he recognised the cloth she'd bought in Jorvik. The woman was certainly industrious when she put her mind to it.

She turned towards him, clearly curious to see who had blocked her light.

'Thorstein…'

She said his name softly, like a sigh and a question all rolled into one. She blinked, as if awakening from a dream, and then her face hardened to a frozen lake.

'Come in or move out of the light. I've got work to do.'

'Rearranging my household. I've heard.'

He stepped into the store and shoved the chest into a nearby corner. She frowned at his placement, and he could almost see her rearranging it in her head.

Magnus followed soon after. He took one look at the married couple's dark faces, then dropped his chest next to Thorstein's feet and walked straight back out with a mumbled, 'I'll get the rest…'

'Who gave you permission to reorganise the stores?'

Her back became rigid. 'I am the mistress of this settlement. I need no one's permission to run my household as I see fit.'

'*Your* household? That is still to be decided, is it not?'

'Only by you. I know my mind.'

She shrugged and turned away, returning to whatever interfering she'd been doing previously.

He looked around the room and had to admit the store was well packed. There was some old shelving here, from one of the other stores, and it seemed to hold far more than he could have imagined. He sucked his teeth with a click of his tongue. He couldn't even criticise what she'd done.

He wobbled the shelf, testing its strength.

She jumped back with a squeal of fright. 'What are you doing?'

'This probably isn't strong enough.'

It was, but Thorstein would be damned if he didn't find something wrong with her high-handed plans.

She covered his hand with her own. 'Then stop shaking it!'

Heat raced up his arm, burning away the distance he'd tried so hard to win over the last couple of days. The air tightened in his chest as their eyes locked. It would be so easy to lean in and kiss her, to feel the softness of that perfect bow against his lips. His hand stroked up her arm from wrist to shoulder, compelled by some unknown force to draw her near. Her breath quickened and he took a step closer.

Magnus entered again, took one look at them, put down the chest he carried and hurried out once more.

With a harsh clearing of his throat Thorstein dropped his hand and stepped back, scalded by the heat between them.

'I'm a competent carpenter. I can build you more.'

Why was he offering to help her? Only moments before he'd been ready to reprimand her for taking over his settlement—now he was offering her aid. Why didn't he just dig up his hoard and hand that over to her as well?

'Thank you,' she said softly, and followed that quickly with an enthusiastic, 'I could do with a loom as well... a big one, for tapestries for the Hall. I'd like to separate some of the areas...maybe create an antechamber like the one Sven has in his Hall—'

Thorstein cursed. 'Do you think such changes are wise? It may be best, in the long run, to make any changes as minimal as possible.'

He'd used his time at sea to consider the future, and had calmly decided that the best course of action would be to treat Gyda as a guest. She could never be his wife. They were too ill-suited for one another. She would realise that eventually.

'But how else can I show you that I'd make a good wife?'

He swallowed the knot in his throat and tried to divert his mind from imagining her peeling off her russet gown and showing him how good they could be together. But lust wasn't the basis for a happy marriage. He knew that first-hand.

With a gruff, 'Fine...' he turned away.

How was he going to survive until Yule?

Well, if she wanted a loom he would need wood. And the best trees were a little further out of the village.

He saw Magnus at the forge. 'Gyda wants wood for a

loom and some more shelves for the stores. Gather your things and we'll head out.'

Magnus stared at him as if he'd grown antlers, 'Now?'

'Of course.'

'But, it's almost time for *nattmal*…and it'll be dark soon.'

'Surely you're not afraid of the dark? Now, hurry. I want a strong oak, and it might take us a while to find a good one. Then you can build that future wife of yours a bed,' he said cheerfully.

Magnus's scowl only deepened as he tossed down his hammer and took off his apron. 'Why are you doing this?'

'Doing what?'

'Ignoring your wife. Treating her like a burden when all she's done is try her best to honour you? She is well-liked, Thorstein, be careful how you treat her.'

He stared at Magnus in astonishment. 'Well-liked? She's only been here a handful of days and she's as cold as a fish.'

His friend raised an eyebrow. 'To you, maybe. But not to us. She has settled in well here. She's a fine mistress and she has already made some significant and positive improvements. You'd be wise to treat her well.'

'Do not get used to her. I suspect she will not be here for long.'

'Why?'

'She will grow tired of this life and will be begging to leave well before Yule. Now, hurry, the light is fading.'

'Why before Yule?'

'Because that's how long she's got to prove we are suited to one another.'

Magnus stared at him. 'She's on trial? You've put a woman like her *on trial*? Are you mad?'

'Do not look at me like that. I am on trial as well. She

may walk away from me at any time. In fact, I hope she does—it would make things far easier in the long run.'

'I'm confused,' Magnus said, scrubbing a hand down his face before counting off on his fingers. 'She's beautiful, intelligent and experienced in running much grander homes than yours. What is there to reject or even question for that matter? And she's been approved by Sven! That alone should be enough for you to accept her. Surely you would not go against Sven?'

'Which is why I have agreed to consider her. Marriage should not be rushed into.'

'Bit late for that—you're already married,' said Magnus as he rolled his eyes, but Thorstein ignored him.

He headed back to his Hall to gather some supplies. How could Magnus not see how ill-suited they were to one another? Yes, she was beautiful, and intelligent, and he was sure she was more than capable of running a small settlement like his. But she'd been so much wealthier before—far more important, and with more power and status than he could imagine. She couldn't possibly want this life with him. She clung to her jewellery and had hopes of fine clothing, by the sounds of her loom plans. Surely she would realise her mistake and move on?

Although if what Magnus had said about her popularity was true, then his plan to treat her as a guest until Yule was doomed to fail. It appeared she wished to prove herself and already had the support of his people.

He pushed the worry from his mind. A couple more days alone would surely make her realise her mistake.

Two days later Thorstein and Magnus drove a cart laden with timber through the village. Gyda smoothed down the apron of her dress and wondered if she should go and greet her husband. Any other wife would not hesitate, but she wasn't sure if Thorstein even considered her his wife.

He stepped down from the cart and passed the reins to Hilda's brother. Was she imagining it, or were his movements more sluggish than usual? She took a few steps forward for a better look. Yes, he definitely looked paler. He leaned against the side of the cart and scrubbed his face with a weary hand.

She picked up her pace and hurried to his side. 'You're not well.'

'I'm fine,' he ground out with a pained expression.

'He's not,' muttered Magnus, as he passed by them on his way to help empty the cart with the others.

'It's just a chill…nothing serious.'

Gyda searched his face. Dark shadows were smudged beneath his eyes and a clammy sweat clung to his brow. She ignored him when he weakly tried to swat her hand away.

'You're hot. Let's get you inside.'

He looked as if he was going to argue, but when she tugged on his elbow he followed with a heavy tread. It spoke loudly of his current state of health that he was willing to do as she asked. That worried her more than his fever.

She hurried him inside the Hall, taking him straight to their private chamber. He flopped fully clothed onto the bed, barely taking the time to kick off his boots before he closed his eyes.

'Just a quick lie-down…' he groaned.

She covered him with fur and hurried out of the room. She had a lot of work to do.

A steaming cup of foul-smelling liquid was pressed against his lips. He sighed. 'I can lift a cup, Gyda.'

'Then drink.' Her smile belied the sharpness of her words.

He drained the cup, passing it back with a grimace. 'I think you're trying to kill me.'

She laughed, took the cup and offered him water, which he downed gratefully.

'Well, I'm doing a poor job of killing you. You look much better today.'

She was right—much to his chagrin. Three days ago he'd arrived home feeling as if he was about to set sail to the afterlife. Several deep periods of sleep and foul-tasting tonics later and he was feeling much better.

But now he was better he found the proximity of her too much. It clouded his judgement and made him question his choices. He'd been lying to himself this whole time. He hadn't been avoiding her to give her time to change her mind, not really. He'd avoided her because he was afraid. Afraid of what getting to know her might mean. Which was stupid. He wasn't a love-struck youth any more. He was a seasoned man with intelligence and battle-hardened skills.

'I grow tired of looking at these walls. I think I'll start preparing the logs for building.'

She grabbed his arm as he reached for the covers, her soft fingertips a silent plea that stole his breath and his plans.

'No,' she said. 'Wait at least another day. Your cough still sounds thick on your chest.'

'I'm fine,' he said sharply, although the force of his statement was somewhat diminished by the hacking cough that rose up from his lungs at this the most inconvenient of times.

She gave him a pointed look and waited for it to subside. Then she tucked him back under the covers like a babe. 'You've developed this chill from being in and out of the elements. I seem to recall you telling me that was how people got chills. Anyway, one more day won't hurt. The logs will still be waiting for you and there are no pressing matters to attend to. In my experience it is better to rest than to return to labour too quickly after an illness. I suggest you take my advice. I know what I'm doing.'

Frustration made him bad-tempered at the best of times, and not getting his own way even more so. 'You're a good healer. I'll give you that. I suppose you have lots of experience looking after the weak and infirm?'

'Yes. I made a point of looking after the health of the families under my care,' she said mildly, and he had a feeling his arrow had failed to strike home.

'And your husband, of course,' he added, unable to help his curiosity. 'He was older than you?'

'Yes. But his health wasn't weak.' At his disbelieving snort, she laughed. 'Oh, but you're right. He was much older than me. Halvor was older than my father, in fact. He'd seen over fifty winters by the time we married. But he wasn't infirm. He died suddenly of chest pains after a hunting trip. There was no long illness.'

'I see.' Although in fact it only confused him more. 'You were married a long time, then?'

'Ten years. Although he liked to spend most of his days at his hunting cabin. At times I felt as if I wasn't married at all.' She gave him a hard look.

He opened his mouth to ask why her husband had spent so much time away from her, but shut it quickly. Hadn't *he* avoided her since their marriage? Who was he to judge her first husband? Maybe he'd been trapped by circumstance as well?

Instead he said, 'I'm sure that worked well for you.

Running an important trading port alone. So much wealth and power at your fingertips.'

'At the time it suited me, yes.' She held his gaze with a firm look. 'That's not the reason I married him, though.'

'And what *was* your reason? Love?' His bitterness twisted into a sour laugh.

She stared at him and took a deep breath, as if bracing herself against a sharp pain. She looked away, lost in thought, and that same grief he'd glimpsed on their trip to Jorvik returned to her face.

'I married to secure my sisters' future. They could marry any man they wanted if my match with Halvor was agreed. So, yes, I offered to marry a man older than my father. The marriage took over five years to arrange… you know how it is with a political match. It is a negotiation, a display of power and wealth. It is a union of families and not hearts. I knew that when I agreed. And I did not mind because I wanted my sisters to be happy. More than anything I wanted them to be happy. I thought I was doing the right thing. I watched my sisters fall in love, marry and then…disappear from this world.'

A bitter sound escaped her lips as she looked back at him with eyes that he knew refused to shed any tears.

'How Loki must have laughed at my twisted fate. They all died before I even married.'

Had she been trapped? That thought made him squirm. He didn't like to think of her like that…as innocent. It put doubt in his mind and made his actions since their wedding seem rude and dishonourable. Even though he'd planned them as a means for her to escape.

'You could have refused the match.'

Even as he said it, he knew that her family's honour would never have allowed it. But to his surprise she nodded.

'I could have. At that point I doubt even my father would have refused me. But I was lost in grief...and anger...so much anger. I learnt of Astrid's death only days before my wedding. Something broke inside me and I...' She stopped, as if suddenly aware of his presence, then shrugged and brushed her fingers dismissively across her skirts with a weak smile. 'Maybe I just wanted to be pampered...looked after. Is that so wrong?'

It was a strange turn in her manner that made him think for a moment that she must be concealing something. But he dismissed it. He'd seen her love of finery first-hand.

He decided to press her on her past no further. It was probably best not to learn more. She'd be gone in a few months. He smoothed back his hair with a rake of his fingers and winced as they snagged on a tangle of knots. He'd not combed his hair in days...it was no wonder it was a mess.

'I should cut all this off. It's got too long.'

'No!'

Her sharp tone surprised him, and he glanced up to catch a blush blooming across her cheeks before she stood up and walked over to her chest.

'I'll get a comb.'

He held out his hand for the comb as she approached the bed, but to his surprise she gathered up her skirts and crawled onto the bed beside him.

'I can do it,' he said gruffly, reaching for the comb she held above his head.

The sight of her crawling towards him had awoken his desire. It seemed even in his illness he could not help but want her.

'Let me do it. I can braid it away from your face.'

He had the sudden and very masculine realisation that

with her kneeling up as she was her breasts were close to his face.

He turned away from her sharply and hunched himself over his knees. 'No braids. I wouldn't want to be mistaken for a woman.'

A soft, feminine laugh rippled over him. 'I doubt that would ever happen. Besides, plenty of men braid their hair.'

She settled herself behind him, resting her hands lightly on his shoulders as she adjusted her position. As she reached forward to gather his hair, the soft scent of heather and sea air tickled his nose. He felt soft curves press against the taut muscles of his back, and had to bite back a groan as desire flooded his veins.

What sweet torture was this?

He wasn't sure if he could bear it.

The comb ran through his hair and he welcomed the sharp tugs on his scalp as she worked on the knots. He wished she would be rougher, so that he could forget about her body being so close, so soft, so warm…

She began to braid his hair.

'I said no braids,' he grumbled.

'Just a couple, to keep it out of your eyes.'

He closed his eyes and dropped his head back. Despite his arousal, he found her touch strangely soothing.

'There! All done,' she said, moving around him to sit facing him on the bed.

He ran his fingers over his scalp and felt smooth woven knots on either side of his temples, the hair below left loose. 'Thank you.'

Her face was flushed, and he wondered if she'd also been aroused by their close proximity to each other. That would certainly make things more awkward between them. He could deny himself if he thought she didn't feel the same, but if she did...

Something about the way her eyes dropped down and lingered momentarily on his bare chest made his pulse race.

With a gruff sigh he shuffled down into the covers. 'Maybe I'll rest a little longer,' he grumbled, dragging a blanket over his head.

Thorstein awoke warm and comfortable. His headache was gone and the painful weight on his chest had lifted. A soft body was pressed against his side, feminine and enticing. Instinctively he moved closer into the curve of her spine, his hand sliding around the dip of her waist to the slope of her belly. He sighed with pleasure. It had been a long time since he'd woken with a woman in his arms.

His eyes snapped open as he came to his senses. He remained deathly still, unsure of what to do.

He listened to her breath. Quiet and even.

Gyda.

He gently lifted one arm and then turned onto his side. She made a small sound of distress that made his jaw clench, and his body responded in spite of himself. He quickly rolled out of bed, using a wrestling move that made him light on his feet, but silently cursed when his foot caught on a discarded boot. He almost fell, and had to clutch the straw mattress to stop himself.

He glanced back, and almost fainted with relief when he saw she was still curled up on her side.

He threw on his clothes and left silently, before dawn arrived.

He didn't know if he could trust himself to sleep another night beside her. He remembered her body pressed to his side. How she'd turned in her sleep towards him, like a flower seeking the sun. How she'd snuggled beside him, breathing in his scent deeply and sighing with pleasure, as if he was everything she wanted, whether consciously or not. As if she wanted him with a deep longing.

The thoughts sent a riot of blood ringing in his ears. Of course they were the stupid hopes of a lonely man.

He needed distance.

He walked towards the old Saxon Hall, which was now filled with timber. Maybe there was a solution after all.

Chapter Fifteen

Gyda had hoped she would see more of her husband after his illness. She'd certainly felt as if they'd taken a step forward. He'd been interested in her past—not the most pleasant aspect of it, she conceded, but it had been a start. Maybe his chill had made him realise how foolish his avoidance of her had been. How they needed to spend time together to see if their marriage would work. She certainly hoped it would.

The settlement families were warm and friendly. This settlement, if Thorstein ever gave it a name, would be a happy home for many generations. She wanted it to be her home too. To dedicate her life to its prosperity and defence.

But since his recovery Thorstein had remained distant. And he'd worked tirelessly for the past two weeks. If he wasn't away hunting or fishing he was in the old Saxon Hall, preparing the wood that had cost him three days in bed.

Those three days had been an odd mixture of worry and pleasure. He'd needed her, if only for a short time, and it had felt good. So good to be close to him.

Elga's teasing voice interrupted her thoughts. 'I think that's enough, mistress.'

Gyda looked down at the piles of venison she'd cut up for a stew. It was a mountain of meat.

She smiled. 'Are you sure? Maybe I should add a bucket of salted herring? Or a goat or two?'

Elga laughed, gesturing at the huge oak table, laden with prepared meat and vegetables as well as a haunch of venison ready for the spit. 'Even your husband's appetite will struggle tonight with this much food.'

Gyda cast a measured eye over the feast. 'You're right…just one more goat.'

Elga shook her head with a giggle. After a pause, she added quietly, 'You know there's no need to do this…? Thorstein only ever has feasts when he has guests.'

'I'm sure that was only while he was building the settlement. It was an oversight I'm sure he's happy for me to remedy.'

Before she'd arrived the families had taken all their meals in their own homes, only coming to the Hall for special occasions. She hoped to increase the number of *nattmals* in the Hall to at least once or twice a week. She'd found it helped to develop a sense of community, but if she were honest, she also enjoyed the company. She missed the families of Njardarheimr. When she'd escaped her stepsons she'd lost more than her valuables—she'd lost her friends.

She looked at the cheerful Elga and smiled. She was already fast becoming a close friend. 'The last two were fun.' She grinned, then added more sombrely, 'It was a shame Thorstein missed them.'

'Yes, but our Chief must ensure we have enough food to eat during the long winter.'

They both looked at the heaving pile of food on the

table. They only had to look around them to see the ridic-
ulousness of Elga's statement. Some of the other women
across from them were making bread, there were bowls
of berries at the ready, as well as apples, quinces and
pears. The larders were full to the brim.

Gyda decided to change the subject. 'A regular feast is
good for community bonds... Forging alliances... Marriages. Is there not a man who interests you? The black-
smith Magnus, perhaps?'

Elga blushed furiously, and Gyda worried that she'd
overstepped. 'Perhaps... Although, I never know what
to say to him. I try to speak, but my mind becomes addled and I can barely say more than two words... Last
time we were together I spent the whole night nodding
at him. Eventually he grew so bored with my silence that
he walked away!'

'Just be yourself.'

'But what if he thinks me stupid? Or I say something
wrong?'

'You have plenty of charm and wit to satisfy any man.
And besides, if a man cannot appreciate you for who you
are then he is not the right man for you. The gods love
brave women. Show him who you are and then at least
you will know.'

Elga beamed happily at her. 'Thank you! You are right,
Gyda.' She wiped her hands on her apron and picked up
two buckets. 'I'll go and fetch the water for the stew.'

Gyda nodded and started to put the contents of the
stew into the waiting cauldrons, making sure to evenly
distribute the ingredients. But as she considered her
words to Elga she began to throw the ingredients in with
less care.

Who was she to advise a young woman on relation-
ships? Be brave? Be yourself? Where had that got her

in the past? Into a hay barn filled with humiliation and regret for what she'd done. What she'd failed to do…

No man had wanted her as she truly was—why should it ever be any different?

She paused and steadied her breath.

But that was the past. She was wiser now. Wasn't she…?

Except Thorstein was still distant.

He'd slept in their bed only a handful of times, usually coming back late at night and leaving well before dawn. He would join her for his evening meal when he wasn't away. But those meals were always quiet and polite. She would ask about his day and he would give vague answers that she wouldn't pursue. It was as if she lived alone, for all that his presence impacted on her.

His behaviour was bizarre and it was beginning to embarrass her. It was obviously to avoid her, and nothing to do with stocking up the larders.

The settlement had plenty of food. There were goats, a few horses, pigs and some cattle. The sea provided fish and shellfish, although whales did not like the waters this far south. The woods behind them offered plenty of game, including boar, rabbits and venison, as well as logs for building and fuel. There was also wool and meat from the sheep, although most of the fleeces went straight to Jorvik without being spun into cloth.

She wanted to remedy that, as it was a waste of an excellent source of income for the village. New looms would be needed, of course, and Thorstein had been hard at work in the old Saxon Hall with the logs he'd brought back. She'd not wanted to pressure him by checking on his progress, but a beautiful new set of shelves had been placed in her storeroom, so she presumed he'd be ready soon.

So far she had put aside the best fleeces for spinning into yarn. She'd been experimenting with some moss and plants to achieve dyes, and had succeeded in creating simple yellows and reds—although nothing like what Edith had achieved.

She also brewed ale and mead—although many of the villagers were more skilled than her in that particular area, and she was grateful for their expertise. She'd even mucked out the animals, being sure to pick a day when Thorstein had been close to home, working the land, and better able to admire her efforts.

Not that he'd paid her any attention.

She sighed miserably and threw more meat into a pot.

The women had laughed at her strange desire to try all aspects of farming life. They knew as well as she did that the lady of the settlement didn't need to go to such lengths. But she'd brushed away their concerns with an easy smile and some nonsense about wanting to know all the chores inside and out.

Well, she certainly knew them now—more so than Thorstein, she'd wager. But he'd not given her a single word of praise for all her efforts, so she'd be damned if she did any more hard labour for him.

No, she would go back to what she did best. Running a settlement. No more 'proving herself' to a man who didn't even notice her efforts.

At this rate it would be Yule before she even spoke to her husband, let alone convinced him she was a favourable wife.

It would be a terrible risk, but maybe she shouldn't guard herself around him any more. Maybe she should show him more of her true self. A woman who enjoyed a regular feast with friends and family. Who, despite appearances, didn't actually enjoy living alone and never had.

* * *

'Tell us a tale, please, Gyda,' begged the child, and Gyda pretended to contemplate the request.

It was *nattmal*, and the people of the settlement were full and languid from the rich venison stew she and some of the other women had made. The fire cast a warm glow over the hopeful faces of the children and one or two of the adults surrounding the fire. Pride swelled and unfurled in her chest and bloomed.

'Hmmm, it is late…maybe we should all retire for the night?' she suggested casually.

'No!' came the shouts of denial from the children, and she failed to smother her smile.

She yawned and stretched, causing some of the adults to laugh at her for teasing the children so mercilessly.

She saw Thorstein looking at her curiously out of the corner of her eye and some of her enthusiasm died.

He was here, watching for the first time, and his presence made her heart flutter with excitement. Her stomach twisted. He would listen to her tales. What would he think? Surely he would like them? Who didn't love the sagas?

She had to take her own advice in this instance. If they were ever to suit each other then he would need to know what their married life would be like, and she'd decided it wouldn't include mucking out the animals. It would hold times like this, when she would help shape and nurture the loyalty of the community.

'Very well…' She sighed. 'A short one… Have you heard of the giant's marriage to Freya?'

A few of the children looked puzzled, and the adults gave each other knowing smiles. The fire cracked and a hush fell upon the gathered children, their eager faces tilted towards her in the dancing light. Gyda loved these moments. She basked in the glory, in the joy of entertaining others with her tales. It was a time of magic and ancient wisdom.

'It all began when the giant stole Thor's hammer, Mjölnir. Which was bad enough! But then he refused to return it unless the beautiful goddess Freya married him...'

Thorstein watched Gyda tell her tale in awe—and he wasn't alone. The whole room was enthralled by her. She used different voices and expressions for each of the different gods and giants, to both the children's and the adults' delight. A dumb slow growl for the giant, a mighty bellow for Thor, a hissing snake-like voice for the trickster Loki...

The children fell about in fits of giggles when she described Thor disguising himself as Freya. They excitedly thumped invisible hammers when Gyda leapt to her feet and threw off Thor's imaginary veil, describing with bloodthirsty pleasure Thor bashing the giant's head in with his hammer.

Thorstein could not have been more surprised if Gyda had revealed herself to be the god Thor himself.

She was usually so controlled...so serious. But tonight she threw aside her cool reserve and carried his people with her through the legends of their homeland as if she were a master of the sagas. Which, in fact, she was!

She had an almost childlike enthusiasm as she told the tale, with no fear of ridicule, and as he looked at the smiling faces of his people he realised they loved her for it.

It was both unsettling and wonderful.

He sat back and looked around the room in bewilderment.

When had this happened?

When had his people become her own?

He'd thought to give her some time to get used to the settlement and her new life, but it appeared she didn't need it. He'd thought she might realise the mistake of their marriage and spare him the trouble of having to wait until Yule for a divorce…

Although that wasn't entirely true.

He wanted her more with every passing day.

At first he'd dismissed it as lust, but he feared it was becoming an obsession.

Whenever she was near, he found himself watching her.

He'd seen her making an effort to help and build a life here and it confused him. She still wore her jewellery, and spent most of her days sitting outside in the sunshine sewing. But he'd also seen her working the land, cooking, preparing ale, and even mucking out the animals.

Oh, the sight of that had almost killed him!

She'd emerged from the stables with her hair stuck to her temples and damp sweat on her brow, and she'd stretched like a cat in the midday sun. He'd decided then and there to go fishing for at least three days.

Now he was back, and here was yet another fascinating glimpse into his wife's character. The storyteller, the matriarch… It left him wondering if she was deliberately trying to confuse him.

Her story came to an end and his people clapped and cheered to show their appreciation. Her cool reserve returned as she gave polite thanks, but her cheeks were still flushed with the joy of her tale.

Soon the conversations and the fire died down low, and the families made their farewells and left. Gyda stood at the door and waved goodnight to the last family before she barred the door and walked across the room.

She looked at him for a moment, hesitating slightly in her step, before she moved onwards towards the bed-chamber.

'Will you join me for a drink?' he asked, reaching for the jug of mead and pouring her a cup.

He wasn't sure what he would ask her, but he knew he needed to know more. To comprehend even in a small way what he'd seen tonight.

She nodded and cautiously took the cup and sat down beside him, her eyes flashing like twin moons in the firelight.

'Is there anything you can't do?' he asked quietly.

She blinked, her lips slightly parted, looking uncertain. 'What?'

'You're a storyteller, a healer, an artisan weaver and a seamstress, you run the stores better than I ever could. Is there anything you can't do?'

He could have gone on, but he realised his praise was taking his heart down a dangerous route. Attraction, admiration...all led to a broken heart.

She sighed. 'Oh, plenty. I can't sing, or play an instrument, I brew terrible ale and, despite these long limbs...' she waved her slender arms and he couldn't help but imagine them wrapped around his shoulders '... I'm clumsy with a sword. I'd make a terrible shieldmaiden. And, as you've witnessed, I can be stubborn beyond reason when it comes to my independence. Even when my life or the safety of others is at stake. There's so much I can't do...'

She paused and bit her lip. When she spoke again her voice was hushed...sultry, even. He leaned closer to her, desperate to know what she was afraid to say.

'I can't make you want me...'

He shifted uncomfortably in his seat, unable to move away or to face her words. The air between them heated.

'Are you happy here, Gyda?'

Why had he asked her that?

But as he waited for her answer, his breath held tight, he realised that he was desperate to know the truth.

'Yes.'

She hesitated for a moment before speaking, but her answer was firm. She moved and the wool of her dress brushed against his thigh. He wished it were her hand, and he clenched his fist against the admission.

'Are you?' she asked, with concerned eyes that searched his for answers.

That shocked him. He blinked away the smoke from his eyes. 'Er… Yes…'

'Good,' she replied, taking a sip of her mead with tight lips and one blonde eyebrow raised.

He leaned back, breaking the invisible connection between them. 'Why wouldn't I be?'

His voice snapped with more aggression than he'd originally intended. The tension between them had set his nerves on edge. She shrugged, and that only infuriated him further. He decided to change the subject.

'You're a good storyteller.'

'Thank you. My mother was the best. I learnt all the sagas from her. We used to sew together for hours, reciting the tales to each other.'

'So you became a master seamstress and a master storyteller. And here I was thinking you spent all your days admiring your jewellery.'

Gyda laughed. 'You have a low opinion of me, Thorstein.' She swirled the mead in her horn cup before she looked up with sharp eyes. 'Why does my jewellery bother you so much?'

He thought of the piles of silver and gold he'd laid at Thora's feet, paid for in blood and death. None of it had been enough to keep her. He'd sworn never to fall down that well again.

'It does not bother me... As long as you know you won't receive any similar pretty trinkets from me during our marriage.'

Her eyes narrowed and then she held out her wrist towards him, her palm facing up in an open and trusting gesture. Her pale skin shone like the moon as the silver and bronze bracelets clicked together softly.

'This bronze bracelet was given to my mother by her sister on her wedding day. I never met my aunt. She lives east of Kattegat. But my mother said her hair was the same colour as polished bronze. She taught my mother how to sew, and so in a way she taught me as well.'

She stroked a silver bracelet, and the runes carved into the metal came alive in the firelight, whispering their magical power.

'This was my sister Inga's. She was always laughing. She was very clumsy—that's why there are so many scratches on it... My mother and all three of my sisters are now dead. Each piece of my jewellery is a memory. They are far more than pretty trinkets to me.'

Heat flared along Thorstein's cheekbones. 'I'm sorry... I didn't realise their significance.'

Gyda nodded, took a breath and turned her wrist. Her wedding ring shone brightly in the firelight.

'Now, this one *is* just a pretty trinket...and not even a very good one.'

She looked at Thorstein out of the corner of her eye, as if she wondered how he would take the insult. His shout of laughter made her grin.

'What about your family?' she asked, easing back into her seat.

'My parents died when I was young. I was brought up by my uncle and his family. They had enough mouths to feed, so I went raiding as soon as I could throw an axe.'

The story of his past rattled off his tongue easily. He'd told it a hundred times over the years, when he'd been asked about his family name and honour. It had come to be far easier to tell it than to have lived it.

'I'm sorry.'

Her words were honest and kind. He looked away, furious with himself. He didn't want her kindness.

They sat in silence for a moment, until Gyda put down her cup and said briskly, 'Sven said you were married before—what happened?'

He hid his discomfort by taking a long draught of his mead. He considered telling her to mind her own business, but what good would that do?

'We divorced.'

'Why?'

'Does it matter? It's in the past.'

She didn't say anything, but she kept staring at him as if she expected more—as if she deserved more.

Maybe she did.

He looked away from her with a muttered curse. 'We married quickly. I had had some success in battle. Thora was the daughter of a camp follower. I think she was desperate for security and an honourable match, and I was desperate for her... She soon cast me aside when she realised we weren't suited to one another. I heard she married a jarl...or a jarl's son...no matter. A man with more wealth and status than I. It was for the best.'

'But you're a chieftain.'

'I wasn't then. First I was a raider and then, after Sven

trained me, I was a warrior in the Great Army. Thora was tired of living in a camp, wondering if I'd ever return. Then, when I came back wounded, she grew tired of waiting for me to die… She left me for someone who could offer her more.'

'She betrayed you with someone else?'

Gyda looked horrified by his confession, her face pale, and he felt the old shame burn once more.

'I know…shocking…' he answered dryly, trying to make light of the pain that scarred his heart far deeper than the brand across his face. 'She had no honour. I only realised it too late.'

He'd thought Thora was like him—a child born in the muck, trying to make a better life for herself and her children. He hadn't realised he'd simply been a stepping stone. He'd been too blinded by lust and loneliness to see.

Gyda swallowed more mead, and then coughed so violently he reached over to thump her back. When she finally caught her breath, she grabbed the sleeve of his tunic, sloshing the remains of her mead onto the reeds. She gripped his arm so tightly he could feel the press of her nails against his skin.

'I will never betray you.'

Her eyes pleaded with him to believe her. It would be so easy to take her hand from his tunic and pull her into his embrace. To kiss the doubt from his mind. But he couldn't bring himself to do it. Thora had been just as convincing with her words of devotion. *Hadn't she?* And hadn't he desired her with the same intense lust he felt now?

'You should rest,' he said. 'You look tired from your storytelling.'

His whole body ached as she leaned away from him, breaking her hold on his arm as she went back to nursing her mead with a desolate expression. He took the empty cup from her limp fingers.

She stood. 'Goodnight... Husband,' she said softly, her hand lingering on his shoulder for a moment as she passed, then dropping awkwardly to her side with a flutter.

He grunted, unable to articulate a coherent response, afraid to look up in case he lost all control and pulled her into his lap.

He wasn't sure what to do, so he remained where he was. She'd revealed so much tonight, and he wasn't sure if it was good or bad. She was not everything he'd presumed. The jewellery was sentimental in value. She wasn't as prideful and as detached as he'd originally thought.

His arguments against her were falling one by one. Leaving him without any defence.

But she was still proud, arrogant and from a wealthy family, he reminded himself. How could he make her happy? She probably didn't even realise what she'd given up by marrying him. She'd be better off in Viken or Jorvik with a rich jarl. She'd realise that soon enough as the season turned.

Somehow that thought did not comfort him.

He waited until the fire had turned to ash and then he too retired, lying down beside his still wife for the first time in days. He prepared for another restless night as he listened miserably to the rainfall and her quiet breath in the darkness.

Autumn had arrived.

Chapter Sixteen

Time and patience had not been enough.

Being herself had not been enough.

She sat up in bed and looked around in dismay. Thorstein's side of the mattress was empty, but sunken. He had come to bed late. She vaguely remembered his weight dropping beside her in the darkness. But he had gone before dawn.

She sighed, weary of this hunt.

Another morning meal she'd have to eat alone.

Last night she'd finally had a chance to talk to him.

Really talk to him.

He'd asked her questions, and in return she'd been gifted with valuable insights into his past. Although she'd felt sick when he'd mentioned his first wife's betrayal. Would he judge her harshly if he found out about her own lack of honour? Dared she risk their future by admitting her past mistake?

When he'd spoken about Thora he'd spoken so matter-of-factly. It had chilled her to the bone. He had been so detached—as if he were talking about strangers from another time and place. It had shocked her because it had been so familiar. It was the same way she dealt with any pain, quietly placing it in a box and burying it deep, pretending that it didn't matter, that it didn't hurt.

She'd felt trapped. Unable to press him further or empathise for fear of revealing too much. She could lose everything. Her new home, her new friends, the children she longed to have.

She shook off the fear that stalked her.

He would never learn of it.

She went out into the Hall. The door was unbarred and empty, but she hadn't expected it to be any different. There were plenty of leftovers from the feast. Thorstein's dirty bowl was the only sign of his earlier presence here.

She chewed on some bread while she tidied up.

She'd come to England for a fresh start. She could be whoever she wanted to be here. She could be free. Halvor and his son Ragnar were the only ones who knew of her past. Halvor was dead and Ragnar was no doubt in Viken, or raiding in Francia. She'd never have to see him again. She had nothing to worry about.

Except Thorstein's continued distance.

Once again she cursed her ability to sleep so heavily. She'd tried to stay awake, but so many days spent working on the settlement had left her tired, and storytelling, in particular, had exhausted her. She loved it, but it was a performance all the same.

She went outside and waved at a few friendly faces. People who were already going about their daily chores. She didn't see Thorstein. No doubt he was on another fishing trip. They'd be eating herring at every meal until the following winter at this rate.

If she was allowed to stay that long…

Last night had proved one thing beyond doubt. She needed to bridge the gap between herself and Thorstein quickly. The leaves on the trees were beginning to yellow and fall, as were her hopes for the future. She could sense the turn of the season in the shifting light. The days were beginning to shorten and the rain last night had been heavy with the kiss of autumn and the impending threat of winter.

If this marriage between them failed, what were her options? She had her jewellery, and Thorstein had offered her the bridal dowry too—although that had been said in the heat of the moment, and men could always go back on their word. Even so, she'd be left with very little. Selling her family jewellery would be like cutting out her heart with a rusty knife. And what silver she might or might not be given for it would only be enough for the voyage back to Viken. She had no family who cared for her there.

She could go to Jorvik. The silver would pay for her food and shelter until she could find herself a new husband. Or Sven could. Another depressing thought. She did not like Thorstein's indifference to her, but he was a good man all the same. Better to have a decent, if indifferent man than risk the whims of an unknown one.

She needed help from the gods if she was going to convince Thorstein to accept her.

She'd thought she'd given him an open invitation last night to their bed, and…nothing.

It wasn't even embarrassing any more. It was just plain depressing.

She had to do something.

Maybe she should make a sacrifice or leave an offering? She'd never done so with Halvor, as it had been her own failure that had caused the rift in their marriage. But she would do so now. Too much was at stake.

However, there was nowhere to leave an offering. There was no family tree, nothing to symbolise Yggdrasil—the great tree of life that connected all nine realms.

Every homestead in Viken had a Guardian tree, close to the Hall or at an important burial site nearby. But there was nothing here—she'd checked.

Well, that would be remedied today. Last night had lit a fire in her belly. The day was cooler after the rain, but the air was still humid and she knew she needed to get to work before the midday heat made her task unbearable. Gyda wasn't yet used to the warmth of Northumbria but she enjoyed it, loving the sunlight on her skin.

It only strengthened her resolve.

They'd reached an understanding last night and, although their marriage was still not consummated, she had to believe that there was still hope for them.

She grabbed a wooden spade from the stable and walked briskly into the woods.

Thorstein stalked his prey. He crawled through the undergrowth, his body low and his movements fluid. His bow and quiver were strapped to his back, waiting until he was close enough to use them.

He'd had to circle the thick patch of bushes in which the dozing boar lay. He wanted to approach the beast downwind. Catch it unawares and have it tied and slaughtered before it even realised its fate.

A snapping sound drew his focus away from his prey and he sucked in a sharp breath that froze the blood in his veins.

Gyda strode through the woods alone, unarmed save for a wooden spade, oblivious to the danger she was in. She was heading straight towards the thicket and the sleeping boar within its hidden depths.

If she was lucky she would scare the boar from its hiding place and it would run towards him instead. Unlucky and the boar would rush her. She'd be skewered by the beast's tusks—a cornered boar was a deadly threat.

The boar awoke; it came screaming out of the undergrowth in a wild rage. The bushes shivered as it ran towards Gyda at a terrifying pace.

Thorstein burst forward at a sprint, grabbing the short axe in his belt as he leapt over logs and thistles to cut the distance between them. There wasn't enough time to notch an arrow.

'Boar!' he roared, praying his charge would redirect the beast.

Gyda stopped and stared at him in bewilderment, her jaw slack. The thundering in the bushes drew nearer and she looked towards them with alarm.

He raised his axe and she raised her shovel high like a club. The axe whipped across the wood and struck true. It landed with a wet thud in the boar's side, throwing it off its feet and onto its side with a crack. The death blow caused the boar to release one last wheezing breath before its limbs fell limply against the earth.

Thorstein ran to Gyda's side and she stumbled back a step, still clutching her spade high, as if she feared the boar would rise once more.

'It's dead,' he managed through ragged breaths.

Gyda lowered her shovel, clearly shaken. 'You're sure?'

He walked over to the corpse and pressed his foot against the boar's stomach for leverage as he pulled out his axe. 'I'm sure.'

She sighed with relief—a rattled, husky sound that she quickly covered with a cough. Why did she always hide her true feelings like that? She must have been terrified. *He'd* been terrified!

Without thinking he strode towards her, attaching

his axe to his belt, and pulled her into his arms. He'd meant it to be a quick gesture of comfort—like something he would have given any of the settlement's children if they'd found themselves in a similarly frightening situation.

But she stiffened in his arms and he remembered how she'd flinched from him on the day of the shipwreck. The idea of her being afraid of him made his stomach sour, and he gently rubbed her back in a soothing gesture.

Had her husband been cruel? He didn't want to know the answer to that question. It awakened something dark and murderous within him. But what did it matter? She'd chosen her fate when she'd agreed to marry for wealth and power.

The gentle curves of her body relaxed and pressed closer against the hardness of his chest. Awareness raced through his veins and his arms tightened, drawing her closer. The scent of her skin washed over him and last night's desire—the desire he'd tried so hard to forget— rushed through him like a riptide.

It only reinforced to him the fact that they needed to take their time getting to know each other. Allow themselves time to consider their marriage carefully. He wanted her to do it without fear of reprisal if she changed her mind… Which she surely would.

She looked up at him through pale lashes, her eyes wide with a possibility he needed only to reach out to taste.

'Thank you, Thorstein. I never expected there to be a boar so close to the village.'

She blushed, as if sensing every indecent thought in his head, and he stepped away from her, unable to think clearly with her in his arms. He nodded and took several steps away, pretending to be scanning the forest for threats that no longer existed.

'These woods are overrun with boar. The old Saxon settlement was abandoned for many years before it was gifted to me. We have spent the last year reclaiming it. You shouldn't come out here alone until we've reduced their numbers.'

'I'm sorry. I didn't know.'

'It's my fault. I should have warned you.'

He would have to remind the children not to play too near the woods too, and he'd go hunting with more men to clear the surrounding area before winter arrived.

'You've been busy,' she said.

He raised his head at the bitterness in her tone. Surely she hadn't missed him? No, of course not. Her pride was hurt, that was all. He'd caught the curious looks from his people when he avoided her.

'I like to have a well-stocked larder for winter.'

She rolled her eyes with a laugh. 'Oh, it's definitely well stocked.'

Heat raced up his neck and he gritted his teeth. She was right and it infuriated him. The larders were groaning with food. He'd been impressed with how Gyda always managed to find more space to organise and store it all.

They had enough herring to see them into next winter, and he didn't even like herring. He was considering a trip to Jorvik to sell it, but then he'd have to admit they had far too much.

'There's nothing worse than the cries of hungry children. Better to have too much than not enough,' he said.

She nodded, her face softening with a delicate frown. 'You've heard the cries of hungry children?'

'I was one of them.'

She gasped, and he wondered what had possessed him to tell her. He concentrated on preparing the boar, brushing aside her concerns before she could voice them. 'It was a long time ago. Not all of us were born into a grand Hall.'

She ignored his jibe. 'I'm sorry to hear that. No child should ever go hungry.'

It was something they both agreed on, and he gave an awkward grunt of assent. He strung up the boar on a nearby tree and allowed the blood to drain from the meat.

'The stores are getting full, though,' she said. 'I wouldn't want anything to spoil. That would be wasteful, which is a crime in itself.'

That made him pause. 'Maybe I should build another store?'

'Maybe,' she agreed, although there was a twinkle of amusement in her eyes. 'Oh! You haven't forgotten my loom? A big one? I want to weave some tapestries for the Hall. There's plenty of wool, and I've started making some dyes...'

He nodded. He'd remembered—he'd hoped she'd forgotten.

'I usually sell my fleeces as they are.' He frowned, not liking the path she was leading him down. It suggested a future he wasn't sure was possible.

'I know, but I can make several tapestries and sell half of them. Or make cloth. That would certainly fetch a higher price than the fleeces on their own.'

She took a deep breath and clasped her hands tightly in front of her skirts. Her stare was firm, but there was a slight tremble to her voice he hated to hear.

'Please... I'm good. I swear you won't regret it.'

He nodded—how could he refuse? It would benefit his people, and he'd feel bad if she couldn't enjoy something she was so obviously passionate about. He would go mad if he couldn't carve or hunt.

He looked at her with new eyes. 'What are you doing out here anyway?'

'I need to find an ash sapling... You need a Guardian tree.'

'I do?'

'Yes! Every Hall should have one. Otherwise you bring bad luck to the settlement.'

He smiled, taking the spade from her fingers. The warmth of her hand next to his made him inhale sharply. 'Then I shall help you. It is another oversight on my part. I take it you want that sapling over there?'

He pointed to the ash that grew just beyond the boar's den and she nodded, her eyes not leaving his until he turned away.

They both walked over to the sapling.

'Can you dig a large circle around it? I don't want to damage the roots,' she said.

She needn't have warned him. He took great care digging out the roots, and in no time at all he was carrying it back home. He called over to two tall youths who were feeding the goats as they entered.

'There's a boar hanging in the north of the woods, five hundred paces east past the stream. Bring it in and prepare it for tonight. We're celebrating the planting of our Guardian tree.'

The youths grinned and ran towards the woods. Unlike Gyda, they had the sense to take pitchforks with them.

'Another feast?'

She gave him a delighted smile that gladdened his heart.

'Why not? I hear our stores are almost bursting with food.'

She laughed, the sound as light as summer rain, and just as refreshing.

'Where would you like it?' he asked, and was gifted with one of her dazzling smiles. Not the coy, calculated one she'd practised on the river, but an honest one that seemed to reach her eyes and her heart.

'I thought that patch of land looked promising.' She pointed. 'It's close to the Hall, but not so close as to affect the building with its roots.'

His heart beat like a hammer in his chest. 'That's where I imagined I would plant one.'

'So you hadn't forgotten? Why did you leave it so long?'

They'd both reached the spot now, and the air was thick between them.

'I was waiting until I married... A Guardian tree for my family.'

He stared at the trampled grass, dotted with yellow and white flowers. Beauty and life were both so delicate and fleeting...

Her voice broke into his thoughts and robbed him further of his certainty.

'I want that too, Thorstein. I want to be your wife, and to raise a family.'

It was not the first time she'd spoken of a desire for children. But he knew her twin sister had died shortly after the birth of Ivar. 'Are you not afraid? Your sister...'

She paused, as if she needed to consider her words, but then she sighed as if it were pointless. 'Yes, I'm afraid. All of my sisters—Astrid, Inga and Sigga—were taken by the birthing bed one way or another. Our fate is woven by the Norns. Should warriors not go into battle because they fear death? Childbirth is a woman's battlefield and

I will not turn away. Not now. I want children... And, more than anything, I want a family again.'

Her words set his broken heart aflame. She was a warrior, with courage fiercer than any man he'd ever met on the battlefield, and if what she said was true, then they wanted the same things in life. But he did not deserve her.

He spoke softly, not wishing to be cruel. 'I could never love you, Gyda. I don't think I could love anyone again.'

'Have I asked for that? Have I ever asked for anything you are unable to give?' She bristled. 'I only want you to try, Thorstein. Try to get to know me, see what kind of a wife I can and will be.'

She paused in her tirade and looked up to the darkening clouds, then back at his face, her eyes filled with injustice.

'You gave me until Yule, but how is that fair if you ignore me? Marriage should be a partnership.'

Silence stretched the air thin. She'd asked for so little and taken so much.

He plunged the spade into the soil. 'I will try,' he said, and she smiled as if her blood sang with triumph.

He'd agreed to try—but what did that even mean?

'Thank you,' she whispered.

He felt as trussed-up as that boar in the woods.

Chapter Seventeen

The boar was being roasted and his Hall was filled with good cheer. Gyda stood in the thick of it all, organising everyone with an easy smile and a cool composure.

He sat by the fire and cleaned his weapons, choosing a seat opposite her so that he could see her better. And as he watched her work, he realised how at home she was with his people.

She was talking to some of the women about Yule, and the things they would need to do to prepare for the celebration. He felt an itch of shame at the long list of things she was discussing. He'd barely done anything these past few years. A small feast at best, with a few gifts for the children...

Gyda, on the other hand, was getting everybody involved and excited about the festival. It would be something to look forward to in the next few months of miserable weather. A beacon of hope in an otherwise dreary season.

If anything, he was the outsider here—not her. He realised that he'd always put a distance between himself and those around him. He'd thought it was because he was their leader and he needed emotional distance to make tough choices. But would he lose their loyalty if he remained isolated?

He wasn't sure how to change, or whether he could. She wanted more from him—but was it more than he could give?

Little Frida skipped towards him, a shy and hopeful expression on her face. 'Chief Thorstein, is it true? Will Old Man Winter really visit us this Yule?'

He glanced at Gyda, who raised a pale eyebrow in question. He found himself unable to deny either of them. 'I… Yes… I think he might manage to visit us this Yule.'

Frida squealed with joy, but he was too busy watching Gyda's reaction to notice. She gave him a secretive smile from across the room and then turned to talk to the woman beside her.

He traced the line of her elegant neck with his eyes, and imagined what it would be like to run his lips down from her jaw to the gentle swell of her breasts. A strange longing rose within his chest, and he dampened it down by focusing on the little girl beside him.

'That's a pretty belt you're wearing,' he said.

He'd meant it simply as something pleasant to say, but as he looked closer he realised the colourful belt she wore truly was magnificent. It depicted tales from the motherland with glorious detail and skill. A prickle of awareness ran down his spine.

'Gyda made it for me! It was a thank-you gift for helping her when she first arrived.' Frida grinned proudly, stroking the embroidery reverently.

Guilt twisted in his belly as he realised the effort and kindness his wife had shown the little girl.

'I hope you thanked her. This must have taken her many days to sew.'

'Oh, I did. But Gyda is so good with a needle… She

made it for me in just one day. The day after her ship sank. She's made one for all of us now. Although all of them are different and I think mine is the best.'

His belly twisted, and it turned to a heavy ache as he looked around at the children and saw the variety of belts proudly on display. How had he not noticed them before? And she'd made Frida's the day after the shipwreck... When he'd thought she'd spent all her time mourning her silver.

Guilt caused knots to form in his gut. He looked over at Gyda. So cool and calm. But her heart and her skills were there for all to see at the waists of the village children. She was not so arrogant nor so heartless as he had first imagined.

Their eyes locked again across the room as Frida ran to play with her friends. His heart beat faster as she stopped what she was doing and made her way over to him. Was it his imagination or did she sway her hips as she walked?

She settled on the bench beside him, the heat from her body warming his bones. *His wife.* A possessive voice whispered the words inside his head, and he struggled to clear the fog that clouded his mind whenever she was near.

'I thought you might like some mead after your hard day.'

Her voice was uncharacteristically husky and he blinked, unsure of what to say. She thrust a horn cup towards him. He'd not noticed it until it was too late.

'Thank you.'

He took the cup from her hands quickly, spilling half its contents on the reeds and a little on her gown. She smoothed her skirts, but that only accentuated the curve of her thigh, and suddenly he felt like a green youth, stumbling with lust.

Was she flirting with him?

The thought caused old fears to raise their heads.

'I'm sorry,' he muttered, not daring to move.

He needed time to think, to understand what was happening between them. He couldn't risk making another terrible mistake.

'It was my fault,' she said. 'I practically threw it at you. I'm glad to be able to spend more time with you.'

Her cheeks were flushed and she smiled, reaching across to squeeze his forearm. Her fingers curved around his muscles, as if to measure them, before slipping away. He stopped breathing. Then she looked into the fire with a light blush on her cheekbones and his breath returned. He choked on it, coughing into the sleeve of his tunic until his eyes burned.

'I have some carving to do,' he said, and stood up.

She gasped, lurching to her feet. 'But...the feast—'

'Save me some leftovers.'

He left as fast as he could without running and made his way to the old Saxon Hall. He needed time to think.

When his mind was troubled he liked to focus on a task—hunting, fishing or carpentry. But she'd already accused him of avoiding her as he focused on stocking up the settlement's larders. Of course she'd been correct in her accusation, but he'd never admit it.

He worked for hours, until the light from the small fire and the torches was not enough to see by, and then still he worked.

He stared at the logs in front of him. There were shavings all over the earthen floor from where he'd been carving all afternoon and now most of the evening. He'd thought to make this old Saxon Hall into a temporary bedchamber for himself. Just until Yule, when he would be finally rid of Gyda. Now making another bed seemed like a fruitless exercise...or did it?

She'd asked only that he try to get to know her better before he made his decision. He wasn't such an animal of the land that he presumed she'd meant rutting. She wanted him to get to know *her*. He shouldn't have slept out here, but it had seemed the easiest choice at the time.

Maybe he would build this bed and offer it to Magnus. It was time for him to settle down.

He continued to chip away at the wood, placing it into position to create joints. Then he faced the bedhead, sanded the top and stood back. The wood was rich and beautiful. He imagined an ash tree carved into the centre of the headboard.

Gyda would love it.

He stared at the headboard, the chisel limp in his hand. Thora had loved his carvings. She'd called him an artist and kissed his fingers after he'd made her an elaborate chest for her jewellery. He didn't bother to make decorative carvings any more. It only made him bitter. But now he was considering it, to please Gyda.

He dropped the tools, took one of the torches from the wall and walked away, shutting the door behind him with a loud bang.

Magnus was passing, weaving on his feet as he stumbled to bed. 'There you are. Why didn't you join the feast? Gyda said you weren't to be disturbed. Are you okay? You look troubled.' His words were slurred, as he squinted into the darkness at him.

Thorstein shrugged, trying to throw off his unease with nonchalance. 'My latest piece isn't going according to plan.'

Magnus looked towards the door with a knowing grin. 'Really? Why am I not surprised? Why would you need to build another bed when you have a perfectly good one in your Hall?'

'You know why.'

'I'm not sure I do.'

Thorstein bit back a growl. 'We'll be divorced by Yule.'

'Possibly sooner if you keep up with this nonsense. Why are you behaving like one of those Christian priests? Do you wish to remain celibate for the rest of your life? Don't look at me so shocked… Women talk. The villagers are beginning to worry about you.'

His scar flared with heat. 'My relationship is no business of yours or the washerwomen!'

Magnus raised his hands in surrender. 'I'm only speaking the truth. Gyda has proved herself more than capable of being the lady of this settlement.'

'It's not just about mucking out animals and running the kitchen. She's my wife—'

'Yes!' interrupted Magnus with a laugh. 'She is.'

He swaggered away, leaving Thorstein reeling.

Rain. Rain. And more rain.

Gyda was bored with rain.

All it had done was rain.

For two days she'd spent her time mostly indoors, sewing, only venturing out to check on the families and ensure they had all they needed. Most of the time she was invited in, to stay and warm herself by their fire, and she always accepted, glad for the company.

Thorstein was busy in the old Saxon Hall, and she couldn't complain as he'd agreed to building her a loom. He always came home covered in wood shavings, so he must be busy with it.

He'd not joined her for the boar feast, which she

suspected was because of her disastrous flirting. She cringed, remembering the look of horror on his face when she'd touched him. A seductress she was not. But they both appeared happy to pretend it had never happened, so there was still hope for them.

He'd spent all day yesterday working on the loom, but he'd eaten with her in the evening. They'd talked about her day and the endless rain until their words had dried up. She'd retired and he'd followed a little after, going straight to sleep as he always did.

As usual, nothing had happened.

Her fingers tapped an erratic tune against her thigh. Maybe she should go and see how far along the loom was. The rain had turned to a slow drizzle. She was sure it would stop soon. Just a quick look, to check it really was a loom he was making and not more storage. Then she would know if she should concentrate her efforts on creating enough thread. Thorstein had been working so late, whatever he was making must be ready in a matter of days. She would hate to look ungrateful by not using her loom for lack of thread.

She walked over to the circular barn and tried to ignore the curious looks from the villagers as she passed. It was one of the few Saxon buildings that remained, and one of the largest. It might have been the Saxon chieftain's home at one time, but it was a poor relation to the Hall Thorstein had built.

As she reached the door she saw one of the men whisper to another behind a cupped hand with worried eyes. Gyda brushed it off. Thorstein hadn't said she couldn't go in. Her palm pressed against the oak door and she paused. But he'd not said she could either...

'This is my home,' she muttered angrily, and pushed against the wood with a firm resolve.

The door creaked as she entered. Thorstein wasn't there, which was odd—maybe he'd finished?

The barn was surprisingly well-lit, due to a hole in the roof at one end. She wondered why he'd not repaired it—but then noticed the number of wood shavings spread across the earthen floor. The light was good because of the hole in the roof, and the rest of the room was dry, despite the continuous rain they'd been having. There were also plenty of torches around the walls, which, when lit, would offer plenty of light in the evening.

It all made for a good workshop. Although Gyda would probably have at least had the roof repaired a little better. There was something quite depressing about the building and the way the rain dripped down through the battered roof above. It felt neglected. She shivered and rubbed her arms against the chill.

She walked further in, towards some large lengths of wood, stripped and roughly carved. The loom would be huge—far bigger than she needed. Why had he made the frame so large? And where were the smaller pieces needed for the base of the frame?

As she walked around the stripped logs she began to realise that these lengths couldn't possibly be for a loom—there was far too much wood.

One piece in particular was a large square that had been roughly carved and sanded, as if Thorstein had been in a hurry to finish it.

She stepped inside the frame that was laid out on the floor. There was plenty of room. She could easily have lain down within it.

'Oh!' It hit her like a kick to the stomach. It was a bed!

She turned slowly, looking at the frame in disbelief. Thorstein wasn't building her a loom.

He was building a bed. And by the size of it she would guess it was for one person—one very tall person.

Her throat tightened and her eyes burned. How could he break his promise like this? He'd said he would try. Was that why he spent so much time here? Not to build her the loom she'd asked for but to build a new bed for himself and sleep separately from her?

The disappointment winded her, and she sat on the floor with a soft thud. The rejection hit her harder than any slap or cruel words she'd received from Halvor. Tears stung her eyes and fell bitterly down her cheeks as she stared at the fresh wood chips around her. He'd been working hard... All so that he wouldn't have to sleep next to her any more.

It made sense now.

He didn't want her.

No one wanted her.

Was she really that terrible a wife?

She began to sob, clutching at her gown tightly until her knuckles became white with pain.

All the misery of her past was coming back to suffocate her. Rough hands and broken dreams. Halvor's look of disgust when he'd found them together. Years of trying to mend her mistake by being the best wife and mistress she could be, only to be shamed and slapped when inevitably it didn't work.

And now it was happening again.

The Oracle's words were a cruel mockery of her life. She would be the queen of no man's heart. She couldn't even entice a man into bed with her.

But something began to unfurl within her. Like a serpent waking from a deep sleep it squirmed and stretched, filling up her wounded heart with a fire that would never be tamed.

Rage.

He was a liar!

She'd thought he was decent and honourable! But he was just like all the rest. She'd thought she was building a relationship with him, and this whole time he'd been planning his quiet withdrawal from her. So much for his promise to try! He hadn't even started to make the loom she'd requested!

'No!' she cried, leaping up and dusting the wood chips from her dress in furious slaps. 'He should be grateful to have a wife like me!'

She shook off the pain like a dog coming in from the rain, although the hands fisted at her sides were still trembling.

She waited several minutes for her tears to dry and her composure to return. She would never cry in front of a man. She'd sworn it.

When she was ready she turned away from the bed, unable to resist kicking the bedhead as she passed. It fell with a satisfying crack.

'Thorstein!'

Her shout caused several people to stop and stare— including Magnus, who turned and jumped over the side of the cattle pen.

'Gyda? What's wrong?' Magnus rushed to her side, his face filled with concern.

'Sorry... I'm fine.'

Gyda took a deep breath, clasping her trembling hands tightly in front of her. She cursed herself for shouting so loudly. Whatever had possessed her to make such a scene? Of course Thorstein wouldn't be close by—he was never close by when she was around.

Bitter tears burned the backs of her eyes again and

her nails bit into her skin. She'd thought she was calm, but it had been an illusion. Her breathing was ragged and shame branded her cheeks as she saw the knowing glances shared amongst the onlookers. They knew the significance of that building better than she did. Magnus appeared to know as well, because he glanced at the open doorway with an irritated suck of his teeth.

She forced her tone to sound casual and mild. 'Do you know where Thorstein is?'

Magnus pointed at the distant figure that was making its way down the cliff. 'A goat became trapped on the cliff. He went to rescue it. It looks like he's on his way back with it. Shall I go and tell him to hurry?'

'No, thank you. I'll walk out to meet him.'

She picked up her skirts and headed towards the cliff path.

'The path's more of a bog after all the rain we've had. Are you sure you wouldn't rather I went to fetch him?' Magnus frowned at the murky path that curved from the settlement towards the surrounding pastures and the cliff.

'It's only a little mud,' she said, and saw that Magnus was too polite to contradict her.

He mumbled something under his breath about Thorstein being as stubborn as an old goat, but it was carried away on the breeze.

Gyda had hoped a brisk walk would calm her nerves. But as she pushed forward, eating up the ground with long strides, she only became more agitated. The beast within her was controlling her more with every step. Her nerves were boiling over into a thick rage that churned faster and faster. She stamped her feet harder into the mud, imagining the earth as Thorstein's face.

When she slipped on a particularly swampy patch, and fell in a sodden heap, she cursed bitterly but picked herself up again quickly. She fisted the rough wool of her dress in each hand and raised her skirts as high as her knees. Unfettered, she walked faster, leaping over puddles, uncaring of the cold water that splashed her legs. She refused to be meek a moment longer. She'd tried being the perfect docile wife and it had got her nowhere. He couldn't avoid her for ever. She wouldn't allow it.

To think she'd thought him kind and considerate.

Ha! How dared Thorstein continue to shame her like this? The man did not want a wife. He wanted a work-horse!

'Pig! Brute! Worm!' she spat, the ground sucked at her feet until it was up to her ankles.

'Gyda?'

Thorstein's quiet voice hit her like an axe to her chest. She stopped abruptly, her skirts still hiked above her knees. She looked up and a shiver ran down her spine, setting her senses on fire. Her toes curled at the sight of him, and her mouth fell open.

He stood watching her, a large goat draped across his naked shoulders, his wide chest dripping with sweat. She felt the same as she had that first day she'd seen him. A primal lust caught alight within her, feeding off the anger and pain of earlier until it burned white-hot and melted her insides.

But the pleasure she found in his masculine form was tarnished by the injustice of his treatment of her. It bored into her skin, insidiously working its way into her soul. She wanted him desperately, in a way she'd never wanted any other man, but he refused even to give their marriage a fair chance.

'What are you doing here?'

Thorstein moved towards her. He glanced down at her

bare legs as he approached, but quickly looked away towards the settlement.

'Has something happened?'

Her fingers clenched and then relaxed as she dropped her skirts to the ground. It irritated her that he so quickly dismissed her body. She might not be his ideal 'sweet woman', but she was not ugly either. Why did he have to dismiss her so easily? It only added to her humiliation.

'I came to speak with you.'

'Then speak.'

He moved past her, casually carrying the goat as if it were no heavier than a cloak, its legs pinned on either side by the firm grip of his strong hands. The muscles rolled beneath his tattooed skin and his back rippled as he moved, the raven wings unfurling across his back. Gyda was lost for a moment by the sight, only stumbling out of her stupor when she saw he'd moved a significant distance away.

Well, no longer! She would force him to honour their agreement.

She grabbed her skirts and ran.

'I will not be humiliated by you any longer!' shrieked Gyda as she ran past him with surprising speed and rounded on him like a she-wolf.

'Humiliated? What are you talking about, woman?'

It was hard enough to walk through the mire as it was. Almost impossible with Gyda running around with her naked legs on display. They were perfect. Long, pale as milk and deliciously curved, like a bow. How would they feel wrapped around his hips?

He stopped and pretended to adjust his grip on the goat as he tried to force the image from his mind. Thankfully she'd dropped her skirts and he was granted a reprieve.

The goat bleated miserably, but didn't struggle. It was still docile and exhausted from its hours stuck on the cliff.

'The bed! The bed in the old Saxon Hall!' she shouted.

And belatedly Thorstein realised Gyda was furious with him. He'd never seen her like this. Her eyes were wild, her face flushed, and there was mud splattered all over her rain-soaked skin and gown. He sighed, the goat suddenly weighing ten times heavier than it had only a few moments before.

'I thought you'd welcome the privacy.'

Gyda's fists shook at her sides. 'Am I so repugnant to you that you must sleep with the cattle rather than in our bed?'

Raw pain burned in her eyes, and it made his chest tighten with guilt. She'd said 'our' bed, and that one word made his knees feel weak. He'd hurt her pride, and it irritated him far more than it should have.

'I meant no insult, Gyda.'

'You said you were willing to try! You said you wished to build a future, a family! But you spend your days and nights avoiding me. You shame me in front of your people by treating me as less than my position deserves. I am your wife! I demand you treat me as such—in all ways!'

Thorstein stared at her, his face numb. 'You demand I bed you?'

Some of the wind went out of her sails, but she quickly recovered. Squaring her shoulders with a defiant thrust of her chin, she looked him dead in the eyes.

'Yes.'

The air became thick. The brisk wind rushed over the moors and blew wisps of her hair out of her kerchief. His heart hammered in his chest, sparking anger and lust in equal measure.

'And when do you want me to bed you, woman? Here and now? In the mud?'

Loki take him! What had possessed him to say that? Now he was imagining rolling around in the mud with her.

Her eyes widened, but to her credit she didn't crumble.

'Tonight, in *our* bed! But...you need to bathe first!'

She flicked a stray hair out of her eyes before she looked him up and down with a dismissive perusal that would have made any other man's member shrivel. Perversely, it amused him.

She spun back towards the settlement with a haughty toss of her head—but she lost her footing and her legs crumpled beneath her. With a cry, she fell and landed flat on her front in a sloppy puddle. The subsequent spray of mud reached up to his knees.

Before he could react she jumped back to her feet before a heartbeat had passed, skidding and sliding in the mire until she steadied herself. He relaxed. She hadn't hurt herself in the fall.

'Looks like I'm not the only one who needs a bath,' he said, and laughed.

Gyda screamed in outrage, flicking him with muck as she shook out her ruined gown, and then stormed away as fast as her angry legs could carry her.

She was right. He'd avoided this long enough. He needed to make an effort if there was going to be a chance of a future between them. He needed to take a risk.

Chapter Eighteen

Gyda sighed as the warm water eased her bruised flesh. If only her pride could be so easily soothed.

Would her humiliation never end?

First she'd let her emotions get the better of her in front of him—she'd practically begged the man to bed her! And then she'd fallen knee-deep in mud and had had to squelch home in a layer of filth. The whole time with him as her laughing shadow.

She'd not actually heard him laugh after she'd walked away. But she had sensed his mirth at her expense and it had made that walk the longest in her entire life. Thankfully, Elga had taken one look at her and dropped everything to organise a bath.

She wasn't sure what he was doing now.

The last she'd seen of him, he'd been returning the goat to its pen and speaking with Magnus.

She lifted her leg onto the rim of the wooden tub, resting it on the soft linen lining. A large bar of chestnut soap sat on a stool by her side and she grabbed it to scrub away the mud.

It was a bit of a stretch to reach for it as the tub was so large. Poor Elga had had to gather several men to help fill it before the hot water could cool. It was far larger than it needed to be, and it reminded her of Thorstein's bed. For a brute, he had a weakness for luxury that would usually have made her smile.

A sound at the door drew her attention and she dropped her leg. The cloudy water splashed around her as he walked in. Her body flushed to crimson. It was the first time she'd ever been naked in his presence, and the knowledge made her sink further down into the milky water.

He closed the door behind him and went to sit on the edge of the bed in front of her. Without acknowledging her he began to unlace his boots, throwing them in a heap on top of her own soiled clothing.

The water lapped at the bottom of her ear. She stayed perfectly still, not entirely sure her husband had even noticed her. The fire cracked and hissed, casting a golden light over his chest and face, but he did not look at her.

'What are you doing?' she squeaked as he made quick work of the ties at his waist.

'Bathing.'

He shoved down his leggings and she quickly looked away, mortified.

'Move up,' he growled, and he stepped into the tub.

Water washed over her neck and face, causing her to splutter. She crawled awkwardly in the tub like a crab, trying her best to avoid looking at him as well as keep her body submerged. She reached for a length of dry linen and draped it across the tub as a shield. It wasn't much, but she was able to sit more upright with it there.

'Why the sudden shyness? Not long ago you were demanding I bed you,' he said with a wry shrug.

'Don't be so crude!' she retorted, her shoulders rising out of the water a little further in defiance.

After a moment she braved a glare at him—and almost choked.

He was glorious. All masculine strength, with a fine dusting of dark hair over plates of muscle and ridges. No wonder he could carry her as if she was a bag of feathers.

She deliberately avoided looking below his flat stomach, but there was definitely something equally impressively masculine there too. The thought sent strange thrills of excitement and fear through her.

He was submerged now, at least, which gave her frantic pulse a little relief. The tub didn't seem so large any more, with his big body in it, and the water barely reached the grooves of his abdomen. She could feel his feet and shins pressed up against her own…

'I only asked you to behave as a husband should.'

'And how should a husband behave?' he asked.

He reached forward and took the soap from her limp fingers. Her heart leapt at his touch and she shivered as she watched him casually wash his chest and arms, the creamy soap gliding over mountains and valleys of bronzed skin.

Distracted by the sight of his lathered body, she struggled to answer his question. 'Well… Firstly…he shouldn't build another bed for himself.'

'Sounds fair… And?'

'And nothing. You should treat me as your wife. Not avoid me, not treat me like a guest…or a burden.'

How she hated that idea. She wanted to be his partner. She was sick of men dismissing her and treating her with contempt. She had value—it had taken her ten years to fully accept that.

He placed the soap carefully out of the way, reached for a bucket of rinsing water and poured it over his head.

The lather washed down his skin in enticing rivers that made Gyda's breath catch and her heart race.

'You keep telling me what I should and shouldn't be doing, Gyda...'

He sighed, placing the now-empty bucket down beside the tub. He used both hands to smooth the water out of his hair and she lost all comprehension and thought at the sight of his biceps and chest flexing. He leaned forward and rested one hand on her knee. Heat rushed down her thigh, causing her to shift in the water.

'Why don't you tell me what you *want* me to do? Tell me what you like.'

'Are you mocking me?' Bitterness boiled in her stomach as she remembered how once before she'd been the victim of a cruel joke.

He blinked. 'Why would I be mocking you?'

She couldn't bear to look at him and instead stared into the fire. How could she tell him? How could she explain to him what had caused not one but two men to reject her? But when she looked up into his eyes, he seemed so kind and patient, as if she could tell him anything.

'I'm not very good...in the marriage bed... It's best done...quickly.'

He drew in a sharp breath, his brow creasing with a frown. 'Is that what you believe?'

'It's what I know. He said my touch left him cold.' She held her breath, hoping he wouldn't ask more. She wouldn't lie, but there were some things she was too ashamed to admit even to herself. Halvor hadn't always been cruel. He'd made mistakes, but so had she.

With a growl of frustration Thorstein rocked back against the tub, causing more water to slosh onto the reeds. 'And he blamed you?'

Shame clawed at her and her cheeks burned. 'Sometimes he struggled to...to respond.'

She cleared her throat, feeling as if she'd swallowed a dozen rocks. She closed her eyes, but she could still feel the shame of the few times Halvor had tried to perform, when he'd ended up angry and violent, slapping her or cursing her when he couldn't summon the lust to bed her.

Thorstein eased back in the water with a shrug. 'He was much older than you, yes? That can affect a man's... virility.'

Her throat tightened again. Now she should tell him—tell him everything. But the words wouldn't form on her tongue, and instead she looked into the fire and whispered, 'Maybe.'

She didn't tell him that Halvor had taken other women to his bed, that he'd shunned her because of what she'd done, that he had never been able to look at her without feeling revulsion, without seeing the mocking grin of his son.

Her stomach tightened and she felt a cold sweat against her skin.

'Gyda...'

His gentle voice pulled her eyes away from the flames. 'I am not your first husband. When I look at you... I want you. I have avoided your bed not out of lack of desire, but because I wished to give us both a choice. Give us time to get to know each other first...to make sure we are suited to one another.'

The waves of nausea abated and were replaced by a spreading blush that heated her cheeks. His words made her light-headed. Did he truly want her as much as his eyes implied?

'But you think we're *not* suited to each other!' Exasperated, she looked away. 'What more can I do to prove to you that we are?'

'Nothing. I should not have asked it of you. I rushed into marriage once before...and it turned out badly for both of us. Do not think I do not want you. I do. Very much so. I have wanted you from the first moment I saw you and threw you into the sea.'

An unexpected giggle burst from her lips and she smiled shyly back at him. She was not entirely sure she believed him completely, but she was hoping desperately it was true. Although she tried her best not to show it.

He looked at her shrewdly from beneath heavy lids. 'When you look at me does it leave you cold?'

Her breath quickened and she felt her nipples tighten under his probing gaze. Did she dare confess the truth? That she wanted him more than she'd ever wanted anyone else in her entire life? That she longed for his approval, his desire, his kindness? Those feelings left her vulnerable and naive. But if she wanted things to progress...if she wanted to have children...

She smothered her guilty secret and managed a barely audible, 'No... I...want you too.'

'Then come closer... Show me.' He gestured lightly with a crook of his finger.

She stared at him, at his golden body so languid in the water. He was an army of muscle and strength, powerfully restrained and under her command. It sent a thrill racing up her spine. She wanted to explore him, to finally touch her husband. She'd never had such control before—certainly never had it offered to her.

She eased forward, saw the water lapping at his belly. With a deep inhalation she slid her legs around, so that she was kneeling in the water, her breasts and stomach exposed to the cool air. It was a wanton gesture that made her insides twist with uncertainty.

I am his wife, she reminded herself, and she was within her rights to please herself. He lowered his knees, watching her with bright, intense eyes, and she gasped at the brush of his legs on her inner thighs.

His bright blue eyes trailed up her body slowly, as if the sight of her was something to be savoured. Her fingers itched to squeeze the strong muscles of his biceps, and after a moment's hesitation she indulged herself, gripping each arm to pull herself closer. She looked down at him, her breath shallow and uneven as she trailed her fingertips over the blue ink of his tattoos, tracing the lines until she reached Thor's hammer above his heart.

He didn't move, his chest rising and falling in a steady rhythm as he allowed her to explore him.

Her fingers smoothed up over the plate of his chest. Up to the thick pulsating cords of his neck. Every muscle in his body was strong and hard, from years of fighting and working the land. It made her stomach clench and her knees weak to touch him. He was everything she could ever desire in a man and more.

She cupped his rough jaw with her palm and brushed her thumb over his full, slightly parted lips. She'd seen him brush his thumb over that spot before and it held a strange fascination for her. She wanted to know how it felt.

She leaned down and pressed her own against them. Unlike the rest of him, his lips were soft. He moaned beneath her and the power thrilled her.

His hands grabbed her bottom and pulled her close in one rough movement. Her aching breasts were pressed against his chest. She could feel his thick length between them, pressed into her lower belly.

Molten flame burst within her and she pressed her lips against his, seeking more. She groaned as his tongue swept into her mouth, teasing and tempting her into submission. He pulled her close and took everything she had to offer. She surrendered gladly, her body melting against his like butter on hot bread.

Their tongues stroked against each other as one of his hands slipped between them. She moaned as his hand cupped her womanhood and his fingers slipped between her silken folds.

'Thorstein!' she cried out, unsure if she was surprised or begging him not to stop.

He trailed kisses down her neck and chest, his fingers stroking at her entrance in a relentless rhythm that made her hips rock and her toes curl. His tongue lapped at her nipple and then sucked the flushed bud between his teeth. She cried out again as a rush of shivers boiled across her skin, setting her world aflame.

She ached for something just beyond her reach that only he could give her. She gripped his arms and held him tight, pressing desperate kisses into his neck as the water splashed around them. *This* was the pleasure her sisters had whispered about. *This* was the connection she'd been missing for all those years. And she wanted it desperately.

She begged with whimpers and moans, rocking against his fingers, hoping it would never end. Her body became as tight as a bowstring as he held her over the precipice with an expert touch. Her hands grabbed the sides of the bath with bone-white knuckles that tightened into the linen draped around them.

She didn't think she could take another stroke—and then her thighs locked tight around him. With a scream of joy her control snapped, and then she unravelled in a molten spiral.

He stroked his hands up her spent body to rest at her waist, and she let out a pitiful whimper.

He laughed—a rich, deep sound. 'Don't worry...it's not over yet.'

He lifted her up with one arm and reached between them. She felt the thick length of his erection pressed between her thighs. A sudden rush of longing made her start to pant. She wanted not only his body but to make him hers, by both law and action. She pushed herself down upon him, slowly and deliberately, allowing her body time to adjust to his size.

It was Thorstein's time to cry out, and he threw back his head and gritted his teeth as she continued to lower herself until she was fully seated on his hips, triumphant.

She had never been in this position before, but she knew what to do. For the first time in her life it was no longer an infrequent, unpleasant chore. She longed to feel him inside her, filling her and possessing her. She wanted to give him the same pleasure he'd given her.

She used his shoulders to push herself slightly up and away from him. To gain better leverage and—if she was honest—to enjoy the view.

He was the most handsome of men...raw strength decorated with symbolic meaning and burned by honour. She enjoyed the sight of his clenched jaw and rippling muscles as she rode him. She felt powerful and in control, and it caused her body to respond once more. The hot ache returned and she leaned closer, pushing her hips against his until she was almost weak with need.

He took over then, gripping her by the buttocks and thrusting into her with a barely contained savagery that sent her body soaring into a climax. He followed shortly after, and her body felt boneless as she fell upon him, spent.

They clung to one another, their breathing ragged as the water cooled around them. Neither one wanted to let go of this moment or each other.

Chapter Nineteen

Who knew love-lust could be so violent?

Gyda had always imagined love to be like a gentle sun, her days filled with simple pleasures. She had never imagined it would burn so brightly or be as tempestuous as a storm. It made her feel naive and vulnerable, and shook the natural order of her life. It was overwhelming, and frightening, and if she thought too long about it a dark hole of despair opened in her heart and she found it difficult to breathe or think.

She'd tasted the possibility of a future filled with laughter and lovemaking, and she'd tasted something far more worrying.

Hope.

Hope for a future with a man who filled her days and nights with joy—who treated her as a respected equal and partner, but also as a desired lover and friend. She wanted that more than anything. Not to be the queen of her lover's heart—not to control or rule over him as the prophecy had stated. But to be seen—truly seen—and loved regardless. Valued above all others and treasured in his heart.

She'd wanted that as a maiden and she'd been foolish

enough to seek it out in a place where it could not exist. This was her second chance, and she'd not failed—not yet.

Their marriage was consummated now. Thoroughly so.

A small giggle escaped her lips and she lay back in the huge bed. The sound echoed and then drifted away, a stranger in her life. She never giggled. But this wasn't the first time—and every time it had been because of Thorstein.

They'd made love again after *nattmal*, in the bed where she'd been alone for so many nights, and she'd had a taste of their future together. Strangely, if she thought about it too long, it made her afraid. Now there was more for her to lose with each day of this marriage, and the Yule festival loomed in the distance like the angel of death, ready with an outstretched claw to scratch out her fate.

Surely Thorstein would not set her aside now?

A dark disappointment settled across her chest as she remembered the last time she'd thought a man would not so easily cast her away. She'd been wrong then—why not now? She tried to brush it away as she reasoned with herself, but it clung to her like a bad smell.

She had proved her capability as the mistress of the settlement, and he had accepted her as his true wife, hopefully the mother of his children. Why, then, did this fear still haunt her, closing in from the shadows of her mind and suffocating the joy she should feel in this moment? Why did she feel guilty about what she'd not said?

It was better to keep her growing feelings to herself. Not to risk her future on girlish dreams.

This was more than she could have hoped for.

She would have a family, a home, a life to be proud of.

She lay on the bed with the sunlight flooding in from

the smoke hole, causing dust to dance in the streams flooding in, and wondered what Thorstein was doing right now.

As usual, he'd risen before her. Would he have gone hunting again? On another pointless fishing trip to avoid her company? Or would he remain for a few days, at least, and join her at night? Sleep by her side and warm their bed?

Her lips ached for him. Her fingers burned to run down his skin. She was obsessed. She wondered if she would be able to wait for the night to fall before she sought him out.

Sighing, she rose from the bed and began to dress. Better to seek out what fate had in store for her than lie in bed wasting the day away.

She found him by the Saxon Hall, the doors thrown wide and his workbench dragged out into the light. Her heart sank heavy in her chest when she saw him back at work. Until she realised he was breaking up the bed… cutting the longer pieces of wood and hammering them into a frame she did recognise.

A loom.

She straightened her shoulders and sauntered over. He brushed the hair out of his eyes with the back of his hand to look up at her and her heart took flight.

'Your new loom,' he said gruffly.

Gyda nodded, casting a critical eye over his handiwork for want of anything else better to do. 'I see… It will be a fine loom when it's complete. Hopefully it will not take up too many of your evenings late into the night.'

He smiled at her teasing. 'The hard work was preparing the logs. That's been done. It won't take long to complete now, and I shall get Magnus to help me.'

'Good. I suppose it will be nice to have your company again.'

He shook his head with a laugh, and she was captivated by the sight of his raven hair as it swept across his sharp cheekbones. She reached out and smoothed it aside, tucking it behind his ear. He sucked in a breath and his eyes burned with blue fire. Then with an arrogant grin he gave her palm a playful nip and her fingers retreated.

'You miss me already?'

Should she beg him to join her once more? Would he come if she asked?

Wanton whore!

The cruel words from the past slammed into her.

Her spine stiffened and her hand dropped.

Thorstein stared at Gyda's sudden transformation in shock and wondered what he'd done to cause it. She was pale, her arms wrapped around her middle as if she were in pain, although her face was devoid of any expression. What had he done to upset her? She'd enjoyed his touch in private—what had changed?

He was about to ask when little Frida came running over.

'Mistress Gyda, Módir was wondering if she could have more of your tonic. She still has a chill and needs it.'

'Of course, Frida. Tell her I'll bring something over straight away.'

As the child sprinted away Gyda turned to him, biting her bottom lip with a frown. 'The stores are running low on healing herbs, and I could do with more lichen for my dyes. Do you think the woods are safer now? You've been hunting so much...surely the boars and wolves have moved further out?'

He paused for a moment. The woods were safer, but

maybe he should spend more time with her. He had a feeling there were aspects of her past that still worried her. And she'd been right. He needed to get to know her better if they were ever going to make this marriage work.

After their lovemaking yesterday he was more than happy to spend time with her. Beneath her cool facade was a woman with violent passions. By Odin! Last night she'd spoiled him for all other women. He could imagine no face but hers, no skin as soft or as radiant...

He shook his head to clear his thoughts. He was behaving like a lovesick pup, and this time he didn't have the excuse of youth. Yet he wasn't sure if he minded. They were married and they both wanted the same things. The misunderstandings of the past were forgotten. Why deny themselves happiness?

A sudden idea bubbled up inside him. 'The woods are safer. But there's a good meadow further into the forest, near where the older trees grow. There's lots of lichen there too, by a rocky stream. You should find everything you need there.'

'But isn't that far away?' She had tensed again.

'Yes...we'd be gone at least overnight.'

'We?'

Some of the tension dropped from her shoulders and she looked at him hopefully.

He couldn't wipe the smile off his face. She wanted to be with him.

'Yes. I can pack a cart with supplies. You won't need to sleep on the forest floor.'

'You will be coming with me?'

'Of course...if that's what you want.'

'Yes!' She nodded eagerly, before twisting her fingers and adding coolly, 'I've never been out in the wild before...overnight. It will be good to have some company.'

That surprised him. He couldn't imagine a childhood without swimming in secluded lakes and hunting through forests. 'What? Never? Not even as a child?'

'It was not something I enjoyed... But I would like to go with you now.'

She blushed, and he found her embarrassment endearing. He would do his best to ensure their trip was as comfortable and as enjoyable as possible.

'Good. After you've seen Frida's *módir*, gather some warm clothes, blankets and food. We'll head out shortly—after I've finished your loom.'

With a nod she began to walk after Frida, but then stopped suddenly and spun on her heel to walk in the opposite direction. 'The tonic,' she muttered, by way of explanation.

He laughed, finding her barely concealed excitement charming. He would enjoy a night under the stars with her...

With Magnus's help it didn't take long to finish the loom and prepare the cart. In what felt like no time at all he and Gyda were headed out into the countryside. The cart squelched through the puddles as they drove through moorland and towards an old forest in the distance. Gyda sat beside him, a bundle of fabric in her lap. He knew she liked to keep her hands busy, especially if she had to be sitting down for long periods of time, like today.

It was slow going at first, and the boggy path was filled with puddles, but soon the road evened out and they made better time.

'Do you think it will rain any more?' she asked.

'Yes.' He smiled when he saw her shiver. 'But not too badly—at least not while we're away. How was Frida's family?'

'Hilda is in bed with a similar chill to the one you had.

It's been making the rounds of the settlement. But her husband is looking after her well, and the children don't seem to have caught it yet. It's a mild illness. I believe it will pass with the right amount of care.'

'You're a skilled healer. Did your mother teach you that as well?'

There was something reassuring about having a lady running a settlement—he'd never appreciated that until now. She would ensure the health and wellbeing of his people, while he would concentrate on their protection and prosperity. They would make a good team.

'She did. She prepared me in every way that she could.'

'She did a fine job. You are a credit to her.'

Gyda blinked up at him, as if he'd said something unexpected.

'So you think I'm suited to your life after all? I'm not a useless waste of your time?'

The question floored him.

Had he really been so hard on her?

Yes, he had.

'I'm sorry, Gyda. I was wrong. You *are* suited to this life. You were willing to give it a chance, at least. It shouldn't have taken me this long to see it.'

'No, it shouldn't have.'

She nodded thoughtfully. Then she peeked at him from the corner of her eye and they both laughed.

'What was your father like?' he asked.

She stiffened and looked out at the purple-tipped moors. 'Why do you ask?'

'You've never mentioned him. You've spoken of your sisters and your mother often, but never him.'

'He was…ambitious.'

'Ah, I see.'

Was that why she'd married her first husband? he wondered. To please her father?

'No, I don't think you do.'

She didn't look at him, just watched the meandering countryside pass them by with a relaxed countenance. He waited, hoping she would say more, and when she spoke he didn't dare look at her for fear of interrupting.

'My father was a man surrounded by women. He blamed my mother for giving him only daughters, and she blamed him for not loving us as he should. Their marriage wasn't a happy one, but they got along in their own way. Their relationship taught me restraint and patience. Halvor was a friend from my father's youth and our neighbour. Father had told us about his prowess in battle and their adventures raiding together—it was clear he wanted an alliance between our families. Astrid had already given her heart to Sven, and Inga and Sigga were so young... I was the logical choice. My mother had hoped and begged for my marriage to one of Halvor's sons...'

Gyda paused, her face pale and tight. Had that been her wish too? wondered Thorstein. To marry one of his sons?

'It might have been possible,' she continued, 'but my father had plans to control Halvor's port through me. His eldest son, Baldor, was already married, and control would not have been possible if I had married a younger son. Besides... Halvor liked the look of me, and so my father agreed for him to marry me. As it turned out fate was unkind. My parents died from a disease that struck their settlement shortly after I was married. Their land was taken by Halvor anyway. My father's ambition led to nothing.'

He waited to make sure she'd said everything she

wanted to say. He was sure there was more. Every time she opened up to him he realised there was a deep well of sadness within her. She was not as shallow as he'd first thought and, more importantly, she was nothing like his first wife.

'No daughter of mine will be forced to marry a man three times her age,' he said firmly.

He might not be able to change Gyda's past, but he could reassure her about the future.

'Even if I give you four daughters and no sons to pass on your name?' she asked mildly, although her eyes still showed that deep well.

He snorted. 'It would be nice to have a son to carry my name. But if my fate is to have a dozen daughters then I will ensure I am the best of fathers so that they will carry my name in their hearts. The men they marry will become my sons, so I will train my girls to be strong and wise so that they choose only the best of men.'

He clicked his tongue at the pony to speed it up. He wanted to reach the forest before dark—it would be safer than being out in the open.

Her fingers wrapped around his forearm and gave it a tender squeeze.

'You are a good man, Thorstein. The gods have been kind to me.'

Gyda sighed, her heart full. He was indeed the best of men, and she was shocked by her change in fortune. To think she'd presumed she'd never be happy in marriage…and yet with Thorstein she dared to imagine a future where she was.

Chapter Twenty

They made camp just inside the forest, away from the sight of the main road, in a little clearing Thorstein had obviously used before. There was the blackened circle of an old campfire and a tripod for cooking, a pile of logs covered with waxed linen and a small shelter.

It was not big enough to be honoured with the name of 'hut', but it was big enough for two people at night, she supposed. Everything was wet from the rains, and if Gyda were honest it looked a pretty miserable place to be spending the night.

Thorstein seemed oblivious, however. 'I'll just go and set a couple of traps…see if I can catch something for to-night. If not, we'll need those supplies of yours for *natt-mal*. Do you think you could light a fire while I'm gone?'

She looked at the pile of logs. There must be something reasonably dry there. 'I think so.'

'Great! There's a stream a hundred paces that way,' Thorstein said cheerfully as he slung a big sack, some quivers and a bow over his shoulder.

She watched him crunch into the woods and waited until she could no longer hear him. Then she slumped down on the pile of logs. Why had she agreed to this? She wasn't suited to the outdoors—she was suited to warm hearths and cosy beds that smelt of fresh herbs.

But Thorstein seemed quite happy, so maybe she should at least try to make the best of it. At least their cart was overflowing with warm bedding and supplies—surely it wouldn't be that much of a hardship?

She stood, brushed down her skirts and got to work on building the fire.

By the time Thorstein returned with a rabbit hanging from his belt the fire was burning well.

'You're back!' she cried, glad to see him. It was getting dark and she was becoming more nervous with every hoot and screech from the forest shadows. 'And you've got a rabbit! That will go perfectly with the root stew I've made.'

'You've been busy.' He smiled as he surveyed her handiwork, causing a bubble of pride to swell in her chest. 'You have even put the bed together!'

She grinned, looking over at the low wooden bed now tucked under the shelter. 'It was quite easy, really. Once I realised what it was and how it all slotted together. It's quite ingenious! A bed you can put up anywhere and then take apart again once you're done. Do you usually sleep on the forest floor?'

'Sometimes I do. But I thought you'd prefer a bed.'

'It's so clever. You really are a talented carpenter. How ever did you think of it?'

Thorstein's cheeks flushed and she wondered if he was embarrassed by her praise. If anything, it made him more endearing.

'I cannot take credit for the design. I have seen jarls with similar furniture while travelling with the Great Army. This is a small and crude version in comparison. I put it together after I'd finished your loom.'

'Then I am even more impressed, because you made it so quickly. Would you mind checking I've put it together correctly? I'd hate to break it.'

He went over to the bed and gave a cursory look over the slotted joints and bed slats. 'Perfect, I couldn't have done it any better myself.'

It was her turn to blush, and she quickly grabbed the massive bundle of furs and blankets from the cart and brought them over to the bed. He took them from her and they began to spread them out.

Now that he was beside her she realised with a little thrill that the bed would be much smaller than the one at the settlement. They'd have to be pressed up against each other to fit.

She imagined their limbs entangled and it made her pulse race.

Unless…unless she was going to sleep alone?

'I'm glad you're back… Honestly, I'm a little nervous about sleeping out in the wild tonight. What if a wolf or a bear attacks us while we sleep?'

He laughed. 'There's no bears here, and the fire would keep them away anyway.'

'Oh, good. All the same, I'm glad you're here. You will be sleeping…here, won't you?' She tried to indicate the bed casually, to make her point clear.

His bright blue eyes followed her movement and he nodded slowly. 'Of course.'

'Good. Now, let's take a look at that rabbit,' she said briskly, walking back to the campfire with a lighter step.

'I'll get you something to sit on,' Thorstein said.

He rolled a large piece of a tree trunk over to the fire, and she sat down with a grateful smile as she began to skin the rabbit. He'd already gutted it, so she was able to add the meat to the pot quickly. She washed her hands in the bucket of water she'd brought especially for cleaning, and then sat down again next to Thorstein, who had already opened the parcel of bread and cheese and was happily nibbling on it while he prodded the stew with a ladle.

She reached over and took a piece from his lap. The forest didn't feel so threatening now that Thorstein was here. She could listen to the chirps and tweets of the roosting birds with an easy mind. With him she felt safe.

It was a revelation that made her pause. She knew so little about his past, and yet she trusted him.

'What was it like being in the Great Army?' she asked.

He bit into a chunk of bread and chewed thoughtfully before answering. 'Exciting at times, terrifying at others, but mostly it was boring. Lots of walking and camping without an enemy in sight. Or waiting within Jorvik for a counter-attack.'

'What happened to your face?'

He looked down at her, and she worried for a moment that she'd offended him.

'I took a risk. The Christians had laid siege, and with some men I crept into their encampment to cause trouble—set a few fires, contaminate their water, that sort of thing. But our leader was hurt and I had to cause a distraction to help him escape. I was taken prisoner by one of the Christians' warrior priests. They tried their best to get information out of me about our defences. They failed.'

'How did you escape?'

Thorstein shrugged. 'I didn't. Sven attacked them with reinforcements in a pincer movement and freed me in the process.'

She ladled out the stew into bowls and handed him one. 'You were very brave. But I thought Sven owed you a great debt? It sounds like he saved your life.'

Thorstein shrugged, taking his time to answer through mouthfuls of stew. 'The leader who was hurt…that was Sven.'

'Ah, I see!' She laughed. 'I think you are the bravest and best man I have ever met.'

'I was reckless and stupid.'

'Why do you say that?'

'Because I didn't do it to be brave or for honour and glory. I did it for a woman.'

'Your first wife?'

'Yes. She wanted me to attain glory on the battlefield in the hope that I would win more silver and gain a better position. So I took risks to please her.'

'But you could have left Sven to die and you didn't. You could have told the Christians about the defences, but you didn't. I think that proves you're a brave and decent man…and, well, you wanted to please your wife. I don't agree with her encouraging you to take risks, but I think your intentions were good even if hers weren't.'

She wasn't sure if he believed her, but she felt better for saying it. He ate some more stew and she plucked up the courage to ask him what she'd always wanted to know.

'What was she like? Your first wife?'

'Thora?'

He looked at her in surprise and she nodded, unsure if she really wanted to know his answer.

He sighed. 'She was beautiful…and shallow. She liked jewellery, silver and fine clothes.'

'You think I'm like her,' Gyda said, and the pain cut deeper than it should.

She took his empty bowl from his hands and dropped it with hers into the cleaning bucket. She would deal with it in the morning.

'No.'

Her eyes snapped to his and he smiled.

'At first...maybe. But not now. I was wrong to think you were the same. In a way, I was wrong to judge Thora so harshly too. She grew up with nothing. Her mother was a camp follower. She probably thought her fate would end up being the same as her mother's, and then I came along and swore that I loved her and wanted to marry her. She must have seen me as a stepping stone to a better life. Who am I to judge her for taking it? I should have known better and not been blinded by beauty.'

'But she left you.'

'And I'm grateful she did. I don't think I would have left her, and we would have ended up miserable together. That was what I was afraid of with us. That we wouldn't be suited...that you would want a different life from what I could offer and that you'd end up being miserable with me. I don't want that. I want a family. If I can't have that I'd rather be alone.'

'I want a family too. And I want a husband who...who cares for me...as much as he can, at least.'

He turned towards her then, the firelight dancing across his scars. 'I care for you, Gyda. Do not doubt that.'

She leaned forward, her hand cupping his face and drawing him close with a featherlight touch. She pressed her lips to his and he kissed her back.

The stars sparkled above their heads and she heard the faint call of an owl in the distance. She felt as if she were living in the magical world of the gods and her heart sang at the promise of his words. He cared for her. He'd not said he loved her, but by the sound of it that was too much to ask. He'd loved his first wife and she'd betrayed him. If he knew the truth of her past, he would assume she'd do the same.

At least she knew the truth in her own heart.

She loved him.

She loved her husband and his affection for her would be enough to sustain her.

It had to be.

She pulled him closer, wanting him to know her feelings but not able to voice them. He picked her up and carried her to the tiny shelter, stooping down low to lay her on the bed. He unclipped the brooches on her gown and she did her best to wriggle out of her clothes in what little light she could see by. She heard him undressing and it made her speed up with haste.

She was naked when he reached for her and she pulled him down on top of her.

The bed creaked and groaned. They both stilled, holding their breath in the darkness.

'Do you think it will hold up?' she whispered.

'You doubt my handiwork?' he asked, his fingers already smoothing down her breasts and her sides, pulling her closer.

'Do you?' She shivered, her breath misting in the air as she wrapped her arms around his chest.

He laughed rich and low against her neck, the sound vibrating through her chest. She bit her lip to stifle a moan as he tenderly nuzzled below her ear.

'We'll just have to be very slow and very careful,' he said.

His fingers stroked between her legs and she moaned, pulling him closer. Her body was drowning in sensation. 'I don't think I can wait.'

She wrapped her fingers around his length and stroked him with a tight grip, triumphant when he groaned against her.

'I have an idea,' he growled, gently pulling her hand

away from him as he trailed kisses down her neck, breasts and stomach.

She squirmed beneath him, the mixture of cool air and burning kisses sending shivers up and down her spine. He moved away from her and went to the bottom of the bed. The fire glowed behind him as he knelt on the floor.

'What?' she asked in a daze of confusion and disappointment.

Was he going to sleep on the floor after all?

His fingers wrapped around her ankles and he tugged her down the bed. She began to sit up, unsure of what was going on.

'Lie back, trust me.'

She lay down, her heart hammering in her chest, shivering with anticipation when his lips kissed her inner thigh and then moved higher and higher, until she was aching with the need for his touch. She felt his tongue slide across her womanhood and she jumped with shock. She'd never thought a man could kiss a woman *there*.

He stroked her leg reassuringly and she lay down again. 'Oh!' she gasped as his tongue began to stroke her in a rhythm similar to the one he used with his fingers.

She began to pant and moan as the rhythm took over her body, until she drowned in the pleasure of his kiss. Her climax was fast and hard. She screamed his name into the cool night air. It was a wordless declaration of love and joy, but only the stars heard her.

Thorstein woke with Gyda on top of him, her long limbs wrapped around him like ropes. It was the first time he didn't mind. He kissed the top of her head and untangled himself to rise. Dawn was only just filling the clearing with its pale light, but he was a man used to rising early. He'd let her sleep longer, get the fire going and some food ready for when she awoke.

He couldn't resist looking back at her after he'd stretched the tiredness from his muscles. She was truly stunning, lying amidst the furs, naked and resplendent. He threw on his clothes to stop the temptation to crawl back into bed with her and make love to her again.

He smiled to himself as he remembered the pleasures they'd taken last night. He was certain she'd never experienced them before, and he felt a smug satisfaction in knowing that he'd shown her the delights of the marriage bed.

By the time she woke the sun was fully up in the sky. She rubbed her eyes and called to him, her hair a messy cloud around her head. 'Thorstein…?'

'I'm here,' he called back, and she smiled her dazzling smile that never failed to make his heart stop.

'You should have woken me,' she said, rising and gasping at the cool air.

He admired her body as she dressed, feeling for the first time that he could. As if they were truly married.

When she joined him, he offered her a platter of bread, cheese and leftover stew. She took it with a shy smile and began to eat. The forest was alive with sound. Birds chirped and he could hear the stream bubbling.

'There's a waterfall not far from here,' he said. 'I was thinking we could walk there. We can wash, gather some herbs and lichen and then head back home. I'm sure we'll find all you need there.'

She nodded. 'Perfect.'

They set off shortly afterwards, leaving most of their supplies at the camp as they wouldn't be gone long. Thorstein led the way, helping her through the thick undergrowth by offering her his hand when she needed it. There was no rain, and she was grateful for that.

The sun sparkled through the canopy above them and she felt at peace walking through so much lush greenery. In Viken the weather would be turning sharply by now. It was nice to still have days when she could walk with just a cloak for warmth. She carried a large basket, and whenever she spotted an important plant she would tell Thorstein, so they could stop a moment while she gathered what she needed.

They followed the rocky path of the stream to reach its source: an impressive waterfall as tall as a dragon ship from nose to tail, covered in mossy rocks and evergreen bushes.

She gathered some more lichen, herbs and mushrooms until her basket overflowed, and then sat on a rock to rest and enjoy the peaceful sound of the waterfall. She watched as her husband stripped naked and then washed under the stream of water.

She couldn't help but laugh as she heard him gasp and grumble beneath the freezing cold spray. She cupped some water in her hands and washed her face with it. It was bracingly cold, and even that small amount made her shiver.

'That will hardly get you clean!' he shouted as he jumped from foot to foot as he dressed, his skin covered in goosebumps.

She laughed. 'This is enough for me.'

He came over and sat beside her on the rock, his tunic damp after his hasty wash. 'It's refreshing. You should try it.'

She eyed the waterfall and the edges of the forest.

'We're alone...the nearest farmstead is ours,' he added. 'Come on, the gods love brave women.'

Her heart stopped and then leapt. 'My sister Astrid always used to say that.'

His grin stilled and then softened. 'She was right.'

Her heart felt as if it would burst, and she shrugged off her cloak and stood. He looked up at her, his eyes full of admiration, as she undid her brooches and let the gown fall...

Chapter Twenty-One

'There!' said Gyda, biting off the thread on the garment she'd been embroidering and shaking it out.

'Finished?' asked Thorstein, looking up from the Yule decoration he was carving—his own evening activity.

On the nights when they didn't open their Hall to the community, they sat in the small section Gyda had blocked off with her new loom. She'd got her antechamber after all, and he had to admit it made for a cosy place to talk and rest before bed. His evenings had never been so pleasant.

'Yes—and I can't wait for you to try it on.'

She held out the garment and it took him a moment to catch her meaning.

'It's for me?' he asked, his surprise quickly replaced by a warm glow.

Ever since they'd returned from their forest trip over a week ago, he'd watched her sewing the blue fabric whenever she had a moment to spare. He'd imagined it was a gown, and had not even thought she might be making something for him.

'Yes. Consider it an early Yule gift.'

He stood up and pulled off his tunic, casting it aside

without a glance to where it fell. She stood up too, and took a step to stand in front of him. Then another, until she was only a breath away from him.

'It matches your eyes,' she said, and pressed the tunic against his shoulders, smiling with satisfaction that she'd judged his size so expertly. She turned her face up towards him expectantly, and he dipped into a gentle kiss before taking the tunic from her fingers.

'Thank you,' he said, and she smiled again.

'I only wanted a kiss as payment.'

He laughed, stroking the intricate embroidery in amazement. There was a family tree growing from the chest of the tunic, reaching its branches up and around the collar, with ravens darting amongst its branches and wolves dancing amongst the purple heather around the cuffs. Between them were runes denoting power, strength and prosperity, scattered amongst the images.

He'd never owned a piece of clothing so beautifully made in his entire life, and it was even more special because it was Gyda who'd made it.

He pulled it carefully over his head and smoothed it down. 'You're talented,' he said, frowning because it seemed such a poor description of her abilities.

'I told you I was,' she said, bristling, and then she laughed with a bittersweet smile that melted his heart. 'Sorry—I'm used to people dismissing my skill.'

Outrage flared in his chest on her behalf, but there was nothing he could do about the past injustices she'd received. He could only help her now.

'Would you like to make another trip to Jorvik?' he asked. 'Just for the day? We could buy more supplies for you. It won't be long until winter makes travel difficult, and this way you'll have plenty of supplies to make your tapestries. You can sell them in the spring, when I next go to the markets.'

'You'd let me sell my tapestries?'

'If you wish.'

'Thank you…' She touched his arm, her eyes bright with unshed tears. 'You don't know how much that means to me—'

She didn't manage to say any more as he cut off her words by crushing his mouth to hers.

The chaos of Jorvik filled his nose and ears, and he longed to go back home to fresh air and his comfortable bed. But when he saw Gyda happily chatting with the cloth merchant, and blushing with pride at her praise of her samples, he knew he'd made the right decision.

He waited for her to complete her business with significantly more patience than he'd felt the first time they'd been to the cloth merchant's stall. He stood a short distance away, watching her. Her face was lit up from within with excitement and confidence as she chose dyes and supplies. She looked happy and it made his blood sing.

So much had changed between them. He could now envisage a future where the two of them worked side by side. Building a life together, having children. He wanted it all.

She glanced over at him, and there was a shy smile on her lips that unravelled him in an instant.

When she came to stand by his side he asked, 'Your business is complete?'

'Yes. I can collect the materials on our way back from visiting Sven and my nephew. She's agreed to sell any tapestries I weave on the basis of the samples I showed her. She's even given me the materials I need at a reduced price. Thank you so much for bringing me.'

He shrugged. 'You can come whenever you like—it's only that winter makes the journey more difficult.'

He took her by the arm and they started towards Sven's Hall.

'Well, I'm grateful all the same. She thinks we'll get a good price for my work.'

'Any silver you make is yours.'

She stopped and stared at him. 'Thorstein, we're married. Our fortunes are entwined.'

'I have no need for your silver.'

She thought for a moment, and then continued walking with an easy smile. 'Then I will save it towards our daughters' bridal gifts.'

The mention of children made his heart soar, and he could only nod in answer.

As they approached Sven's Hall, they met Ivar outside.

Gyda took a step forward, but hesitated, her manner cool and collected, as it had been when Thorstein had first met her. Gone was the excitable woman from only a moment ago.

Ivar smiled at her. 'Aunt Gyda! Will you be staying long?'

Her shoulders relaxed slightly. 'I'm afraid not. But I hope to visit Jorvik regularly in the future. Maybe I can see you then?'

'I'd like that.'

The naked pleasure on her face reminded Thorstein of how early and fragile her relationship with her nephew was.

He gave Ivar a friendly pat on the shoulder. 'You are also welcome to come and stay with us, Ivar. I can always do with an extra pair of strong arms to work the land. As long as your father agrees, of course.'

Gyda reached out and squeezed Thorstein's arm, her

fingers tense. When Ivar grinned, her fingers softened and became a loving caress.

'We'd love to have you visit us,' she added softly, her tone barely concealing the hope she felt—or at least he could hear it. His understanding of her manner was so much better now.

They'd reached the square and Sven's Hall and Ivar nodded. 'That would be great. I'm sure my father won't mind. We can ask him now. He's talking with your stepson.'

Gyda gasped and her step faltered. Her face drained of colour and Thorstein felt his stomach tighten with concern.

'Are you well?' he asked, but she ignored him.

Her spine had straightened and her hand dropped from his arm. 'My stepson?' she whispered.

'Yes, Ragnar Halvorson. He arrived a moment ago. Come in!'

Ivar swept the door to the Hall open and Thorstein saw Gyda reach out towards him, as if to stop him. But the door was now open and her hand dropped to her side. That mask of cold politeness returned, causing a wave of unease to wash over Thorstein.

His beautiful wife had disappeared before his eyes.

Chapter Twenty-Two

She was drowning again. Only this time she wasn't in the North Sea. She stared at the golden-haired warrior in front of her and the air was stolen from her lungs and replaced with ice.

He was as handsome as ever and, judging by his cruel laugh, she'd guess he was still proud and arrogant too. The golden hair was intricately woven and a thick beard was cut short at the sides, tapering to a neat plait. His expression, always jovial, masked the cunning she knew was behind those sea-green eyes. He wore a scarlet tunic and gold brooches, his boots were of the finest leather and his cloak was made of bear skin.

He was every inch the wealthy son of a jarl, and long ago the sight of him had made her heart flutter. But that had all changed when she'd realised what kind of man he really was. He was stuck in the past, and until his elder brothers died without issue, or he was brave enough to fight his siblings, he would remain just that—the wealthy brother of a jarl. Not a true and deserving leader like Thorstein.

'Módir!'

He laughed, his arms spread wide in a joyous welcome

that pricked her skin like a dozen rusty blades. Needless to say she did not walk into his embrace.

'Ha! Well, isn't this a pleasant coincidence? How strange that the fates should weave us together once again, Gyda. The threads of our lives seem always to become entangled, don't they?'

She felt the urge to scream, but managed to choke it down with a strangled cough. She could feel Thorstein's eyes on her but she couldn't face him—she couldn't face either of them.

Sven looked between them with a frown. She wondered if Ragnar had ever told him. But they'd not been close friends in Viken, and surely Sven would never have helped her if he'd known the truth.

'Come, everyone,' he said. 'Let's sit by the fire and drink a cup of mead together.'

They sat around the fire, each taking a cup from the waiting servants.

'Where's Brunhild?' asked Gyda, hoping for an excuse to leave this terrible situation.

'Helping Eric Bloodaxe's wife deliver her child.'

'Oh...' Bile filled her stomach. She always found the birthing room difficult, but she'd prefer anywhere to here at this moment. 'Shall I go and offer my assistance?'

Ragnar feigned surprise, his eyes sparkling with mischief. 'So you have overcome your fear of childbirth, then? I am pleased to hear it.'

She opened her mouth to speak, but as always Ragnar ignored her.

'I remember her fainting at the first birth she attended. It was most fortunate that she never had to worry about such things herself while married to my father...what with his advanced age. It is good that you have overcome your fears. Especially now that you have remarried.'

'I didn't faint. I just needed to sit down for a moment… It wasn't long after I'd heard of Astrid's death,' she answered weakly, her resolve to stay strong crumbling like sand beneath her feet.

'Ah, yes. Your sisters were taken far too soon. Tragic…' Ragnar sighed, staring her down, and she looked away.

How she loathed those deceiving eyes. There had been a time when those eyes could have begged her to do anything and she would have obeyed gladly. Now they left her cold. She longed for the warmth of sky-blue eyes.

She glanced at Thorstein, but he was watching Ragnar with suspicion and it caused the bile to churn once more in her stomach, until she feared she would be sick.

'What brings you to Jorvik, Ragnar?' asked Thorstein, his tone menacing.

It was then that she noticed both Thorstein and Sven were scowling at Ragnar. It lightened her heart a little to know they supported her.

'I have come to trade. My brothers have had difficulty securing new agreements with our neighbours. Once I return to Viken, I'm sure I can settle the dispute.'

Her heart smiled at that news. Her stepsons had always been happy to travel and indulge in their father's power, taking no interest in how his wealth had been made. She was not surprised that with her gone some of their alliances had faltered. Neighbours in Viken were always potential enemies, and Halvor's sons—Ragnar included—were not the most reliable of men. At least it meant that Ragnar wouldn't be staying long.

Ragnar's voice interrupted her thoughts. 'I'm sorry you were given so little after my father's death. I also received very little. My brothers were promised almost everything. Then again, we were never the favourites of my father, were we, Gyda? But a devoted wife deserves more than the scraps from the table… You know that if I'd been free to come home I would have ensured you were well tended to…as I have in the past.'

She said nothing. Thorstein's fists were clenched on his thighs and she felt waves of shame threaten to swallow her whole.

The gods love brave women.

'I came to England for a new life, a fresh start…and I found it with Thorstein.' She raised her chin and looked at her husband as she spoke. She wanted him to know that despite what Ragnar said she was living for their future together. She would not allow her past to ruin it.

Pride shone in his eyes and some of her courage returned.

Ragnar gave her a smug smile as he rocked back in his seat and took a sip of his mead. 'Sven told me… To think you're a simple farmer's wife now. I'd never have imagined it. But do we ever truly know a person's heart?'

Thorstein leaned forward, his voice low and his eyes hard. 'A warrior's heart is only revealed by the axe. Call me *simple* once more and I may be tempted to reveal yours.'

Sven bellowed a laugh and slapped his thigh. 'You deserved that, Ragnar! Chief Thorstein was an exceptional warrior in the Great Army. He is a trusted advisor and most importantly a close friend of mine. Their marriage binds Thorstein to my family.'

'My apologies, Chief Thorstein,' Ragnar said, with an inclination of his head. 'I meant no disrespect.'

Thorstein didn't respond, and Ragnar was the first to look away.

The tension between the two men made Gyda feel sick with anxiety. She smoothed her skirts and tried to pretend indifference, but her fingers trembled and she had to clasp them tightly in her lap to stop from shaking.

'What are your plans?' asked Sven mildly.

'After trading here I will go and help my eldest brother settle matters back home,' Ragnar replied. 'Then I plan to go raiding. There is little opportunity left in England. Even less now that the treaty has been signed. I will try Francia. Paris has been plundered, but there are other places still ripe for the taking, and I plan to own land soon. I will win it with steel and blood—in the old way.'

Thorstein seemed to ignore the implied jibe, but his eyes narrowed and his hand rested lightly on the axe at his belt. Gyda could barely conceal her own distaste. If Ragnar had truly wanted to be a Viking then he would have done so in his youth, like Thorstein had. Ragnar was an opportunist, not a risk-taker. He wasn't brave, like Thorstein, and he only wanted glory—not land, as he claimed.

She knew him well and the knowledge made her sick. If only she'd had the gift of foresight back then.

'Any man can steal land. It takes a warrior with strength and wisdom to keep it,' she said, finally finding her courage now that Thorstein's reputation was being played with.

Sven sloshed mead on the floor as he pointed at her in triumph. 'Well said, Gyda! Now, I'm afraid I have business at the docks. Will you be staying here tonight, Thorstein?'

'No, we'll be returning now. Gyda only wished to visit her nephew.'

Ivar spoke up from the side of the room where he'd been standing. 'Thorstein says I can go and work on his settlement. If you agree…'

Sven nodded. 'I wouldn't object. In the spring, though.

Now I want you by my side. You should learn the politics of rule.'

Ragnar stood, dropping his cup on the bench with a dull thud. 'I must be getting on myself. I have business with an old friend that I need to attend to. Farewell, Jarl Sven... Chief Thorstein...'

He stopped in front of Gyda and gave her a warm smile that worried her more than any cruelty he might have spoken.

'Gyda, my brothers were wrong to let you go. Know that I would never have allowed it if I'd been there. You will always have a home in Njardarheimr.'

'That is...good of you to say. However, my home is now with Thorstein.'

Ragnar gave a wicked grin and nodded. 'Of course it is. Goodbye, Gyda.'

He walked out of the Hall, and she hoped with all her heart and soul that he was walking out of her life for ever.

In no time at all they were going through the winding paths filled with workshops and stalls back to the docks. Sven and Thorstein walked slightly ahead of her, deep in conversation about the new treaty and current opposition to the King's plans. She was grateful for the time alone. She wasn't sure what she should tell Thorstein about Ragnar, but she knew he would ask her.

She needed time to think before she faced him.

Thorstein and Sven had turned a corner, and then a strong arm grabbed at her from between two stalls and pulled her into the shadows beside a workshop. She gasped in surprise, but her scream was cut off by a sweaty palm across her face.

'Hello, sweetling,' Ragnar said, and his deep, sultry

voice was an echo from the past that she'd hoped never to hear again.

Her breath left her lungs in a rush, as if someone had punched her in the guts. She glanced over his shoulder as he removed his hand, but she could see nothing. His big body was a wall of muscle, blocking her path. Thorstein and Sven walked on ahead, oblivious.

Horror overwhelmed her. Surely this was a nightmare and it would end soon?

'You seem to have married well.'

Ragnar reached out, and before she could object he scraped his fingers against her collarbone as he touched the amber at her neck.

'Mine,' he said.

'It was a gift from your father.'

Hot bile rose in her throat. There had been a time when she would have craved such a touch from him. Now she saw it for what it was—manipulation.

'A gift from my father? Then it is definitely mine.'

With trembling fingers she tugged it over her head. 'Here—take it. Just leave me alone.'

He didn't take it from her, but smiled thoughtfully, like a cat playing with its prey. 'I wonder what else you have of mine...? It was bad enough that you ruined the relationship I had with my father.'

'You seduced his bride—of course he disowned you.'

'I remember it differently. The smell of hay in your hair...the sweat on your skin. You begged me to take you. Distracted me as you're doing now. Trying to make me forget my birthright. Shall I tell your husband the truth? Or Sven and Ivar? What would they think of your adultery? Sleeping with another man after your marriage to my father was agreed, after you'd sworn to marry him the next day?'

His words were poison. This was how she'd ended up in a hay barn, her maidenhood cast aside for weak promises he hadn't been able to keep. Only this time she wasn't a doe-eyed maiden. Yes, her long betrothal had meant that her unfaithfulness would have been viewed as adultery, and the fact it had been with her future husband's son had made it doubly shameful. But the truth was she had thought by giving into Ragnar she would have avoided the marriage completely and a new alliance could have been agreed instead.

She'd been wrong.

Her mistake had only tightened the noose around her neck. As keeping it a secret from Thorstein had now trapped her in a cycle of deceit.

'No! Don't! And that's not what happened!'

He'd been the seducer…he'd implied promises of marriage. But, as always, she began to doubt her own memory. *Had* she flirted? Maybe a little… She'd hoped for a way out of marrying Halvor while keeping the alliance intact, and Ragnar's attentions had given her hope. She'd been young and naive.

No, he was wrong. She hadn't seduced him. He'd been rough and quick, taking her consent with pressured words and sweet promises. How could she doubt herself? But Ragnar had always had that effect on her…twisting her words and thoughts until she was lost at sea.

'I wonder…what would you give for my silence?'

'I owe you nothing. Get out of my way, Ragnar! Unless you wish for my husband to split your miserable face in two.'

She shrugged out of his grasp.

'Really? Do you think he would kill me? *I* was not an adulterer… I will be passing Thorstein's settlement at dawn in two days' time. I expect to find you waiting for me. I shall leave a boat for you at the water's edge, where the river is narrowest. Do not pretend you have nothing. Sven reassured me of your security by telling me of all the silver he gave you. Or I shall warn your husband that he has married an adulteress…just like his first wife.'

Ragnar chuckled as she pushed past him.

How she hated his name. It held a double meaning for her. He was her *ragnarok*—her end of days. There was no escaping her fate.

Chapter Twenty-Three

Thorstein glanced behind him and stopped dead. Sven walked a couple of paces ahead before he stopped and turned as well.

'Where's Gyda?'

Thorstein waited for three heartbeats, in case she turned the corner, and then he ran.

People dived out of his way as he charged through the crowd. Any who were too slow were shoved aside.

How long had she not been with them? He'd last seen her as they'd passed through the wood-turning district. She'd only been a couple of steps behind them.

Then he saw her, walking out from behind a workshop. She looked fragile and tormented. Her face was pale, her shoulders were hunched and his beautiful regal wife looked half her size.

Then she saw him.

Her eyes sharpened, her back straightened with defiance, and she strode towards him with purpose. She was strong and powerful again, and it made him ashamed to have worried about her in the first place.

She was a Valkyrie, a goddess, his everything.

He saw the flash of a gold and scarlet tunic moving in the opposite direction. 'Is that…?'

She grabbed him by the arm and dragged him with her. 'I'm sorry. I was distracted. Let's go home.'

He looked over his shoulder but the man he'd thought he'd seen was already gone.

They walked on, back to the boat. Her steps faltered as they reached it and he worried that she was hesitant about leaving. What would he do if she wanted to stay? Wanted to seek out Ragnar and travel back to Viken with him?

'Are you ready?' he asked.

'Yes.'

He smoothed his hands down to her waist and then lifted her up onto the boat.

He followed her shattered gaze to a couple walking together, hand in hand. A babe was strapped to the mother's back, a little boy on his father's shoulders. A happy, healthy family.

Was she afraid?

He looked at her closely. Yes, he could see that old grief behind her eyes. The fear.

He thought for a moment and then touched her chin to draw her back to him. 'Stay here. I need to do something. I swear I won't be long.'

'What…?'

'I swear. Stay here with our men.'

He nodded to his warriors, who inclined their heads. He knew they would defend her to the death—not that there was any fear of that here.

He turned and strode away. He would do all that he could to remove the fear from her eyes.

He was back before the sun had set on the river. But it could have been a thousand years for the way she glared at him.

'Where have you been?' she barked, her foot tapping on the deck with a steady beat.

'I got another tattoo.'

Her foot stilled. 'Well, that's not what I was expecting.'

'I know—and I'm sorry I kept you waiting.'

He held out his palm, where a dramatic rune was marked across his skin, still red and tender.

'My uncle had this rune on his palm. It was for my aunt… She struggled with the birth of my eldest cousin. It took several days to deliver him, and both she and my cousin nearly died. My uncle asked a priestess for a protection rune—she gave him this symbol. She told him to hold her hand during every birth. That the magic of the rune would give her his strength. My aunt never struggled again. I know you are not yet carrying my child, but when the time comes I want to be ready. I will give you my strength… You have nothing to fear… You will not face your battlefield alone.'

She took his palm in her hands and kissed the rune. When she looked up, she blinked back tears and cleared her throat with a nod.

'Thank you,' she whispered, and then she turned away from him.

His heart broke, and he wondered if she would ever reveal her true thoughts and emotions to him.

Thorstein stared at Gyda from across the fire. There was something wrong, but he couldn't understand what. She'd closed a door in her mind to him and he suspected he needed to tread carefully where she was concerned.

There was no settlement *nattmal* tonight—no stories or laughter as there had been before they went to Jorvik. She worked on some Yuletide decorations, while he carved little gifts for the children. But she was distracted, her needle constantly pausing as she looked towards the fading light.

He could only think that meeting her stepson had unsettled her. Did she fear she'd made a mistake in marrying him?

'Gyda, let's go to bed,' he said, standing and feigning a stretch.

'It's not that late,' she whispered, her eyes darting to the door as if afraid of the darkness outside.

He moved to her side and stroked his fingers down her arm. 'Are you avoiding our bed now? I thought that was my job?'

'No!'

She laughed, and the knots in his shoulders loosened a little.

'You know I'm not.' She smiled, leaning into his embrace. 'I always crave your touch. Sometimes I long for the day to end so you can take me to bed.'

A shiver ran down his spine and he felt his body stiffen in response. 'That's good to know...' He smoothed his hands against her sides, worshipping the smooth curves beneath his callused fingers. She was perfect. 'I am the luckiest of men.'

'No, I'm the lucky one,' she said, and she tucked the hair out of his eyes, causing his skin to tingle across his face.

Her blue-grey eyes watched him, quiet and hesitant, as if there was something else between them—some other obstacle.

'Since Jorvik—'

'Let's not speak of it,' she whispered, gripping his face tightly in her hands and pulling his lips close.

The kiss was deep and urgent, as if he was about to

go into battle and not to bed. She tugged on his hand and led him to their bedchamber.

He closed the door behind them. The fire he'd lit earlier had burned low, so he put another log on as he passed. She moved away and removed her jewellery, placing it in her chest carefully, her fingers brushing tenderly over the engravings and stones of each piece, as if she were saying goodnight to each memory.

Now he knew its significance, her care for the jewellery didn't bother him as it once had. It was a tender and sweet act of love, not avarice.

He undressed and got into bed, settling himself down for the pleasure of watching her undress—his favourite time of day.

She closed the lid on the chest and gave it a pat, as if to check the lid was secure. She turned away and the sadness in her eyes turned to honey in the light of the fire as she drank in the sight of him in their bed. She smiled and he felt his breath catch in his throat.

She kicked off her shoes and unravelled the wrappings around her calves. Her eyes barely left his as she moved, and it made anticipation grow heavy in the air. Slowly she untied her gown, letting the fabric drop to the ground. She didn't bother to fold it before she undid the linen shift beneath. Then it dropped too, and she was completely bare, stepping over the discarded linen to reach their bed.

She stopped at the foot and climbed on top of the covers. Crawling towards him on her hands and knees, she stalked him like a she-wolf, a seductive glint in her eyes. He had to claw his fingers into the fur covers to stop himself from reaching for her.

'You're teasing me again, woman.'

She pouted playfully. 'It's you who teases me. I cannot stop thinking of you…of your touch. I ache for your lips, your fingers, your tongue.'

She'd reached him now and she settled on his lap, her long hair curling lightly around her breasts as she nipped at his mouth.

A helpless groan escaped his throat as she rubbed against him. He gripped her by the waist and tossed her to the side, rolling over her until she was pinned down on the bed.

She gasped with excitement, her back arching to meet the heat of his chest. 'I want you…so much,' she moaned.

His throat choked on the words he wanted to say, longed to say. But the shadow of doubt stopped him. He looked into her silvery blue eyes and saw longing, and lust, and a hint of sadness that he couldn't understand. That he was afraid to understand.

He kissed her. Abandoning his mind in pure sensation and lust. Hoping to tell her with actions and touch what he couldn't express in words.

She wrapped her arms around him and pulled him close, as if she never wanted to let him go.

Pleasure and desire were never in doubt between them. They ignited a fire within each other and it burned with ferocious greed as they came together.

He took his time. Teasing her as she'd teased him. Kissing and nipping at her neck, tasting the tenderness of her flesh with long, languid strokes of his tongue, up her neck and down her breasts.

She wrapped her thighs around him, cradling him to her, hips seeking hips and building a glorious heat between them.

He slipped his hand down, stroked her wet opening and groaned with satisfaction at her needy whimpers as she rocked against him with ever-increasing rhythm. Unable to resist any longer, he pushed inside her with one hard thrust. Her back arched and she cried out, her body squeezing him rhythmically with her pleasure.

He couldn't see her face as she came, because she buried it against his shoulder and neck. He wanted to see her face so desperately, but like so many things she hid it from him.

It caused him to pause, and he held her close for a moment.

'Thorstein?' she murmured, her voice muffled against his neck.

It sent shivers of longing down his spine.

'Please don't stop.'

A surge of lust slammed through his body like a stampede of wild horses. She needed him and he would do anything to please her. He began to move, slowly at first, then increasing the pace as he cradled her arching body in his arms, sensing another climax was drawing near. He gritted his teeth, determined to prove to her how much he cared, how willing he was to chase any doubts from her mind.

She gripped him by the hair and dragged him down to her mouth, and then to her breasts. Her body was riding him just as much as his was riding hers.

Her body stiffened with a wild cry of abandon and then she rippled with pleasure. A tear escaped her eye before she turned her face into the furs and moaned. He kissed her cheek, hoping to turn her back towards him, but as he moved to her side she turned away.

At a loss, he reached for her, and was comforted when she pressed her back to his chest and pulled his arm around her waist, cradling him to her. He breathed in the scent of her hair and sighed...

* * *

Gyda didn't sleep that night. She waited for Ragnar's dawn to burn a line under her door.

When the darkness turned to milky light, she carefully rose. She dressed quietly, so as not to wake Thorstein, picked up her jewellery chest from the table and slipped from the room.

She stepped out into the cold light of dawn, the box clutched to her chest. She wished she didn't have to give it up—especially to Ragnar, who deserved nothing. She would rather have thrown it in the sea, but she would not risk her marriage with Thorstein for anything.

She strode forward, pulling her cloak close against the bitter wind as she made her way into the woods. She would have been afraid if there hadn't been a greater threat waiting for her. She would have walked through a hundred woods if it meant she could keep her husband.

Thankfully the woods were calm, and it didn't take her long to reach the narrow part of the river and find the little rowing boat Ragnar had left for her. Ragnar's longship waited for her, its scarlet sail down for lack of wind and his men waiting at the oars, ready to depart.

She didn't look back and see that Thorstein was following her.

Her gaze was set on the ordeal she had yet to face.

After a few strokes of the oars to get her out into the river she took a deep breath and stopped rowing. Let Ragnar Halvorson come the rest of the way to meet her. She would not waste any more energy on him. She hoped the sea god Aegir dragged him and her chest beneath the waves, to face justice for his crimes. But she doubted fate would be so kind.

The dragon ship began to move towards her.

At least soon she would be free of him and his threats.

He would go back to Viken, or go raiding, or whatever he had planned, and she would be left in peace to live with Thorstein for the rest of her life.

The jewellery was a small sacrifice to make in comparison to a lifetime of happiness.

Chapter Twenty-Four

Ragnar looked down at her from the serpent-headed longship as he approached. She wobbled in her rowing boat as his longship pulled up beside her.

'Welcome, Gyda. Let me help you aboard.' The softness of his voice caused a hundred snakes to slither down her spine.

'No need—here, take it,' she said, holding up the chest as she struggled to stay balanced.

'Nonsense, come and join us.'

'Hello, Aunt Gyda!'

A familiar blond head peeked over the boat's side, causing her blood to freeze.

'Ivar, what are you doing here?'

Ragnar leaned down and pulled her up onto the deck of the longship, his fingers digging into her arms with bruising strength. She wasn't far from his height but he was still a warrior, moulded for battle.

'Why? Why would you bring him?' she cried, thrusting the box at Ragnar's chest.

'I wanted to see you before you left,' answered Ivar.

'Left...?'

'With Ragnar... He said you're leaving Thorstein.

Going back home… I wanted to say goodbye.' He looked between them, uncertain.

Ragnar cocked an eyebrow and she knew what he'd done. This had to be a manipulation—to force her to return with him to Viken. He would not become the Jarl if he didn't challenge his brother, and he would gain approval from Halvor's loyal men if he were married to her.

'Does your father know where you are?' She took a step towards Ivar, and spoke quietly, her eyes never leaving Ragnar as he watched in smug satisfaction.

'Yes… Well, I told one of my friends to let him know.'

'Quick, Ivar, get in the rowing boat!'

'What?' Ivar stared at her in dismay, his face pale.

He took an uncertain step towards the boat, but at Ragnar's nod a warrior blocked him. Gyda watched helplessly as the rowing boat floated away.

'Let's eat first,' Ragnar said briskly. 'There's plenty of time for Ivar to be dropped off before we leave. Or, if you do not come with me, maybe Ivar would like to join me raiding in Francia?'

'We're both going back,' she said, turning towards her nephew, who looked very young and very frightened.

Hard fingers gripped her by the arm and pulled her back. 'No. I've lost you once. I won't lose you again.'

Gone was the softness of earlier, and in its place was a far more familiar cruelty. She threw off his hand with a defiant shrug and stood beside Ivar, placing an arm around his shoulders. She let her voice carry strongly across Ragnar's ship, hoping his men would see sense.

'You have abducted the wife of Chief Thorstein the Burned, as well as the son and heir of Jarl Sven Leifson, a valued advisor to the King! Take us both home now, or suffer the wrath of Jorvik!'

Ragnar smiled, although she saw some of his men wince.

'Ivar wanted to come. I have a witness who will say that he left with me willingly. Now…' He stepped forward and whispered closely in her ear. 'Ivar will be returned safely if you agree to come home with me and become my wife. But make your decision quickly, Gyda. I do not like the look of this weather and…as you know…terrible things can happen at sea…'

Her heart sank. 'Why are you doing this?'

He looked at her then—really looked at her—and the smug mask faltered ever so slightly for a moment. 'Because I love you. I have always loved you. And now we can finally be together. Is that not wonderful? I will defeat my brothers and we will rule the port together. As we always should have.'

As he spoke he reached towards her, pulling her close, and she balled her fists against his chest. She would have clawed out his heart if she hadn't feared for Ivar's safety.

He leaned in to kiss her and she screamed in frustration, slapping his face as hard as she could. He let go of her and she stumbled back to Ivar, years of bitter anger fuelling her words.

'That was not love! *This* is not love! You wish to win! That is all. You don't want me—you never have! You wanted to win against your father, and now you wish to win against your brothers. I could never make you happy—not then or now.'

His face hardened to stone, and it reminded her of Halvor so much it made the air choke in her lungs.

'You will come with me. Or I will kill you both!'

She took Ivar's trembling fingers in her own and squeezed them gently. 'Then I have no choice.'

'Good. We'll be passing a bend in the river shortly.

Thorstein's settlement is nearer on foot from here. I take it you're a strong swimmer, boy?'

Ivar swallowed nervously, but jerked his head in a nod.

'No! Land him on the shore at least!' said Gyda.

Ragnar gave a dismissive snort and walked towards a tented area of his ship. 'If he can't swim he's not Sven's son.'

Ivar looked up at her with defiance in his eyes. In a hushed voice he said, 'I have swum this river with my father and Thorstein many times. Do not worry. They will come and save you.'

'I'm sure they will,' she said, patting his cold hand gently.

Obviously Ivar's voice had not been quiet enough.

'No, they will not!' Ragnar roared, turning on them both like a wounded beast.

He loomed over Ivar with such cruel rage that Gyda stepped in front of her nephew to shield him, her hands outstretched in a silent plea.

Ragnar stopped short of striking them, his chest heaving with anger. 'Gyda has left Thorstein for ever! If I hear that Thorstein or Sven are coming for her…even if it's just a rumour…your aunt will die! Do you understand? If anyone asks, she left willingly! She supports my claim of inheritance and she is *delighted* to be a jarl's wife again. Understand? If you say anything different, she dies! I have friends in Jorvik and they'll let me know if you have deceived me!'

'Yes,' squeaked Ivar, blinking back tears.

'This is close enough. Goodbye, Ivar.'

Ragnar jerked his head at a warrior Gyda had not realised had moved behind them. The warrior grabbed Ivar in a tight bear hold, picked him up and tossed the child overboard.

A scream was ripped from her throat and she fought several strong arms as she tried to save her nephew. Then Ragnar's arms locked around her chest with crushing force. But instead of pulling her away, as she'd feared, he took her to the side of the boat so that she could see what was happening.

'He's fine!'

He laughed, and she sagged with both relief and despair when she saw Ivar's blond head bob up. He trod water for a moment, watching her, and then he turned and with steady strokes swam towards the riverbank.

He would be safe. That was all that mattered.

Thorstein stared at Ragnar's longship as it sailed towards the mouth of the river. Madman that he was, he'd followed her.

She was leaving him.

He'd known it when he'd seen her take her jewellery with her. She'd walked through the woods to the river, taken a rowing boat and met Ragnar's longship. She had betrayed him as Thora had done, lured by the promise of power and status.

It was what he'd wanted, wasn't it? For Gyda to realise they weren't suited? For her to leave?

And yet he hadn't been able to stop himself. He'd followed, watched and waited. Hoping for some kind of clue as to why she would do this. Some sign that he'd been mistaken in his recent change of heart towards her.

Except this was Gyda—cool, calm Gyda—who'd burned like the Northern lights beneath him last night, who told stories to children and sewed happily for hours, just content to be by his side. He *knew* her.

But he also knew that his beautiful wife kept dark secrets from him…that she was haunted by her past.

With every passing moment he was left more and more confused. Soon he would have to make a decision. The river would twist and wind before it switched back towards his settlement and the sea. If he left now he could be back at his settlement and raise the alarm before Ragnar's ship reached the mouth of the sea.

He just needed a sign.

Then he saw it.

A boy had been thrown from the ship.

He leapt forward to the edge of the trees, but stopped when he saw that Gyda had been grabbed by rough hands. The boy began to swim and he realised it was Ivar.

He stared at the ship as it sailed onwards. That man held power over his wife. The pain stabbed him in the heart, causing his nails to scratch into the bark of a nearby tree.

She might not trust him with her secrets. But he loved her anyway.

Thankfully, Ivar was a strong swimmer, and was approaching the riverbank. Gyda was fighting, and it took all Thorstein's strength not to wade out to her. All he had was his axe and a knife, while Ragnar had a dozen warriors and a ship. He needed help, and he would raise an army to save her.

He waited for Ivar to enter the woods before he revealed himself. The boy jerked in fright, and at the sight of a familiar face his composure crumpled.

'She's *delighted*...to be the Jarl's wife,' he said, and then burst into gut-wrenching sobs.

Thorstein wrapped his arm around the shaking boy and held him tight. 'It's all right. You're safe now.'

Ivar's spine straightened and he took in one deep breath. When he looked up his jaw was firm and his silver-blue eyes strong.

'I lied! He's taken her. But there's still time. Ragnar is a poor helmsman. His ship is barely moving. There might be time for you to launch an attack. You can save her! What are you waiting for?'

'Can you run?' asked Thorstein.

Ivar thumped his arm, just as his father, Sven, would have. 'Not as fast as you. Now, *go*!'

He handed the boy his knife, his axe and some flint. 'Stay here and build a fire. I'll send someone for you.'

Ivar nodded solemnly. 'Please help her,' he said, but Thorstein was already running.

A shout from one of Ragnar's men had drawn his attention away from her, and he'd left the tent. Gyda followed immediately. Whatever had distracted Ragnar, it might give her the opportunity to jump from the ship and swim to shore. He'd not left her side until now, and she'd cursed every moment she'd spent in his foul grip.

They were almost out to sea now, and the cliffs of the harbour were shining like bone in the morning light. The wind whipped at her hair and she had to scrape it out of her eyes to see clearly.

She saw that the raiders had pulled their shields from the hooks on the side of the longship and were raising them in a line. On top of the cliff the women and youths of Thorstein's settlement ran forward with arrows notched, a dozen bows aimed at the longship and its crew.

'Shields!' shouted Ragnar, although they were already raised.

He was all bluster and no bite. He got what he wanted through manipulation and deceit. He was the opposite in every way to Thorstein.

'Hold!' shouted Magnus from the cliff top. 'Chief Thorstein wishes to speak with you.'

Ragnar cursed as he looked behind him. Thorstein was advancing quickly in a longship, his boat heavily armed with warriors.

Her world split in two. What would Thorstein say when he found her on Ragnar's boat, presumably leaving England?

She walked to the side of the ship and watched her husband approach, with her knuckles white and a bitten lip.

He reached them quickly, thudding into the side of Ragnar's boat with a harsh crack that made the deck rock. In no time at all Thorstein had boarded, his mighty axe and leather-covered shield in his hands. Gyda wanted to run to him, but the rage in his eyes made her hesitate. Would he blame her for this, as Halvor had done?

'You wish to steal my wife, Ragnar Halvorson?' he shouted, his voice as heavy and as savage as thunder.

Ragnar laughed. 'I was born to be a jarl, farmer! I plan to rule, even if I have to kill my brothers for it. Do you think I'm afraid of a man like you? Gyda will be *my* wife, not yours. As it always should have been!'

'Shut your *mouth*!' she cried, striding past him towards Thorstein, her heart aching with hope. Her next words were spoken directly to her husband. 'I am leaving with my husband, Ragnar. I will tell him everything. As I should have done from the start.' She spat the last words in disgust. 'You are a snake. No! A *worm*! And I will *never* marry you!'

She reached Thorstein and placed a tentative hand on his shoulder, begging silently for him to leave and take her with him.

'So your husband knows nothing about us?'

The satisfied smugness of Ragnar's voice made her stomach heave. She spun to face him, feeling contemptible secrets ripping apart her insides. She couldn't contain them any longer. Her fragile happiness was pouring through her hands like water.

'There is nothing to tell.'

'Ah, so he knows nothing of how you betrayed my father?'

'The only person who betrayed your father was you, Ragnar!' she cried out, all her hope for pride and dignity blown away with the sea breeze.

'That's not what he said when he found us together on the morning of your wedding!' Ragnar said, looking triumphantly at Thorstein.

Thorstein's jaw locked, but he said nothing.

She looked between the two men, her face numb, as if she'd been struck by a hammer. Then fiery rage burst forth, flooding the cage of her heart with years of shame, grief and torment.

It was happening again.

Ragnar was ruining her life all over again!

A shot of clarity flew up her spine and exploded in her mind. *Not again!* She would not allow this to happen again.

This bitter, spoilt man-child would not steal her hard-fought-for happiness and pride. She now knew true love, and she'd never felt it before.

'Oh, please!' she said, her voice dripping with disgust. 'I was a young girl, filled with your romantic lies of love and whispered promises of marriage. You planned everything! I see that now. You seduced me. You plied me with strong ale and silly dreams. I may have willingly lain with you…once…but you were the one who planned it. I bet you even arranged for Halvor to find us together. You knew how much it would hurt him, you knew that he would never forgive me, but you did it anyway. You destroyed your father's marriage before it had even begun and, fool that I was, I thought you would marry me afterwards! Hah! You just wanted to spite your father and damn the consequences. You are a pathetic excuse for a man. Remember, Ragnar, there's a reason I only lay with you *once*!'

'Because you did not wish to shame yourself further...' Ragnar spluttered in outrage.

'Enough! Believe that if you wish. I am older and wiser now. I am no longer swayed by honeyed words.'

She turned away from Ragnar and looked down at Thorstein's waiting longship. She clutched her trembling fingers in front of her in a strangled grip. Now the ugly truth was revealed, what would Thorstein think?

'Will you take me home, Thorstein? Please.'

She waited, her breath held. She didn't dare look him in the eye. She'd promised she would not betray him, and here was proof that she had kept secrets from him. Would he view that as a betrayal? Would he hate her for what she had done in the past?

'Give Gyda back her property.'

'What?'

Gyda and Ragnar both said it at the same time, equally dumbfounded.

'You heard. Give my wife her property back. Now. Or I will let loose a hundred arrows upon your head. If you are blessed by the gods and manage to survive, then I will take this axe and remove your miserable head from your miserable shoulders. I am tempted to do that anyway, after what I have heard.'

'Take it. I have no use for pathetic trinkets!'

Ragnar grabbed the chest from the floor and tossed it at Gyda. She just managed to catch it before it fell, and she hugged it tightly, staring at Thorstein in amazement.

Ragnar's cruel laugh followed, his ridicule the only

weapon he dared to use against them. 'I can understand your anger, Thorstein. It must be hard to learn both of your wives were unfaithful liars.'

The blow cut her deep. Her worst fears had been spoken out loud, made into monsters of flesh and bone that would wreak havoc on her marriage for years to come.

Her step faltered and she clutched the side of the boat to steady herself.

Thorstein did not look at her and it broke her heart.

'Get into the boat, Gyda,' he murmured, and she obeyed, her whole body shaking.

She jumped across to Thorstein's ship, crumpling onto the deck where sympathetic eyes and gentle hands lifted her up. She thought she heard a thud and shout of pain, but she wasn't sure if she'd imagined it.

Thorstein joined her shortly, his eyes raking over her body with thorough care. 'Were you hurt?'

She shook her head, feeling pitiful. His kindness was another lash of shame across her back.

Chapter Twenty-Five

Her heart drummed in her chest to an ever-increasing beat as she watched Thorstein from beneath her lashes. It was full daylight now, and the autumn sun sparkled off the dark water as if treasure and not sand lay on the seabed.

'Why take such a risk?'

Thorstein's voice was quiet, and the steady beat of the ship's oars cutting through the surf was in complete contrast to her erratic pulse.

She looked around her at their people, rowing or lining the clifftop, arrows notched and ready to let loose on the now retreating longship with the scarlet sail. She could see Magnus and Elga. Elga had never used a weapon in her entire life, as far as Gyda was aware, but she stood amongst them, her bow steady. Gyda's throat tightened at this display of loyalty from her people, from her friends and family.

Why? It was such a simple question, but she had a thousand answers.

'Does it matter?' she whispered, looking away from Thorstein and her people to the never-ending sea. She didn't deserve any of them.

'It matters to me.'

Her eyes were dragged back to his face. To the hard set of his jaw as his scar flexed in the morning light. He was impossibly calm. After what she'd done she would have expected him to rage against her deception. But he watched her and waited, his eyes as sharp as a wolf's as it waited to pounce.

'I am your wife. I wanted to remain that way.'

'But why...? You could have been the wife of a jarl. You could have returned to your wealthy port and had children there. You could have easily divorced me... You wouldn't have been the first.'

She blinked at him, suddenly realising the pain she must have caused him. It cut her heart deeply. 'I wouldn't do that.'

'Then why? Why were you willing to give up so much to stay with me, a simple farmer?'

'You are *not* a simple farmer! Stop saying that. You're better than Ragnar. You must know that!'

He gave a dismissive snort. 'Anyone is better than Ragnar. But why do you want to stay with me? Why were you willing to pay a man like him to keep quiet about your past? Why do you care so much about what I think? I agreed to marry you. You haven't been unfaithful to me with Ragnar—'

'Of course not!' she cried, her skin crawling at the thought.

'So why go to such lengths? Give up your sisters' jewellery...?'

Emotion and uncertainty raged within her, and she swallowed a painful lump in her throat. The people stared at them, and although they could not hear her she felt their eyes all the same. Watching and waiting.

Could she face the ridicule if she told the truth? Could

she live with the disappointment if he didn't feel the same way?

No, she couldn't bear it.

She stared at the only thing that made the madness make sense. Thorstein's blue eyes, which were looking at her with open pain.

'Tell me why, Gyda? You owe me that at least.'

'Owe you?' She laughed sourly.

She owed him everything, but words were beyond her. Her eyes burned with unshed tears. She would not cry in front of a man. She'd sworn it all those years ago in the barn. But there was nowhere for her to go. She was trapped.

Thorstein raised his hand and the men stopped rowing. The boat bobbed on the peaceful waves. 'Yes. If we are to move on after this then I must know why you wish to stay with me.'

Her heartbeat stumbled. 'We can discuss it back at the Hall.' She felt hot and cold, as if she were coming down with a malignant fever. She needed privacy...a moment to compose her thoughts and emotions.

'No, tell me *now*,' Thorstein growled, frustration making his scar ripple across his clenched jaw. 'Why did you choose me?'

The walls of her control crumbled. 'Because...' She lost her nerve and shrugged.

His scowl darkened. 'Why, Gyda?'

'Because... I...*love* you!' she shouted, and her soul curled up to die as she heard the words echo across the deck.

Panic blazed through her veins and she felt faint. His eyes had widened. But she couldn't bear to see the mocking pity in them, so she stared into the sea instead, and choked on the tears that fell in an endless torrent down her cheeks.

She'd sworn never to cry in front of a man again, and yet here she was, as stupid and as vulnerable as the maiden she'd once been a lifetime ago. He'd caught her in his trap. But he'd asked for the truth and he was right. They couldn't move on until she admitted it, however painful and humiliating it might be.

She continued to speak, even though each word was like probing an open wound. 'I love you, Thorstein… With all my heart. I would have given up everything I owned if it meant I could keep you with me. I thought if you knew about…about how I betrayed Halvor with his son before my wedding…if you knew the real reason why he shunned me as his wife and yet refused to divorce me…it would be an excuse for you to leave me, and I couldn't bear it.'

Her tears were falling in full force now, a storm that she could no longer contain, and she felt as if she were drowning in them. Her breath was ragged and lurching.

Thorstein closed the two steps between them and she squeezed her eyes shut, wishing for it all to end.

'Gyda…'

His voice was soft and gentle, and it hurt her more than any of Halvor's harsh words or slaps. His palms cupped her face and she flinched, pushing against him with a weak smack of her hands against his solid chest.

The boat shifted and Gyda grabbed tightly on to the tunic she'd sewn him. The boat rocked again, but she didn't care. She wished they would capsize—anything to end this humiliating torment.

'No!' she sobbed, punctuating her words with a weak thud to his chest with her clenched fists. 'No, no… Please don't! I can't stand it. I can't stand your pity. I know you can never love me. Especially not now, after you know what I did. I understand, and I can live with it. Just don't ask me to leave. Please! You're my only family now. Without you I'd wither and die. Like a tree robbed of sunlight. I don't care if you don't love me, but I *beg* you... Please, *please* don't cast me aside!'

She forced in a breath, and then another, each one calming her as she forced cool resolve into her mind and voice. She opened her eyes, but her vision was still blurred by tears.

'It will pass...you'll see. I'll be fine...just give me a moment.' With another shaken inhalation she was sure she would survive the pain this time. 'I will be fine... honestly.'

He opened his mouth to speak, but her words rushed forward like a cresting wave.

'I don't expect anything, but you're right. You have a right to know. And...you're not like Halvor. I was wrong to even think you could be. You won't hold my feelings against me. I know that... But you are wrong. You have so much to offer me... You're kind, loyal and the best man I have ever known... I consider myself lucky to be your wife. Even though you don't feel the same way.'

'Oh, do shut up, Gyda!'

The force of Thorstein's exasperated words shocked her. Her eyes locked with his piercing blue ones. She could feel his breath on her face. It was uneven and light. It gave her a glimmer of hope she'd never dared imagine.

'I do love you. I was an idiot to think I couldn't fall in love with you. My feelings for you surpass anything I have ever felt for anyone else. I don't think I really loved my first wife, because what I felt then was nothing compared to what I feel for you now. I think I loved the idea of her, but she wasn't real. Not like you. I love you with all my heart and soul. If I told you every day from now until the end of this world and the next, it would never be enough.'

Her heart unravelled like a broken thread, until her painful emotions were lying in tatters at her feet. Only joy and bright love remained. She leapt forward, crushing her mouth to his with the same force as the first time she'd kissed him.

But he knew what to expect and he was ready, holding her firmly to him as the boat rocked and cut through the waves. A cheer sounded in the air all around them, from their people in the boat and on the cliff, to lift their joined hearts, which soared into the endless harvest sky.

Chapter Twenty-Six

The Yuletide celebration

'Remind me why I'm doing this again?' Thorstein grumbled.

'Because Gyda asked you to…and there's nothing you wouldn't do for her,' Magnus replied, shoving a big glob of foul-smelling glue onto Thorstein's eyebrow, followed by a fluffy cloud of wool.

'This best not take off my eyebrows.'

Magnus only chuckled, and hooked a waist-long woollen beard over Thorstein's ears. 'There. Come on, then, *Old* Man Winter!'

Thorstein scowled and wrapped the heavily hooded cloak around his shoulders. Gyda had made it especially for him. It was the colour of midnight and embroidered with silver runes that put the Yule night sky to shame.

He mounted the awaiting horse and waited for his men to gather. They walked ahead, chanting and beating drums, heralding his arrival.

He passed the sign that carried the name of their home in runes: The Ash and the Burnt Oak. Their settlement was named after the scorched oak that guarded the pale stone cliffs above, and the family tree at its heart. But to Thorstein's mind it also represented their new life together. He was the burnt oak, struck by lightning and changed for ever by his beautiful ash blonde wife, who would always represent his heart, home and family.

His heartbeat joined the steady beating of the drums as they approached his Hall, where the glow of light surrounding the closed doors was a welcome sight.

The doors opened and she stood framed in the doorway, a dazzling smile on her perfect face—the smile he lived and breathed for. The chanting came to an end, and she stepped forward, her pale gown swirling in the frosty air.

'Welcome, Old Man Winter! Come feast with us. We will not turn you away.'

Her voice sang out as a clear promise of the spring to come. He jumped down from his horse, and she smothered a laugh with a delicate hand.

Oh, yes! He was meant to be old!

He gave a loud groan and hunched over, rubbing the small of his back. He heard a few sniggers from the crowd, but they were nothing compared to Gyda's giggle, which made him grin every time he heard it.

He shuffled towards her, clutching on to anyone and anything he passed, playing his role as best as he could. When he reached her she took his arm and led him into the Hall. The children gasped in awe as he entered, and gathered around him to touch his cloak. He smiled. Gyda had been right. Traditions were treasured memories that built communities.

He shook off the frost and drizzle from his boots. 'Take me to the hearth, kind mistress. May the light of the sun shine upon your family this Yule season.'

Frida stood a little distance away, unimpressed. 'It's just Thorstein!' she grumbled in loud outrage.

Her mother shushed her, and Gyda laughed again. She pressed a finger to her lips and winked at the little girl. 'Don't spoil it for the little ones,' she whispered, and Frida smiled, obviously proud of her wisdom.

'Children, do you have hay for my horse?' Thorstein asked. 'He is tired from his long journey across the world.'

Several children ran forward with boots filled with hay. For the end of the feast he and Gyda had prepared sweet treats and little toys to fill the empty boots with. He couldn't wait to see the children's faces when they saw them.

The sight of his decorated Hall made his heart swell with pride. She'd outdone herself in such a short time and now her beautiful tapestries hung on the walls. He would never grow tired of admiring them.

There was a tapestry of her shipwreck, broken against the rocks and illuminated by the oak burning on the cliffs. Another depicted their family tree, crowned with a golden *kransen*.

Her loom stood in front of the doors to their bed-chamber. The half-finished work stretched on its frame was going to depict the wolf Fenrir, fighting his chains. It was a gift for Sven, Brunhild and Ivar when they saw them next.

The Yule log burned in the hearth, the magical runes he'd carved into its side long ago transformed into smoke. There were wreaths of holly and evergreens hung from the beams, representing the circle of life and the seasons.

Gyda had spent hours not only decorating the Hall, but decorating the evergreen trees surrounding the settlement, with ribbons and embroidery, carvings of small gods and runes. He'd carved each one, and Gyda had arranged them with great care on each tree of eternal life that defied the brutal season.

She led him to a chair by the fire, and he couldn't resist squeezing her bottom as he took his seat. She gave him a playful swat on the arm. 'Behave! I'm a married woman.'

'Your husband must be very dim-witted to leave you alone at Yule.'

'Oh, he is. But I love him anyway.'

Magnus and Elga were kissing passionately in a dark corner, and Thorstein couldn't help but laugh at his friend. He'd always thought they would make a happy couple, and he suspected there would be another union to celebrate in the new year. Magnus would need that new bed after all! He couldn't wait to tease him about it.

He smiled at that, and then the feast began.

The Yule boar was delicious, its sacrificial blood having been given to the fields earlier that day. The men and women drank, ate and sang until the Hall practically shook with love and joy.

The children had fallen asleep, clutching the straw toy goats made especially for the occasion. Thorstein took off his itchy beard with a sigh of relief and pulled Gyda into his lap. She curled against his chest with a happy sigh and nuzzled the sensitive skin beneath his ear.

'The year is almost at an end,' she said.

He leaned back in the large armchair he'd carved so that they could sit beside the fire in each other's arms. He kissed her forehead and pulled her close.

'This is the best Yule I have ever had. You are an incredible woman.'

'Thank you. I wanted it to be perfect.' She sighed happily, but he saw her eyes still washed over the celebrations, looking for any fault.

'It is perfect. The first of many,' he reassured her.

'You're sure? Maybe we should have roasted two boars?' she said, with a bite of her lip.

He felt a shadow race across his mind and he sat up taller in the chair. She yelped and clutched at his tunic in surprise.

He cupped her face and raised her eyes to his. 'Are you worried about something? If it's about Ragnar, he will never return to England. He will not risk my displeasure. And Sven has heard news that all his brothers are against him.'

'No, that's not it—I couldn't care less about him.' She took a deep breath and met his eyes. 'There is another reason why I wanted this Yuletide to be perfect.'

'There is?' he asked.

'I wanted the gods' blessings for the new year.'

He shrugged. 'Well, I'm sure you've achieved that. We'll not have to venture out of our Hall until late spring at the earliest. And our crops and animals are all thriving.'

'Oh, yes. But let's maybe not wait that long…there's only so much I can do with herring.'

He laughed. 'Then why else are you seeking favour from the gods?'

She took his hand in hers and laid it against her stomach. 'For our child.'

He stared at their hands, entwined over the pale cloth of her gown. His rough and hers smooth. He wouldn't have had it any other way.

'You're sure?'

She nodded, her face breaking into a dazzling grin.

He jumped up with a shout, cradling her body in his arms as he bellowed, 'We're to have a *babe*!'

The resounding cheers of their people echoed in his ears, matching the joy in his heart.

The feast was revitalised by the announcement. More ale and mead were poured and songs were sung, their people settling in for several long nights of feasting.

He moved gently back in his seat, cradling her lush body to his chest and revelling in the soft scent of heather and herbs on her skin. She'd taken to pampering herself with scent and he did not complain. He'd always had a weakness for pleasant-smelling herbs, and he suspected she knew it.

'Are you afraid?' he asked. He already knew the answer, but he needed to hear her say it.

She turned over his hand and traced the rune on his palm with tenderness. 'When you have crowned me as the queen of your heart? And protected me with your strength? What have I to fear?'

She reached up and stroked along his jaw, following her touch with the searing heat of her lips. 'I am yours and you are mine. We possess the greatest treasure there is. The gods have been kind. I only wish to thank them.'

Epilogue

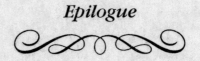

Three years later

Her daughter giggled as the crown rested askew on her shining raven curls. 'Do I look pretty, Módir?'

Gyda grinned at her eldest as she winded the grizzling Inga in her arms. 'You look beautiful, Astrid. Fierce and beautiful.' Her daughter was everything she'd dreamed of and more.

'Good. Shield wall!' cried Astrid, jumping to her bare feet and slashing at the air with her wooden sword.

The sword banged against the trunk of the ash tree, causing a couple of leaves to fall softly on Gyda and Inga's heads.

'Careful of our family tree,' said Thorstein as he approached from the boats.

Gyda laughed. 'Your daughter is a fierce shield maiden…if clumsy.'

'I will be a warrior queen, Father!' Astrid shouted, and then charged out to do battle with an errant chicken.

The chicken squawked and fluttered out of the way, and Gyda began rearranging her skirts so that she could stand.

'Need a hand?'

'Yes, please,' she said, with a grateful smile as her husband helped her up.

'How are you feeling?'

'Good.' She smiled, leaning into his embrace and kissing his scarred cheek. 'Although your daughters are exhausting! Especially Queen Astrid.'

'Ah, but I am the one you should pity. I am ruled by women who own my heart,' he answered with a sorrowful shake of his head.

Gyda roared with laughter. 'You love it!'

His arms slipped around her. 'I do.'

* * * * *